Totally Tossed

PROSPER ANDRE BATINGE

Archway Publishing books may be ordered
through booksellers or by contacting:

Archway Publishing
1663 Liberty Drive
Bloomington, IN 47403
www.archwaypublishing.com
844-669-3957

ISBN: 978-1-6657-3754-8 (sc)
ISBN: 978-1-6657-3753-1 (e)

Library of Congress Control Number: 2023901093

Print information available on the last page.

Archway Publishing rev. date: 01/23/2023

PROLOGUE

America wakes up to a mournful morning: Monday, October 23, 2017.

Fox is streaming it live. CNN is streaming it live. ABC is streaming it live. NBC is streaming it live. MSNBC is streaming it live. Beyond America's borders, BBC is carrying it live. So is Sky News as well as Aljazeera. Everybody is carrying it live on Facebook, Twitter.

The earth, it appears, pauses on its orbit.

She douses herself with gas. Then opens the lighter. She is burning. The image of a burning woman on live TV pauses the usual activities of this mournful Monday morning. Viewers watch in complete dismay. The otherwise talkative morning cable network anchors are too numb to comment. When news anchors manage a comment, a choked whimper echoes. Like their viewers, the anchors sit in disbelief and watch. It's like an Oscar winning movie. Only this time, it isn't a movie. It's real.

Ms Corell Woolsey is self-immolating. She burns herself in the full glare of the public. Up until now, Ms Woolsey is unknown. Even in the office where she works, until fired a day ago, few people know her. She's reclusive. She stays her lane. She minds her business. Her personal business is one: cater for her two kids and a sick, bed-ridden mother.

This mournful Monday morning, America watches as Ms Woolsey burns. And so does the rest of the world.

Helplessly.

1

THE COMPLAINTS

THE COMPLAINTS STILL SIT ON the desk of the head of HR. Ms Woolsey reports that her supervisor sexually harasses her. Management "looks" into her complaint and finds no merit. Management warns Ms Woolsey for her frivolous claims and for tainting the reputation of one of the rainmakers of the company.

Ms Woolsey makes another complaint after the same man abuses her several times again. And again, management "looks" into her complaint, and again, management finds no merit. This time, Ms Woolsey gets more than a warning. She gets a final warning: another frivolous complaint, she's out of the door! Lots of people desperately need her job. Ms Woolsey is ungrateful. If she doesn't want to work here, she should go. Her petty lies are distracting the productivity of the company, management concludes.

The sexual assault finds a new reckless confidence with the "findings" of no merit in her complaints. Her supervisor doubles down on his pervert excesses. Her supervisor knows that his bosses have his back. His bosses' hands are as dirty as his. The bosses have his back.

But Ms Woolsey doesn't want to lose her job. She has a young daughter, a breastfeeding son as well as an aged and sick mother in the hospice. All three vulnerable persons depend on her sweat. She mustn't lose her job; she silently tells herself. But even a caring mother and dutiful daughter like Ms Woolsey has a breaking point as we all do. Sometimes human resilience can't withstand evil.

Ms Woolsey does well. She takes the abuses for a while. She won't complain again. She doesn't want to lose her job. Regardless, she is still fired when her supervisor no longer finds her attractive. She packs her things home. She won't give up. She'll look for another job.

But this morning: Monday, October 23, 2017, she changes her mind. Ms Woolsey can't continue. She comes to the end of her endurance. She decides to end it all. Sometimes human resilience can't withstand evil. With gas and a lighter, she sets herself on fire at Central Park. Ms Woolsey brings her heroic life to an end in the most painful of deaths–self-immolation.

She drenches herself with so much gas. The inferno takes one minute to envelope her and five minutes to completely burn her into ashes.

2

WHO IS SHE?

THE MUTE ANCHORS FIND THEIR voices after the fire dies down. Is it suicide? Is there a suicide note? What could cause a woman in her prime to end her life in so barbaric a manner? Answers aren't forthcoming.

Ms Woolsey is a quiet citizen. Works quietly. Pays her taxes quietly. Doesn't care about politics. No presence in social media. Takes care of her daughter and son and dying mother. She's friendless.

Media producers try in vain to unveil Ms Woolsey's identity.

As well, media producers struggle in vain to find doyens on self-immolation to bring their expertise to bear on the event of this mournful Monday morning, which might well prove the event of the year, probably of the decade. It isn't easy finding self-immolation experts. Not even self-styled connoisseurs. For once, the media doesn't have experts on an urgent issue of utmost public interest.

3

SUICIDE NOTE

MS WOOLSEY INDEED LEAVES A suicide note. A signed letter in a white envelope tied to the right hand of her still sleeping son. The police finds it in her apartment—now a crime scene.

The new find is leaked to the press. She dies because of workplace sexual assault. The abuses span over the past decade. When she reports these abuses, she gets a severe reprimanded instead, then, a sack eventually. So she decides to end it all.

The suicide note ends with an apology. She apologizes to her daughter and son and her mother for failing them. She apologizes for her inability to keep a job to cater for them. She is sorry, the suicide note ends.

4

THE EFFECT

MS WOOLSEY'S GRUESOME DEATH CATCHES on like an angry, wildfire across the Amazon. Women mass up in every nick and crony of the United States of America. Crowds gather in every space, protesting sexual harassment.

Women start speaking. They speak about their own experiences of abuses. Nobody knows until now that many women are abused. Victims are dropping names of sexual predators faster than the pull of gravity on a gargantuan, falling rock.

The anger is profound and palpable. It vibrates the United States of America, the most powerful surviving republic on earth, the like of which no living person remembers.

A national demonstration is planned in Washington D.C. in the coming days. An ad hoc leadership of women are tasked with harnessing this unexpected energy for a cause they have been fighting unsuccessfully for years. Given its suddenness, they don't know exactly what to do. But massive demonstrations emerge all over the nation.

Meantime, photos of Ms Woolsey's two-year-old daughter and six-month-old son as well as her fifty-nine-year-old dying mother go viral. They are the new martyrs of the evil of sexual abuse. The pictures of a feeble, bed-ridden mother and helpless kids whose sole source of survival is forced to commit suicide pierce even the most hardened and uncultivated hearts. Evolved and civilized conscience is fuming with rage.

Sexual predators must account!

5

THE CURIA

LIKE THE REST OF THE world, the self-immolation of Ms Woolsey interrupts the quotidian strict routine at the Jesuits, the nickname of the Society of Jesus (a Catholic Religious Order), curia in Manhattan, New York City. Usually, the five priests at the curia, the nerve center of the Jesuits in New York, New Jersey, Washington D.C. and Maryland States are up and about their core business of coordinating the missions of Jesuits in these states and beyond by 5:00 am. But Monday, October 23, 2017, isn't an ordinary day in American's history. So this mournful Monday morning isn't an ordinary day for the Jesuits in the USA, more so for the Jesuits at the Manhattan curia.

At the pinnacle of governance of the Jesuits in these states is the provincial, Father Anthony Cantwell, SJ. Father Cantwell lives in the curia with four advisors–consultors–: Father Burle O'Connor, SJ, Father Andrew Clovis, SJ, Father Paul Aronson, SJ, and Father Thomas Procopius, SJ. The five priests all sit clued to CNN. Listening. Listening to one of their alumni, Rall Dover–a graduate of Fordham Law School, a Jesuit law school–try, unsuccessfully, to make sense of what's happening. They listen in complete silence. These five Jesuits are listening to their inner selves than they are to the usually livid CNN morning host anchor, Dover.

One question is on the mind of these Jesuit priests with administrative duties. What does the self-immolation of Ms Woolsey mean for the works of the Jesuits in New York, New Jersey, Washington D.C. and Maryland? What does this mean for their colleges, high schools, parishes, hospitals, refugee centers, and many others? Ms Woolsey doesn't set herself on fire, she sets the world on fire. How can this fire be harnessed for the common good and the greater glory of God? These Jesuits wonder? But these Jesuits are also concerned that this fire might burn them.

But the provincial, Father Cantwell, has an additional issue on his mind. More immediate and important for Father Cantwell is what this means for the fate of one of his charges: a fine and resourceful young Jesuit priest. Not one given to emotions, the stoic Father Cantwell wipes suspicious moisture from his eyes. Honestly, not so much for Ms Woolsey or her dying mother or helpless daughter or hungry son who wakes up today to no warm natural breastmilk. Father Cantwell, weeps for a young Jesuit priest whose fate Ms Woolsey just might have sealed, and, not in a good way.

Ms Woolsey has never met Father Priestley Plusbriuschola, SJ, a priest-professor of Ethics and Philosophy at Harvard University. If she had, she would have loved this remarkable priest and great teacher. But Ms Woolseys's self-immolation appears to seal the fate of this young and enterprising priest-professor.

Father Priestley Plusbriuschola, SJ, is totally tossed.

But in the design of divine providence, there are no coincidences. This is one of Father Cantwell's unyielding creeds.

6

THE HOLY MOUNTAIN

THE IGNATIAN HOLY MOUNTAIN IS ordinary at the nave.

Not so at its zenith. The top compels the gazer to look again. And again. And yet another sustained look again. The cross sits at its apex. And because the canopies of trees give the buildings a dark look, the lights are on day and night, especially, during winter, ensuring that the place is as bright as noonday, even at night. The view of the Ignatian Mountain, commonly called the Holy Mountain, is a big-lighted Christmas tree.

The towering sight is certain to draw the average casual looker to want to know more. The road up is not difficult to find. Except you want to climb the 11,000 feet on foot, which few do, a helicopter is the preferred means up.

The Jesuit Spiritual Center, which the Holy Mountain houses, gazes down at the small town of Rochester from its gilded perch at the edge of a cliff. Located at the out shirks of New York State, the remote town of Rochester surrounds the Holy Mountain. The Rochester Fall runs down the Holy Mountain through the little city, finding its way many miles later into the Niagra Fall.

The falling spring is not seen from the town, but its sound massages the ears. The sound compels the listener to want to hear more. And more. And a step a little closer even deepens the desire to want to hear more. The road to the spring side is not difficult to find, either. Another helicopter is ready to pull tourists up.

The breathtaking view of the Ignatius Spiritual Center reminds the keen historian of *Earthrise*–the photo of the earth that astronauts took on route to the moon on the Eve of Christmas in 1969. *Earthrise* reveals from space a blue ball so peaceful and so perfect. The beautiful, blue planet would have compelled, Michael Collins, Edwin "Buzz" Aldrin, and Neil Armstrong, the astronauts from the earth on their way to the moon, to re-route to the earth if they were not citizens of the earth and knew it very well.

Earthrise didn't reveal the turbulent events of that year: the cold war was dividing Europe; the Vietnam war was ongoing; and in America, we slain Dr Martin Luther King Jr. as well as John F. Kennedy. All on this beautiful, blue earth. But *Earthrise* reveals part of a cosmic beauty that is nothing but peaceful. 1969 is the year the Jesuits bought the mountain from native Americans and christened it St. Ignatius Holy Mountain, now popularly called the Holy Mountain.

Likewise, within the calmness of the Holy Mountain are wars and turbulences of a different sort: people seeking the face of God in their troubled lives. The beauty of the Holy Mountain and the silence of its guest retreatants conceal any internal turbulences on it. Like *Earthrise*, which of course portrayed the beauty of the earth, some retreatants radiate the goodness of God. Others radiate with gratitude God's blessing. But quite a number are troubled souls seeking meaning and direction in life.

On October 29, 2017, at the Holy Mountain is a worried man. A Jesuit priest who until now was also a philosophy professor at Harvard. It has been excruciating weeks of waiting for him. The allegations are very damming, especially, if proven true. He won't recover, either, if they're proven false. So he is caught between the devil and the dead sea. He is totally tossed. The accusations take a toll on him.

Of course, none of these troubles are seen in his outward calmness—like *earthrise*— he is perfectly calm. The archbishop of Boston, the Most Reverend George Gaskell, orders him to stop teaching while the committee of investigators do their work. And he has also been asked to stop saying the Holy Mass until the investigations are concluded. Both deprivations do a terrible blow to Father Priestley Plubriuschola, SJ. He can't say Mass as a Catholic priest; he can't teach as a Harvard professor. The priest-professor is a fish out of water. And so seeks solace at the Holy Mountain.

Sometimes, Father Plubriuschola wonders which suspension is more severe: The teaching at the university or the saying of Mass at the parish. He loves both the classroom and the alter. He loves being a professor and a priest. The former allows him to engage younger and adventurous minds on the ultimate questions of life as a professor of ethics and philosophy in the leading university of the world.

The latter rekindles his life of faith as a priest. In fact, the two professions, nay, the two callings, are essentially the same for Father Plubriuschola. The teaching is faith seeking understanding; the Holy Mass is faith in action. He takes both callings—a professor and as a priest—seriously. That is his life. His only life.

The investigations are snailing on forever. Slower than the slowness of Rome in canonizing saints of yore. So Father Plubriuschola waits in great pain and anxiety for weeks now for a verdict that is a significant lost for him whichever way it goes. It's a situation of complete hopelessness. Father Plubriuschola is done and over. Totally tossed.

But Father Plubriuschola is a man of great hope and faith. A hope and faith almost incompatible with his great intellect. The truth, he knows, always has the last say. But he isn't naïve. The truth could take too long to emerge, sometimes a millennium. Sometimes not in a man's lifetime. And while waiting for the truth to surface, an innocent life could be destroyed.

7

THE CALL FROM THE CURIA

THIS MORNING, FATHER PLUBRIUSCHOLA GETS a call from the Jesuit curia in Manhattan, New York City, summoning him to a meeting with the provincial, Father Cantwell, SJ, the following evening at 5:00 pm. The provincial's secretary delivers the message in a weeping tone over the phone. Many love Father Plubriuschola. And the allegations against him disappoint so many; and deeply sadden those closest to him. Father Plubriuschola's teaching assistant faints and is taken to the hospital upon hearing the news. Much of Father Plubriuschola's pain is the pain of others rather than the pain to himself.

Upon receiving the call, Father Plubriuschola goes straight to the chapel to pray. On his knees, Father Plubriuschola prays as is his habit, but especially, during moments like this.

The following afternoon, Father Plubriuschola emplanes from Rochester to Manhattan for the decisive meeting. His guts tells him it is over. Yet, his faith tells him God would never forsake him. Father Plubriuschola, a flightphobic, doesn't know when the plan takes off from Rochester and lands at the JKF airport in New York City. And neither does he recall how he gets from the airport to the curia in Manhattan. But as always, Father Plubriuschola arrives one full hour ahead of schedule.

8

THE MEETING

THE MEETING STARTS WITH THE Provincial, Father Cantwell, SJ, rumbling on and on in his opening remarks. Father Cantwell is visibly saddened. It appears that this might be the most difficult decision he's making since assuming duties as leader of Jesuits of the four states. Still rumbling on, Father Cantwell, SJ, expresses his gratitude for Fr. Plubriuschola's cooperation, obedience, and openness during the investigations.

Father Cantwell, SJ, eventually brings the turbulent plane to a sad landing: he is compelled to have to let Fr. Plubriuschola leave the Jesuits as well as recommend to Rome that he leaves the priesthood because of the gravity of the allegations against him.

Yes, Fr. Plubriuschola is fired. De-roped. Laicized. Defrocked. He's no more a Jesuit. He's no more a priest.

The promise of Melchizedek—you are a priest in the order of Melchizedek, and it is forever—isn't true for Father Plubriuschola. Or so it appears at the time.

Father Plubriuschola isn't expecting this decision. He doesn't even think of it as one of the reasonable outcomes. He's dazed. He hears Father Cantwell but isn't listening to him at this point. The provincial mentions something about the growing spat of scandals after scandals in the Church in the United States and the larger world. Father Cantwell again mentions the current climate of sexual harassment. Father Cantwell emphasizes the recent self-immolation of Ms Woolsey. And also mentions that people think that the Church is covering up for offending priests. The Church must do something. The Church must set some examples.

Father Plubriuschola has always wanted to be a priest all his life. He has always wanted to be a Jesuit. In fact, he has no other alternative vocation to the priesthood. And he never thinks of himself leaving the priesthood. Nor that he might be defrocked one day. Hence, the decision leaves him genuinely confused about what to do with his life. He always considers himself dying a priest. Often, he jokes that he would like to die in Rome and be buried next to the saints. He considers his teaching job an extension of his priestly vocation. He can't think of an alternative life to a priestly life.

More troubling is the directive that he packs out of any Church, Jesuit residences immediately. The provincial agrees that he be gone by morning the following day. Just like that, twelve years preparing to be a priest, five years of serving as a priest, and he can hardly be allowed another day in residence. God, this isn't fair. Fr. Plubriuschola tells the crucified Christ on the cross. The bleeding crucifix replies: Look at me, they aren't fair to me, either. But Fr. Plubriuschola takes no consolation in that reply. For the first time, he feels that Jesus is dumping him.

That night, Mr Plubriuschola, who can't believe the sudden change in his identity and social status, is consumed with one question: where to go from here? For the first time in his life, he has no practical solution to a question so simple and mundane. Admitting defeat, he leaves the question for tomorrow. A new day might bring an answer. A new beginning.

9

STILL A SENSE OF GRATITUDE

BUT THAT NIGHT, HE KNOWS what he must do the following day.

At the Holy Mountain is Father Petrus Mentor, SJ, whom he confides a lot in during his excruciating period of waiting. Father Mentor becomes fond of the troubled, young priest. Fathers Mentor and Plubriuschola talk about deep things during the waiting period. Father Mentor is his consolation during these dark days, the dark night of his soul.

So he plans to say thanks to Fr Mentor, SJ. And Plubriuscola wants to do so in person. So he must travel to Rochester.

After the thank you visit to Father Mentor, he will figure out where to stay and what to do with his life. He isn't in a hurry. One day at a time.

One day, the sun will surely rise and shine again after this grim winter.

10

MENTOR PONDERS

FATHER PETRUS MENTOR, SJ, GETS the news of the double defrocking of Father Priestley Plubriuschola, SJ, from the priesthood as well as from the Jesuit Order last night. The Provincial, Father Cantwell, SJ, exercises the discretion of telephoning Father Mentor with the unfortunate news first. Father Cantwell waits to tell Father Plubriuschola before announcing his departure to the other Jesuit companions. So last night, Father Mentor, SJ, goes to bed in very low spirits and wakes up this morning without his usual sense of high enthusiasm.

At five o'clock this morning as is his habit for decades now, Father Mentor sits in prayer in his quiet room. The departure of fellow Jesuits from the Order is never easy for him. Father Mentor has seen numerous departures from the Jesuit order. Jesuits depart from the Order for several reasons. But anytime a close and talented companion like Plubriuschola leaves the Jesuit Order for whatever reason, Father Mentor is left a deeply sad man. These departures are like deaths to him, deaths of friends and brothers that he shares a kingship of the mission of Christ with.

Father Mentor's prayer this morning is full of the moments of grace shared with the young, departing priest. The two bond tightly during the period of waiting. Father Mentor now knows the heart of the young priest. He's a good man.

While preoccupied with the departure of Father Plubriuschola, Father Mentor can't help but recall the departure of his closest friend when he was a scholastic (one in training to be a Jesuit). This close friend is (and they are still friends) Mr Sparkman

Schola. Two weeks to their ordination as deacons and six months to their ordination as Jesuit priests, Sparkman Schola decides that a Jesuit priestly life isn't suited for him. Sparkman Schola's leaving leaves Mentor friendless for some time. It takes a while before Father Mentor recovers from his loneliness and isolation that his friend's departure induces.

The two—Priestley Plubruischola and Sparkman Schola—are as different as two persons can be in temperament and taste. The priest is calmer, calculated, and reserved with a deep intellect that leans itself to manifestation only when solicited. Sparkman Schola is, however, rash, blunt and action filled; he acts before thinking. Now well on in years, and honed by years of experiences, Sparkman Schola has learned to be reflective and restrained.

Father Mentor always thinks about Sparkman Schola anything he encounters Priestley Plubruischola. The two are quite similar in several ways, however. Plubruischola has his name abbreviated over the years to Schola. Few people know him as Plubruischola. Even official Jesuit documents refer to him as Schola. Everybody now calls him Schola. And of course, Sparkman's surname is also Schola. The two have come to share a common surname though they are biologically unrelated.

But beyond the sameness of surnames, the two stand up to bullies. They are quick to come to the defense of the underprivilege. They truly care a lot about the well-being of the poor. Service to the poor pull both men to the Jesuit Order.

As well, the two have what is called authority problems. They question authority. They simply won't do things because the order is from above. This attitude gets Sparkman Schola in trouble on several occasions with his Jesuit superiors. Priestley Schola questions authority in a manner that isn't obvious because of his reserved demeanor. Many had thought Priestley wouldn't last long in the Jesuit Order—an ecclesiastical order that values obedience—because of his authority problem. But he makes it through twelve years of studies to ordination and lasts five years teaching at Harvard, allaying such fears. Almost.

Just when many think that all is well with Schola, he comes in five months ago to wait for an investigation into an allegation of sexual harassment against him at Harvard where he teaches. And now he ceases to be a Jesuit. He ceases to be a priest. He ceases to be a professor. None of this makes old Father Mentor a happy priest this morning. But Father Mentor is a man of faith, of deep faith.

So this morning, Father Mentor thanks God for the life of Father Schola. And prays for Schola in his new life outside the Jesuit Order. He also prays for whomever Schola might have hurt. He prays for the person's forgiveness and for the person's healing. Father Mentor wonders what Schola would now do with his life.

And it's this last point that worries Father Mentor. Few people know that Father Schola, now Mr Schola, is familyless. Barely a year ago, he lost his entire family parents and a sister—in a boat disaster off the coast of the Atlantic that left no survivors. The tragedy bears so heavily on the young priest. And just when he is about recovering from the misfortune that nature visits upon him, this new misfortune comes along.

Father Schola's family wills everything to him, being the sole heir of the family. And then Father Schola in turn gives his entire inheritance to the Jesuits. All of it.

So it troubles Father Mentor that Schola might have a problem finding a home. Even more troubling for the older spiritual priest is that Schola might feel unloved now. This time, unloved by God himself. Father Mentor prays for him, employing God to guide Schola's steps. Father Mentor wonders whether he would ever see Schola again. That wonder is answered that very morning.

11

THE GOOD BYE

MR PRIESTLEY SCHOLA LEAVES NEW York City for Rochester to say goodbye to his friend and teacher–Father Mentor–without knowing where he goes from there.

It's late afternoon when Schola arrives at the Holy Mountain. Father Mentor is excited to see him even given the circumstances. And ever hopeful, the two make light comments. When the thank you visit ends, Father Mentor asks Schola where he's going to stay and realizes he has no place yet as feared.

Father Mentor thinks seriously for a while. Gets up. Goes to his printer. Brings out a paper. And writes a note. He addresses the note to one Sparkman Schola in Fort Wayne, Indiana. Father Mentor is clear. Schola must hand deliver the note in Fort Wayne, Indiana.

A confused Schola doesn't know what to do. With all that's going on, he's made a postman.

"Father Mentor, I should apply for a job with the post office," Schola remarks upon taking the letter.

"This's probation. Deliver the letter and see whether you like the job," Father Mentor returns the joke.

Beneath the laugher and lightness are two troubled men, wondering what the future holds. An unexpected future is thrown at one of them. A future never expected and never asked for and not deserved. Yet here. God's God. Father Mentor has long come to the firm belief that God does not make mistakes. God's never wrong. During his sojourn at the Holy Mountain, he tries teaching young Schola this basic truth of the faith. Given the events, he won't blame the young man if the lesson is lost on him.

"How's your faith in all of this?" Father Mentor asks, breaking the silence.

"I don't think I've it again," Schola replies, most honestly and pithily, as is his custom.

"Never let it go. Hold on to it. Never let it go. No matter what. Hold on to that faith. And keep moving. One foot in front of the other. Keep moving no matter what."

Those are the last words of Father Mentor before Schola leaves to deliver the letter. In Schola's dazed mind, the faith left him, he didn't leave the faith.

12

THE GOVERNOR

GOVERNOR SPARKMAN SCHOLA, THE TWO-TERM governor of Indiana, wakes up this morning to the melodies of birds outside his Range. The early morning natural choir of the birds is one of the attractions of the former Governor's Range in the out skirts of Fort Wayne. Since he ceases steering the ship of the Hoosier State, one of the luxuries he indulges in is to wake up whenever he pleases. But the latest the Governor is out of bed is 6:00 am. Even without an alarm, the sixty-nine-year former Governor doesn't sleep beyond this time. But in spring and summer and autumn, the sounds of the birds call the governor to take on the day: carpe diem. The Governor, each morning, responds gladly.

As is his habit each morning, Governor Sparkman Schola gets up and walks to the window. Draws the curtail. The melodies are now more audible. And since this year's spring ushers in warmer temperatures—even when winter hasn't disappeared completely—he draws the windows up. The melodies are even more audible with the windows drawn up. The sounds please his ears. And the burgeoning greens please his eyes, too. He stands. He listens. He looks. Over the years, Governor Schola tries counting the different sounds from different species of birds. But the different composures blend so seamlessly that the Governor believes that the birds agree to compose a single song. For they sing different parts of the same song. The Governor loves his natural choir.

Life is beautiful.

Governor Schola might have been beaming in happiness—admiring nature—for an hour or so. The lady sun still sleeps when the Governor goes to the widow. But now, the sun hears the birds, too, and is gradually drawing her curtains to listen as well. But in attending to the sounds of the birds, the sun, unlike Governor Schola, fails to hide herself. Her rays cast through the trees and forages. And the birds, thrilled by this, sing even more. The Governor smiles. He's glad at heart.

Life is beautiful.

He serves his people well. And his people are grateful. And the Governor is humbled by the chance to serve. He is commonly referred to as the most successful Governor in the recent history of Indiana. Mr Sparkman Schola didn't set out to win accolades. His heart was for ensuring that the people get what they need to flourish and prosper. His tenure, though a Republican, ensures that the poor are given a good shot at life. He is pro-poor. He is too liberal for a Republican, especially, in a deep red state such as Indiana. Political pundits often wonder how he won two terms as governor in Indiana given his liberal policies and leanings. The governor wonders, too. One thing is certain, he loves serving his people. Probably, that's it.

Beyond the care of others, Governor Schola does well in business. His business conglomerate – The Schola Group consists of a farm, an investment bank, an audit firm, a law firm, and the third most circulated newspaper in United States, *The World* – is growing. The Schola Group churns out profits every year. He has made money. He's a billionaire. His rankings in Forbes have consistently improved over the years.

Beyond wealth, Governor Schola takes even greater pride in the fact that he employs thousands of Hoosiers and beyond in his businesses. And he continues to employ on a daily base with his ever-expanding businesses. For over two decades he has been ranked the employer that pays the most minimum wage in the entire United States—$25 per hour. Hoosiers love to work for Governor Schola. The Governor pays better and treats employees with respect.

The sun's smiley rays are becoming too overwhelming for the aging eyes of Governor Schola. So he closes the window and goes down to the kitchen for breakfast. Typically, he would be out running or working out in the gym first thing in the morning. But he falls recently and has a shoulder surgery. The injury is no big deal. His doctors are just overly cautious, he reasons. So he puts his daily exercise on hold, for now.

Life is beautiful. The Governor is glad at heart.

13

THE BREAKFAST

THE GOVERNOR'S BREAKFAST IS RATHER Spartan. A cup of coffee with nothing in it. Just dry coffee. And two slices of bread. Just dry bread. Nothing on top. Every day, that's all he eats in the morning. That's, if he happens to eat. Unusual breakfast for a billion, many are quick to remark.

His domestic assistant, Ms Rosa Harvanet, brings him the papers. She admonishes the governor: "You shouldn't be walking about with that injured shoulder. You sit straight up as if nothing is wrong with you. And please go to bed after the breakfast and rest. Rest is good for healing. And here are pancakes and an apple." She takes the cup of coffee away from him and throws the bread in the dustbin. She then places the pancakes and fruits in front of him. And pours him a glass of natural fruit juice.

But Ms Harvanet knows that the Governor will retrieve his beloved dish from the dustbin. So she makes sure she takes the black bag containing the discarded bread away as she leaves. The Governor casts a menacing look at her as she walks away. The Governor is compelled to consume a breakfast that is alien to him: pancakes, a glass of tasty juice, and an apple. It tastes far better. But as he has been trained, if he stops eating what the poor eats, he will soon forget how the poor feels. And with that, he might cease to care for the poor.

Ms Harvanet is a middle-age African American woman. With an undergraduate degree from Indiana University and a Doctor of Jurisprudence (JD) degree from Notre Dame, Ms Harvanet is intelligent and highly accomplished. Governor Schola recruits her to be his Chief of Staff when he was governor because, including her brilliance, she tells authority what she thinks. She fears not. She has malice toward none. But she worships none. Not even the man that Hoosiers pall praises on.

While most subordinates keep leaders in the dark and feed them with what they know the leader likes to her, Ms Harvanet speaks her mind. When the Governor vacates the governor's mansion after his second tenure as governor and moves up to the Range, Ms Harvanet decides to employ herself. And she runs the Range, runs people who wish to see the Governor, and runs the Governor himself.

The joke among the Governor's close associates is that Hoosiers answer to Governor Schola and the Governor answers to Ms Harvanet. That is the hierarchy in the Schola dynasty.

"And by the way, the College wanted to come in this morning to disturb you," Ms Harvanet returns after throwing out the coffee and bread to tell the Governor about a meeting the College is asking for. The College of Presidents refers to the presidents of all the Governor's major corporate entities. The College only meet the governor when there is something of the utmost urgency. Otherwise the College of Presidents meets twice a year.

"Did they tell you what they wanted?" the Governor asks. "No. I don't care what they want. They want to talk. Your health is more important." The de facto chief of staff answers. The Governor knows that she knows the agenda. If it's crucial, she would bring it to his attention, immediately. Besides, the Governor has complete trust in his top lieutenants and believes that they would always make the right choices. The Governor carefully chooses them for their competence and integrity and loyalty to the cause of our common good.

At least, today, the Governor has an official assignment. He meets with the College of Presidents. He hasn't seen them in a while. He looks forward to the meeting.

Life is beautiful. The Governor is glad at heart.

14

THE BUS TRIP

THE LETTER DELIVERY BUS TRIP doesn't make sense to Schola. Father Mentor, SJ, personally drives him from the Holy Mountain to the greyhound bus terminal for the ride to Fort Wayne, Indiana. Father Mentor thinks that traveling by air is faster and, perhaps, more comfortable. But since spring is just springing up and summer is almost in sight, Schola could enjoy the scenery that a greyhound trip from Rochester, New York State, to Fort Wayne, Indiana, offers. Fr Mentor is right. As always.

In all, Schola changes five buses. The scenery along the journey is unbelievable. The green hasn't fully emerged yet on account of it still being the start of spring. But few leaves and flowers can't wait for summer to emerge from their holdings. Their sights are inviting. Schola can't take his eyes off nature. The rivers are peaceful, flowing along with the moving car. And the mountains come into view every now and then with greens here and there, a preview of coming beauty in the summer.

The seats are almost empty. Schola has the perfect ambience to introspect as there's less noise. The silence is another added value of the trip. Something Father Mentor, probably, knows but didn't mention. It's a trip to see beauty and clear the mind. It's therapeutic. Exactly what Schola needs. Schola reflects on his former life as a Jesuit. His life now. And wonders what the future holds for him.

Half way through the eight-hour or so trip, he elects to reserve the ultimate question—what is he to do now?—for another day.

He has no idea. Even more pressing is where to stay in the interim. He has no relatives. He has nobody in the world who has his back. Or so he believes.

Disgraced former priest. Expelled Jesuit. Fired Harvard professor. Poor Priestley Plubruischola. Is that who he is now? Completely screwed. Finished. Totally tossed.

Schola is surprised Father Mentor doesn't discuss his future with him. Or even where he'll be living. Father Mentor knows Schola's familyless story very well.

Schola's entire family perished in a boat off the coast of the Atlantic about a year ago. Schola misses his mother, especially. She would have embraced him and told him: "don't worry. You'll be fine." His father would have sat silently, evaluating the situation with viable options ready in the next day or two. His sister would just have been too happy to see him and care very less about what people are accusing him of. Schola misses his family. Father Mentor knows very well that he has no family to go to. But doesn't ask.

Does old Father Mentor forget, or he doesn't' care? None of the two. Father Mentor never forgets important things—no matter how they seem unimportant to others. And God, he cares a lot. So the failure to bring it up can't possibly be because he doesn't care.

Instead, he makes Schola a postman. Schola chuckles loudly on the thought of his new job as a postman. He's lucky the bus is virtually empty. He would've been judged mad for laughing aloud for no reason. But probably, every poor, homeless person has a mental problem.

15

SCHOLA MEETS MS HARVANET

MS HARVANET, THE SELF-APPOINTED AND de factor chief of staff of former Governor Schola, rarely receive guests that she doesn't know. Or guests that she doesn't expect. The guests know better. So the receptionist's message that she has a guest waiting in the lobby rattles her a bit. Because she's gainfully employed, and most of her friends are out of jobs, occasionally, they would come around for some financial help. But she warns them never to come to the office. She wonders which of them is violating this sacred decree.

Ms Harvanet walks into the lobby and doesn't see anybody resembling her kin. So she goes back to finish her work. And there's always a lot to do for Governor Schola. After fifteen minutes with Ms Harvanet's guest unattended to, the assistant thinks that she needs reminding. This time, she doesn't walk in but calls her on the phone, forcing Ms Harvanet out of her office into the lobby in search of her guest, again.

"Who is waiting for me?" Ms Harvanet asks. Schola looks up and doesn't think the question is for him. Schola expects to see a man. The letter he holds is addressed to a man. "The gentleman seated," the assistant says, pointing to Schola. The two look at each other in utter surprise. Schola gets up.

"Please I've a letter for," he looks at the envelope and said: "Mr Sparkman Schola." Ms Harvanet is even more confused now.

"Please do you work for the post office," she asks.

"No," Schola replies.

Ms Harvanet takes the letter. Her face tightens as she looks at it. She sees the initials at the edge of the envelope–AMDG–turned upside down. In the Governor's affairs, the initials AMDG signals the most secrecy and importance. She repeats them. Schola smiles. And Ms Harvanet knows that her guest is from one of the Governor's inner circles. She takes Schola to her office. And she thinks it best that Schola should deliver the letter directly to the Governor since he comes all the way from Rochester for the purpose. But that means an hour's drive to the Range. Schola doesn't mind. He's all the time in the world.

Since Ms Harvanet doesn't know what the letter conveys, she suspends work that day. She drives back to the Range with this unusual postman.

The Governor is a mixed of excitement and expectation and a bit of anxiety upon seeing the handwriting. Petrus, Petrus, he keeps saying while opening the envelope with excited hands that can't wait to unravel the content therein. He finally gets the arduous task of opening the white, manila, envelope done and smiles again. Yes, it's Petrus. The Governor reads the letter to himself with a mix of seriousness and lightness. The Governor looks at Schola and reads the letter again. And smiles and nods his head severally. Gravely and understandably.

"And how is Petrus holding up on the Holy Mountain?" the governor asks of his old Jesuit classmate.

"Very well, you know the old rock." The two ex-Jesuits laugh.

"Great. Great. Great." The Governor says. The governor is a happy man. As happy as he wakes up this morning.

Life is beautiful. The Governor is glad at heart.

"The first year was very difficult for me. The second year was less painful. And the second year even less painful. And then you finally find yourself. You'll be fine. Please you can stay here as long as you want. This's your home. Figure out what you want to do or what you don't want to do. Money wouldn't be a problem at all." And with that the Governor decides the question of where Schola should live in the interim.

"Rosa, please Priestley Plubriuschola is now part of my family. Show him his room. Make sure he is comfortable. And open an account in his name tomorrow. Spending money." The Governor directs his de facto chief of staff.

Turning to his guest, the Governor says, "unpack and come down for some drinks. We have a lot to talk about. I like to know the state of the Jesuits. How the missions are doing. How the Soldiers of St Ignatius are setting the world on fire these days."

"Sure," Schola replies and wonders whether he would ever in essence leave the Jesuits or cease to be one.

16

THE COLLEGE OF PRESIDENTS

THE MEETING WITH THE COLLEGE of Presidents is scheduled for 6:00 pm on the day of Schola's arrival in Fort Wayne. Members of the College of Presidents are the chief executive officers of the Governor's various business firms and companies. Most of them—seven males and a female—are at the Range not later than 5:00 pm. Individuals of remarkable professional and personal achievements, they bring years of learning, expertise, and vast personal experience to the College. And given the cruciality of the meeting this evening, their punctuality must be indicative besides.

The first to arrive is Mr Plater Post, the President of the *World*, Schola's major daily newspaper. The *World* circulates in Indiana and beyond. It is the second most circulated newspaper in the United States, saddled between the *Wall Street Journal*—first place—and the *New York Times*—third place. It sells three million copies a day, churning out five million dollars daily profit, minus expenses. Many turn to the punchy editorial pages of the *World* for deep insights on the rule of law, politics, freedom of speech, democracy, education, free market, foreign affairs and other important themes that interest or ought to interest the well-educated as well as the curious citizen.

The President of the *World*, Mr Post, is quite a remarkable man. He's a school dropout who self-taught himself. His lack of formal education doesn't reflect on the sage editorial pages of the *World*, however. Instead, the prose that Mr Post produces daily on issues of national relevance in the editorial pages of the

World is unparalleled. A recent survey shows that subscribers and readers of the *World* prefer its editorial pages to the other sections of the paper. Mr Post is now well on in years, almost eighty, fifty years of which were spent laboring at the *Wealth*. He might need replacing soon. Mr Post has surrounded himself with a crop of erudite, passionate, and ambitious young editorial editors. And when the time arrives for him to bow out of the editorial pages of the renowned *World*, the Governor has no doubt that a competent editor would be placed in his stead.

While waiting for the rest, Mr Post updates the Governor on the world of media and journalism.

Next to join them is Mr Koskinen Kendrew, president of Schola Oil, by far the most profitable of all the Governor's businesses. Schola Oil operates in Saudi Arabia, Angola, Nigeria, and in recent decades in the newly discovered oil fields in Ghana. Mr Kendrew flies in with one of the company's Gulf Streams from Arizona. Schola Oil drills and ships crude from its outsources and refines them in Arizona. The refined products are then sold both in the US and around the world.

A very reserved man, Mr Kendrew takes a seat beside himself. The Governor notices that Mr Kendrew is in a hurry to leave. Evidence that the meeting isn't business related, yet crucial to compel the attendance of the president of Schola Oil. What is it about? The Governor wonders.

Conventional protocol requires that nobody informs the Governor of the agenda in emergency meetings like this when the agenda isn't previously communicated to him. Regardless of this rule, Mr Post would often hint the Governor of the agenda. But Mr Post declines to do so for this meeting, leaving the Governor completely in the dark and out in the open sea. Understandably, the Governor is alarmed and can't wait to hear from his top lieutenants.

The presidents of the Governor's Law cum Investment/Audit firms are next to make their entrance charged with grandeur:

Two luxurious limousines rolled through the gates of the Range. Dr Devlin Dingell and Mr Cotton Dodge shake hands with those Presidents present, make light jokes and take their seats next to each other. They continue their elevated chat.

Dr Dingell just returns from Washington, D.C., where he argues a case before the federal Supreme Court. The Governor is in a hurry to get the erudite and learned attorney's take on what the outcome might be. But Dr Dingell learned only early in his career not to predict the outcome of cases the Supreme Justices are reviewing. Every year, the Schola Law Firm targets making an appearance before the Supreme Court of the United States, championing issues of constitutional and national consequences. For the past twenty-five years, they have met this rather ambitious target. And this year, they have three cases in the highest Court of the land. Impressive. The law firm is doing very well. Its newest associates are the most paid in the country—$250,000. Every attorney in the US wants to work for Schola Law.

Dr Custor Ewell is the president of the Schola Foundation. A charitable organization that attends to the poor needs of Hoosiers. Among other things, the Schola Foundation operates soup kitchens across Indiana—the Daily Bread Soup Kitchens. It offers educational scholarships to promising students whose only way through college might be taking predatory, private loans.

But the hospital is by far the most expense driven of the Foundation's undertakings. Its medical services, mostly, to poor Hoosiers and residents of Indiana is hugely subsidized by the other profit-making entities of the Schola Group. The Schola hospital saves lives daily.

Mr Dodge, the president of the Investment and Audit firm often collides with Dr Ewell on the expenditures of the Schola Foundation, especially, the hospital. Mr Dodge tells Dr Ewell to find creative ways of cutting cost while remaining efficient. But if anything, the expenditures of the Schola Foundation keeps climbing, taking up a chuck of the profit of the other firms and companies. Mr Dodge can't bring himself to tell the Governor to ask the hospital to be self-reliant. But the Governor knows that Mr Dodge thinks this point. The Governor also knows that Dr Ewell is doing her best. Some people are simply too poor that to pay all their essential bills. The tension between Mr Dodge and Dr Ewell is a necessary one.

Arriving about twenty minutes to the start of the meeting is Professor Methodius Meliton of Notre Dame University. He is a professor of political philosophy, jurisprudence as well as constitutional law. A global scholar per excellence, Prof Meliton serves both as an advisor and a think tank to the College of Presidents. Smart, intellectually curious, and conscious of the pulse of the nation, he rarely speaks, but when he does, his advice carries weight. Professor Meliton is a Noble Laureate and the Pope recently appointed him a member of the Pontifical Association of the Acts and the Sciences. Professor Meliton is engrossed in a book while waiting for the meeting to start. The Professor appears impatient.

The Governor also owns a basketball team. Hoosiers pack the stadium when the Pacers plays, especially, in Fort Wayne The team has won a number of titles. Mr Joule Lodge, a former head coach of Indiana University is the President of the Pacers. His arrival completes the full complement of the College of Presidents.

17

THE MEETING

THE GOVERNOR IS THE PRESIDENT of the College of Presidents. The Governor appoints the other Presidents often with the informed advice of others within and without the college.

In a recent meeting, the Governor makes the Presidents speechless and the room silent when he declares that the Schola Foundation is the soul of the Schola Group, and without the hospital operating as it does currently, the other businesses would collapse. The evidence points otherwise. The other entities serve as the cash cow for the Foundation. But the metaphysical point was not lost on the eminent personalities gathered in that room.

All too soon, it is time to find out why all the entire College of Presidents calls a meeting whose agenda the Governor is not privy to. Apart from the regular meetings, it's often the Governor who calls meetings without communicating a prior agenda. It appears the Presidents are learning from their President, beating him to his own game.

The Governor clears his throat and begins: "I hear that I have been summoned to be impeached," the room rewards this opening remark with a light laughter. And Mr Dingell, the President of the law firm with the gift of the rhetorical virtues doesn't wait. He stands up to speak. The Presidents often sit and make their interventions, except in extraordinary situations. Mr Dingell stands on this occasion. Again, indicative that this isn't an ordinary matter.

"Governor, the proposal we have for you is worse than impeaching you." Mr Dingell opens his remarks and waits for the laughter to die.

"Just a minute," the Governor interrupts him. "I'll like someone to be part of this meeting."

At this, a confused Priestley Schola is invited in and introduced to the group as a new member of the Schola family. Schola is given a seat with the eminent men and woman. Schola feels completely out of place. The Governor and Schola are the only ones not suited and tied up.

"Sorry about that Mr Dingell, you were saying?" The Governor yields the floor back to Mr Dingell.

"We think you should run for President of the United States of America." Mr Dingell is pithy when the occasion calls for it.

The Governor and Schola laugh. But nobody else sees a joke. The Governor realizes the gravity of the moment. The Governor's face is a mixture of surprise and betrayal and annoyance.

"I like crazy ideas and adventures. But this crazy one is well out of the league even for this group. Suppose I agree to run. I have no viable path to winning even the primary in the Republican Party." The Governor manages to say.

"Leave that to us to worry about," Mr Post, President of the *World* intervenes.

"Just consent to run and we will take care of the rest," Mr Dodge adds.

"And if I lose?" the governor says in bewilderment.

"You have never lost an election," Dr Ewell says to the surprise of the Governor. The Governor doesn't know Dr Ewell for her passion in politics, and her comment amazes him.

"By the way, when did you fear losing a fight. Please just run. Now is the time," Dr Ewell concludes.

The Governor turns to Mr Post and feels betrayed that Mr Post fails to alert him before this ambush. And Mr Post looks at him and smiles shamefully. "They," pointing to the rest "warned me not to leak this one." Mr Post chuckles as the rest do. But the gravity quickly settles in again.

Mr Post continues: "I have an editorial already polished that suggests that you are running."

"You dare not publish it." The Governor is serious, and Mr Post knows it.

"Folks, running for president of the United States is a different animal. It's nothing like running for governor or a senate seat." The Governor attempts to educate these men and woman who have never run for elected office. But he finds his education heedless.

From nowhere and even without realizing that he is speaking, Schola says: "This might be one of the most important decisions, if not the most important in the Governor's life. Please give him time to pray about it."

The meeting ends with Schola's suggestion. The Governor is grateful to his friend, Father Mentor, for bringing this young man into his life at this point.

The College of Presidents takes note of this new voice that brings crucial meetings to an end.

18

RIGHT TO A JURY OF HIS PEERS

THREE QUICK YEARS PASS SINCE Priestly Plubruischola makes that bus trip to deliver a letter in Fort Wayne, Indiana. Out of the many options generous Governor Sparkma Schola unveils before Schola and out of all the virtually unlimited resources to support any chosen option, Schola decides to go to law school instead.

Schola graduates from Loyola University Chicago Law School and is admitted to practice in the State of Indiana as well as the two federal district courts that Indiana envelopes. But he isn't too sure what to do as an attorney. He inclines more towards his old profession, teaching, and hopes to teach constitutional law someday. The Governor doesn't care what Schola does as long as Schola is happy.

Wait when you are not sure is another of Schola's maxims. He decides to wait on his next course of action. In the meantime, he tenders the farm as he has been doing in the last three years when he is home on holidays from law school. Schola beams and sweats in the outdoors. Schola is a happy man. The pains of the event of the past three years seem to substantially fade as manifest in his delightful demeanor as he drinks his morning coffee.

Schola again examines the contents of the opinion article he's about dispatching to the *New York Times*. He submits the same article to the *World*, and the feedback is reproach. The consistently conservative newspaper won't publish an opinion that appears to support a sexual pervert.

Schola tries his luck with the *New York Times*. Before submitting, he concludes that given the public outcry against Senator Cornelius Conner Jr., the Senate Majority leader, the *Times* like the *World* won't publish his opinion and will, probably, give him a lesson in sexual morality. But there's no harm in submitting a piece to a newspaper and receiving a reject for your efforts, especially, once the opinion is already written. One can never be too sure of an outcome is another of Schola's maxims. So Schola submits his opinion on a controversial matter that pervasively dominates the news in the last month.

Senator Conner is a celebrity politician of multi-faceted faces: actor, before that a veteran with the marine corps, a past CEO of a fortune 50 company, and until the continuous scandals caused his resignation, the majority leader of the United States Senate. And, he's wealthy, too. Before his recent troubles, Senator Conner was considered the most viable Republican presidential candidate in the next presidential election, having come in a respectable third place in a previous GOP presidential primary.

The story, which the print and cable media extensively cover and, which is the most talked about topic in the myriad of social media platforms, has it that Mr Conner has been assaulting several women in the course of his public careers. About two hundred women have gone public with complaints of sexual assault against Senator Conner. The number of accusers keeps growing and growing. It's widely believed that several other victims are still silent. So the number of women that Senator Conner abuses over the course of his rather robust careers remains unknown. But the number of known allegations against him is alarming, bordering on incredulity.

The discussions on the sexual sins of Senator Conner always harken back to the self-immolation of Ms Corell Woolsey three years ago. In fact, since that unusual act of protest against sexual abuse, juries across the United States and the world have convicted dozens of sexual predators.

Somehow, Senator Conner keeps the faucet on his sexual scandals tight. Almost. That tight tap now loosens. The victims are accusing him of the same crime. Senator Conner himself pays off many of his victims in millions of dollars according to the stories, and his past employers also pay off victims with several millions in settlement offers. The total amount in pay offs and settlements is staggering, more than the average GDP of a poor country in the developing world.

With three years to the end of his senate term, the Senator is hoping to wait out the pressure until his tenure runs out. The GOP bosses in the White House and Congress have a different view. The Senator brings disrepute to the Republican Party, a party that continuously lauds its conservative principles, its public purity in moral principles. He's also a constant distraction to the work of the Senate. He must go. And so the Senator under duress from the White House, the Senate Republicans, and conservative puritans, resigns his senate seat last month. A disgraceful end to his once promising political career.

But quitting the Senate doesn't quite quiet things down. The Indiana attorney general is gathering evidence and witnesses in view of an anticipated prosecution. A grand jury is assembled, several witnesses subpoenaed to testify before it, and its recommendation is that the evidence exceeds reasonable doubt, more than enough to hang Senator Conner. The Indiana Attorney General is charging the Senator for sexually assaulting Ms Larnage Pincus. In fact, the Senator is arrested and detained, but released on bail pending the commencement of hearing in the coming weeks.

Legal pundits and commentators hold that the prosecution has a very strong case against the Senator. The experts recall examples of even comparatively tenuous evidence that juries depend on to incarcerate many powerful men following the Ms Woolsey protestation in self-immolation.

Civil society groups, especially women groups, have been calling for the head of the Senator. They call him a serial predator, a rapist, and a perverse whose rightful place is behind bars. People that once matter in his life begin distancing themselves from him. The Republican Party bosses, the President, Senators and Congressmen and women to whom Senator Conner once gave money for their campaigns condemn him in public. The media covers their condemnations unreservedly. Everybody now condemns Senator Conner.

"The public," as Schola sees it, "charges, tries, and sentences Mr Conner to perpetual damnation without a trial." It's this presumption of guilt even before trial and the fact that many of the Senator's friends and loyalists desert him in his sexual scandal storm that prompt Schola to author the piece he's about submitting to the *Times*. Schola argues two main points in his opinion piece. The first argument is purely procedural, the Senator should be presumed innocent—*in dubio pro reo*—until the judicial process had reached its completion. The principle of *in dubio pro reo* is grounded in the federal Constitution of the United States of America. The federal Constitution mandates that an accused be presumed innocent until proven guilty. This federal constitutional safeguard has its corollaries in all the state constitutions, including Indiana. Further, the Seventh Amendment guarantees the accused a right to a jury of his peers in cases were legal remedies are adequate. Hence, Schola concludes that the Senator shouldn't be treated as a guilty person until a jury decides the Senator is indeed guilty.

Schola's second argument advances the *audi alteram partem* principle, one of the twin principles of natural justice. This principle provides that the other party should be heard in his defense or admission before judgment is passed.

When Schola dispatches the email to the *Times'* opinion editors, he doesn't even expect a reject in the form of a reply.

But within four hours after the piece goes out, it is accepted with very minor editorial changes bordering on style. By the evening of that same day, the piece is published in the online version of the *Times*; albeit, it's the only lone and sympathetic voice in support of Senator Conner. No, its support of the Senator is a timid recommendation that it is unconstitutional to treat and call an accused, Senator Conner included, a criminal when a trial is yet to be had.

The comments to Schola's article are uncharitable, to put it mildly. Though Schola recognizes them as argumentum ad hominem, some of the negative comments get to his skin. Just a little bit. The first time he is publicly criticized. These aren't intellectual disagreement with his position. The authors don't like his view and express their dislike in unambiguous and insulting ways. The one sure solace is that for the first time, he publishes in a newspaper. His first legal view on a matter of public interest. His first public act that draws on his training as an attorney. But the comments and the overall tone of the discussions surrounding his piece suggest that Schola supports a serial sexual predator. Sadly.

It's still a dream this morning when Schola holds a hard copy of the *Times* in his hands. To be sure, Schola published in numerous academic journals as well as numerous books when he was a priest professor. He published mainly on philosophy and ethics. But never in a national daily newspaper. This's his first. Don't let the disappointments veil the triumphs, another of Schola's maxims. And over coffee, he reads the other condemning opinions on the Senator. Schola is the only dissenting opinion in the collective condemnation of the Senator. Schola feels so lonely, epistemically.

So absolved is Schola with the *Times* that he doesn't notice the persistent calls on his cellphone. Over ten missed calls from an unknown number. Luckily, the caller leaves a voice mail: "This is Senator Conner." Schola listens to the voice mail: "If this is Mr.

Priestley Schola, this is Mr Cornelius Conner. I call to thank you for your sympathetic article in the *New York Times*." The voice pauses and continues: "I understand you were recently called to the bar in the State of Indiana. I'll like to meet with you this evening. I live in Washington." Schola doesn't believe what he's hearing and misses the last part of the message. So he replays it to the end: "I'll have you flown into Washington today for dinner."

Schola sights and wonders what he has gotten himself into.

19

SCHOLA RETURNS CONNER'S CALL

CHOLA RETURNS SENATOR CONNER'S CALL after listening to the voice mail again. Schola isn't dreaming. The Senator indeed calls and looks forward to dinner with him that very day in Washington, D.C. Also revealing, the Senator offers to fly Schola over in his private jet, which apparently flies into Indianapolis, Indiana's capital, for some business and is flying back that afternoon. But the jet can make a stop in Fort Wayne for Schola to join the trip back to D.C. Now Schola knows that the Senator has private planes, including a Gulf Stream. But Schola rejects the offer on the grounds that he isn't worth detaining a private jet in Fort Wayne that is en route to D.C. This strikes the Senator as strange. Many jump at the chance of travelling on a private jet.

As a substitute, one of the Senator's assistants will touch base with Schola for his details for a ticket. Within an hour, a Ms Ananda Stokes emails Schola for his name and the time he likes to take off from Fort Wayne. And within the hour, Ms Stokes secures a first-class ticket with American Airlines scheduled to arrive in D.C. at quarter after 5:00 pm that day.

Honestly, Schola neither knows what to pack for this trip nor how long he would be in D.C. nor the purpose of the trip. But as typical of his Jesuit upbringing, he travels very light, carrying only the essentials. So in less than five minutes, a small, black carry-on bag strolls into the sitting room. Schola is ready for his flight. At this point, Schola recalls his flight three years ago—in that fateful flight from Rochester to Manhattan for that fateful meeting with his provincial, Father Cantwell, SJ. Yes, three years ago. *Tempus Fugi*! Schola inhales as he murmurs to himself in Latin: Time flies, indeed. Surely, this meeting will be nothing like the meeting with the provincial three years ago.

But the similarities of the two meetings aren't lost on Schola, nonetheless.

It dawns on Schola that his parents won't be home before he leaves for D.C. He decides to leave them a note as to his whereabouts. For the first time, he's genuinely out in the open sea as to what to tell them: Why is he going to DC? And for how long? And even where will he be staying in DC? It's reasonable to presume that they aren't even aware of his opinion in the *Times*. Schola decides on this NOTE:

Please see today's NYT page 29…. Apparently, Mr Conner read my piece and asks that I meet with him in D.C. this evening. Mr Conner bought me a ticket for the trip. Will give more details when I arrive in D.C. And see you soon. Signed, PS.

Schola is flying first class for the first time in his life. The Senator pays for this historic flight. A deplorable man in the eyes of the American prurient public pays for this historic flight. A man he knows nothing about until the past few months pays for this historic flight. A man with whom he shares the only kinship that sometimes people are wrongly accused and unfairly punished pays for this historic flight. A man he believes has a right to be heard in defense before he is set off to the gallows as the *audi alteram partem* principle of natural justice requires pays for this historic flight. A wealthy man who owns his own private jet and can afford to buy a first-class plane ticket pays for this historic flight.

Ms Stokes personally goes to the airport to welcome Schola. Schola is surprised that the beautiful, blown girl doesn't ask who he is. Instead, she says, Professor Priestley Plubriuschola, this way, the limousine is waiting. Schola is all goose at the title, professor.

He hasn't been addressed as such in three years. Some of his then students at Harvard call him Professor Schola while others – mostly the Catholics – call him Father Schola. But that's all in the past, three years ago.

Once they settle in the black limousine, Ms Stokes reveals that Schola taught her at Harvard five years ago when she was a law student. Now Schola recalls that his Jurisprudence or the Philosophy of Law for graduate students in the philosophy department attracted several law students as well. But Schola can't recollect the face of this student, Ms Ananda Stokes, now a full-grown woman in her prime. Perhaps, she was a full-grown woman then. Schola won't know, for he then—as is the case now—keeps away from women. Ms Stokes speaks very little, if at all. And Schola decides it best to also say very little, if at all. He is here to listen to Senator Conner, not talk.

The silence makes the relatively short journey from the airport to the Hyatt Hotel a bit awkward. The two aren't sitting face to face, but Schola employs one of the tactics of his priestly training–custody of the senses–to look away from the beautiful legs on the other side. Just such attractions are the cause of the fall of a lot of men. Just these kind of legs (allegedly) caused the Senator's present sad predicament. Ms Stokes realizes the unease and does her best to hide her legs. But those beautiful and exposed legs are in plain sight. And what's in plain sight is seen even without a search. Schola is forced to see what he doesn't want to see.

If Ms Stokes is irresistible while sitting, she is even more so when she walks. Schola wonders why he didn't notice her when he taught her five years ago. But that class was very large. And he was a Roman Catholic priest who did his best to avoid looking at the delicate features of women.

Thus, at the Hyatt Hotel, instead of walking ahead of Schola as the duo make their way to the room, Ms Stokes walks beside him, almost behind him. Considerate and sensible woman, Schola concludes of Ms Stokes. The elevator at the Hyatt takes them to the 8th level and Schola is ushered into room number 808. Ms Stokes leaves him and leaves her cell phone number in case Schola needs anything before dinner with the Senator at 7:00 pm.

Shortly after Ms Stokes leaves, an attendant knocks on the door and asks whether Schola needs anything before dinner. Schola, ever frugal, believes that he has indulged a lot for one day–an expensive first-class ticket, exotic food on the plane, and an expensive hotel–and so he decides that needing anything before dinner will be the very definition of gluttony, a sin. Such consumerism is a large cause of our current economic woes. Despite his refusal, the attendant returns with a trolley of bottles of wine, exotic food, and desserts and much more that Schola sees for the first time.

Schola examines the wine and is amused upon discovering that one was made about 50 years ago by monks. He chuckles at the thought of monks making wine instead of praying. Monks produce and farm all sorts of things including coffins and honey to support themselves. Work and prayer are the binary operations of the monk, both medieval and modern. While a Jesuit priest, the only wine that Schola tasted was during Mass. And that wasn't wine so to say, but the Blood of Christ. Hence, after he was defrocked, there was no need to sip wine or drink any liquor. Schola examines the rest of the content on the trolley and is amused how the rich live their lives.

But as 7:00 pm draws nigh, Schola is admittedly nervous. For the first time in his life, he meets a man despised by nearly everybody. While a priest, he heard a fair share of the acts of sinful men and women in the confession box. Very few sinners are as despicable, if the accounts making the rounds are to be believed, as the man Schola meets soon. For the first time in his life, he's heading for a meeting that makes no sense to him. As with the meeting three years ago, Schola's guts tells him that this might be a life changing encounter.

The Senator shouldn't reasonably think that a newly admitted attorney to the bar holds any keys to his tightly locked and guarded legal dungeon. A person's sympathy towards an accused doesn't save the accused from the prosecutorial claws. No, not at all. The Senator needs a seasoned, criminal, defense attorney, a criminal defense Messiah of sorts. And also, prayer, surely.

Schola is hardly a defense lawyer. He is yet to handle his first criminal case. And that first legal test cannot possibly be this one. Never. And if this is the Senator's way of thanking him for his sympathetic piece in the *Times*, then, the Senator's gratitude is expensive, a misplaced priority given his challenges. Ms Stokes's voice follows the knock on the door at about ten minutes to 7:00 pm, announcing dinner. Soon, Schola will know why he is in D.C. His first visit to the nation's capital after he graduated from law school a few months ago.

20

REACTIONS —JESUITS AND PRESIDENTS

THE JESUIT CURIA IN MANHATTAN is the nerve center of the governance of the Jesuits in New York, New Jersey, Washington, and Maryland. From the Jesuit curia in Manhattan, the provincial directs, controls, and manages the Jesuits and their missions within and outside these states. The curia doesn't miss two dailies – *The Wall Street Journal* and *The New York Times*. To competently care for their flock in the USA, the Jesuits take a daily pulse of the feelings and aspirations of the nation as reflected in its diverse publications. The *Journal* and the *Times* embody the diversity of opinions and feelings in America. But the Jesuit fathers at the curia are often so busy that they skim the papers except where a peculiar story or opinion arrests their interest, connects with their mission or informs a potential cause of action. Though some of them are addicted to columnists such as Ms Peggy Noone of the *Journal* and David Brookes of the *Times,* and so read these columnists religiously.

It's the name that first catches the attention of Father Burle O'Connor, SJ, the socius, that is, the assistant to the provincial, Father Cantwell, SJ. A Mr Priestley Schola, an attorney, authors a piece in the *Times* in support of the disgraced Senator Conner. The said author, Schola, titles his piece: "Even The Deplorables Are Presumed Innocent." This can't be former Father Schola, Father O'Connor murmurs to himself as he devours the 1,500 words piece in less than a minute.

Father O'Connor sits to ponder several lines in the article. One of which reads "all too often, we sent the innocent to the gallows only to realize our error in hastily convicting them." Another reads "many are those who are wrongly accused and continue to suffer irreparable consequences." These and similar lines occupy the thoughts of Father O'Connor who is on his way to fetch a document from the printer for the signature of Father Cantwell, the provincial.

In the other room, Father Cantwell waits for the document from Father O'Connor to append his signature. The document is scheduled to be released that afternoon. The document will announce that all DACA students in Jesuit Schools in the United States won't receive any different treatments because of their DACA status. Given the cruciality of the document, Father Cantwell doesn't understand why his top lieutenant isn't back yet with it. So he chases him to the printing room. Father Cantwell is surprised to see Father O'Connor seated ponderously on the coffee table, instead.

"Please is Father okay?" Father Cantwell announces his presence in the coffee room.

"One of our own who left us three years ago is most likely a lawyer now and writes in the *Times*, cautioning the media trial of the former senate majority leader, Mr Conner," Father O'Connor informs Father Cantwell. Quite a number of Jesuits leave the order every year, so the information isn't particularly helpful. Father Cantwell grabs the *Times* and locates Schola's name. Reads the piece and is convince that, that is their man.

After reading, Father Cantwell re-reads certain portions aloud: "all too often, we sent the innocent to the gallows," Father O'Conner interrupts him to complete the sentence "only to realize our error in hastily convicting them." Both men look at each other with one question in mind which they're afraid to ask.

Ms Harvanet brings Schola's article to the Governor's attention. The Governor reads it and is proud of the young man he considers his son. The mark of a great man is his ability to swim against all currents no matter how strong when convinced of his destination and direction. Schola has this conviction. Not afraid to incur the wrath of almost everybody in the Conner's scandal. The Governor is proud of his son. The Governor is ever grateful to his Jesuit classmate, Petrus.

The newspaper sits on the Governor's laps when the presidents start calling. First is Mr Plater Post. He tells the Governor to bring Schola to order. Schola's reckless opinion in the open might harm the reputation of the Governor if people know that Schola lives under the Governor's care and protection. The other presidents – except for Mr Koskinen Kendrew, President of Schola Oil – note that Schola's piece is very concerning. The Governor notes their concerns but says nothing. And decides to do nothing, either.

Of course, the other person besides the Governor who doesn't see Schola's piece concerning is the disgraced Senator and members of his legal team. The Senator is surprised that someone dares condemn the media trial and tersely suggests that he might be innocent. The Senator's gratitude to Schola is immense. And the Senator knows how to express his gratitude. The Senator, with unsolicited impetus from Ms Stokes, does everything to bring Schola to Washington for dinner with the lawyers on the case. The Senator intends Schola to remain an active part of his defense team. This Schola guy is one of a kind. The Senator can see greatness even in the tone of the piece. He can't wait to meet this guy with a rather curious name. The Senator often relies on his guts. His guts tells him he is right about this Schola guy.

21

MEETING

DINNER IS ON THE FIRST floor of the hotel in an exclusive executive suite. This executive suite is for the exclusive use of the Senator and his likes. To get to this classic suite, the first-time guest passes through an equally exclusive conference room. Schola is experiencing most things for the first time in his life today – flying first class, riding in a limo, staying in a five-star hotel and now dinning in an exclusive suite of a five-star hotel in D.C.

Upon entering the large suite, the Senator's loud voice beckons Schola to the right table. "Here, Mr Schola," the Senator bellows. The Senator gets up and welcomes Schola to his exclusive world with a warm, big handshake. To Schola's relief and added confusion, another man unknown to Schola dines with them as well.

"Please meet Mr Hiss McGinley, lead counsel for my current legal headaches," the Senator introduces and sits down.

"Current legal headaches," the Senator has a thing for euphemism, Schola thinks to himself and stretches his hand to greet Mr McGinley, the lead counsel.

Mr McGinley rises and greets Schola: "Professor Priestley Schola, it's great to personally meet you."

"How do you do, Mr Hiss McGinley?" Schola returns the greeting. "And please call me Schola," Schola adds.

"Please sit gentlemen," the Senator commands. "Please waiter, get our guest something to drink," the Senator calls and orders.

"And what will you drink sir?" the attendant asks of Schola."

"Some water will do, ma'am," Schola replies; and "thanks so very much," Schola adds. The perplexed waitress doesn't leave. Rather she throws a genuine, warm smile at Schola, leaving Schola even more confused.

"Schola, what the [obscenity] are you?" the Senator queries. "I hope you aren't a [obscenity] mormon?" The Senator registers his displeasure of having dinner without wine. Before Schola answers, the Senator orders: "Get the man some great wine. I'm not having dinner with a [obscenity] mormon. Go get him a bottle of wine."

Schola begins to believe that maybe the Senator doesn't need a trial to be judged guilty on account of his completely unmeasured utterances. But Schola keeps his new opinion, albeit unsupported by law, to himself.

Mr McGinley notices the salient protest on Schola's countenance and intervenes. "So, we think it will be an immense pleasure to get to know you better." Mr McGinley hints at the likely purpose of the meeting. "You graduated from law school this summer and admitted for practice last week?" More of a statement than a question from Mr McGinley.

"Yes. That pretty much sums it up." Schola replies. There's an awkward pause. Schola decides he needs to add more to the pithy introduction. But he doesn't know where to start. Schola reaches for some water to fill the awkward silence. He realizes that what's in his hand is a glass of wine. He puts it down. Reaches for the water in the vase and pours himself a glass. He takes a big sip and clears his throat.

"Yes." Schola tries to expand on his pithy self-introduction. "I graduated from law school this summer and was called to the Indiana Bar last week."

"Before law school, what did you do?" Senator Conner is impatient. His impatience notwithstanding the agreement reached with Mr McGinley to let him, Mr McGinley, do all the asking and answering.

"Before law school," Schola inhales deeply and takes another sip. "I was a priest. A Catholic priest. A Jesuit priest." The two men frown at the mention of Jesuit. Forcing Schola to take another sip. Both the Senator and Mr McGinley are in fact alumni of Jesuit colleges –Georgetown University and Boston College respectively. "Before law school, I was a professor of philosophy and ethics at Harvard. Schola takes some more water. "I taught at Harvard for five years." The two men wait patiently for Schola to reveal himself to them.

"After one of my female colleague professors accused me of sexual assault, I was defrocked and laicized and released of my priestly as well as teaching duties." The typically stoic Schola concludes, wipes suspicious drops from his eyes and asks to be excused. Schola goes to the washroom. The two men wait in silent bemusement and understanding.

His honesty and straight forwardness puzzle them. They both trust him at this instant.

Upon Schola's return, the three eat in silence. Schola declines dessert. He has had enough extravagant life for a single day to last for a year.

During dessert, Mr McGinley decides to complete the rest of Mr Schola's resume, the parts that are unknown to anybody including google. "Our checks reveal that you speak thirteen languages with two PhDs?"

Schola is taken aback. "Checks …," Schola decides not to question the questioner. Schola elaborates on the language part. "Well four of them – Latin, Greek (ancient), Hebrew, and Aramaic – aren't, strictly speaking, spoken these days – they are mainly written and read." And yes, in addition to Italian, I also speak German, Arabic, Portuguese, and Swahili." Schola feels bad about what he considers to be boosting. But is compelled to conclude: "And of course, Spanish, French, and some sort of English." The three men laugh.

Mr McGinley clarifies further: "And you also have two PhDs before you went to law school?" "Yes, I studied for a PhD in philosophy at Vanderbilt University before obtaining same in Biblical Studies from the Biblicum in Rome." And since Mr McGinley doesn't know that, in fact, Schola has a third PhD in Ethics from the Pontifical Gregorian University, Schola omits to mention his third PhD.

Mr McGinley's curiosity isn't over yet. "And you taught at Harvard for five years?"

"Yes, I taught a few courses there – undergraduate logic, Social and Political Philosophy, and Ancient Greek Philosophy. For graduate students, I offered various electives – Jurisprudence, for example ..."

"And for all summers while a law student, you worked for the ACLU who, among many things, sees to the representation of prisoners on remand without counsel?" Mr McGinley requests for confirmation again.

"Yes, it was quite an epiphany of our justice system. Our justice system presumes most accused persons guilty. And our society is even worse at that." Schola argues from his experience of working with prisoners. "It'll amaze you how many innocent people we incarcerate daily. Mostly the poor and blacks and people of color."

The Senator and Mr McGinley look at each other in utter surprise.

"Do you have a job offer or any job plans?" The Senator breaks his vow of silence again.

"Nope." Schola answers with a puff of his lips.

Dinner has been going on for two plus hours now. Ms Ananda Stokes walks to announce that another meeting is due for the Senator. Schola returns to his room. The three men will meet the next morning for breakfast at 7:00 am.

So Schola repairs to his room not any less confused than before. But before he leaves, the Senator is sure to query him. "I don't appreciate your not drinking. You didn't touch your wine. What are you, a [obscenity] bird?"

"I will do better in the future with the wine Mr Conner," Schola promises, believing that there won't be much of a next time between them.

On his way to his room, Schola is convinced that the Senator might be guilty of many things that don't need a trial for conviction. Two of which—arrogance and self-importance—Schola just experienced. Both aren't crimes in America, however. Both are, in fact, sort of very American.

22

ROOM ABOVE SCHOLA'S

MS ANANDA STOKES LIES AWAKE on a bed in room number 909 on the ninth floor of the Hyatt directly above Schola's. She can't believe what's happening.

In her third year of law school, she enrolls in a certain Father Priestley Schola's jurisprudence course after she couldn't help her attraction for him. As a Mass-going Catholic, Ms Stokes has been a consistent congregant of the St. Aquinas Church on campus – the Catholic campus ministry at Harvard. She likes Father Schola's homilies: Reflective, intellectual, yet pulses with the daily struggles of students, staff, and faculty. And his brilliant homilies are delivered in the best of voices: His deep baritone and evenness of tone can move even the devil.

Ms Stokes' emotional crush on Father Schola is intense. She sleeps thinking about him. Wakes up thinking about him. But because priest can't marry or even have normal dates, Ms Stokes keeps her feelings to herself. What else could she have done?

In one of his homilies, Father Schola says he never asks God of something which is refused him. And when God doesn't grant him what he pleads for, Schola preaches, it's because God gives him something far better instead. There, Father Schola challenges his congregants to humbly ask of God something that they have been deeply desiring. There and then, Ms Stokes asks of God to give her Father Schola as a husband. Ms Stokes laughs her wish off. Even the almighty God can't fulfil this one. Do it if you are indeed God, she dares God. Let me marry this priest.

That semester of her unusual wish, Father Schola goes missing at Harvard. Stories about his whereabouts are varied and even at odds. Some say he is in Rome. Others that he is somewhere in Africa–for Schola loves African and was in Ghana for three years as a seminarian. Others that he is in Jerusalem where he once did some research. And still others that he isn't a priest any longer.

Today, after graduating from law school and practicing law for almost four years, Ms Stokes sees an article in defense of a repugnant client that her firm represents. Ms Stokes can't believe the author is his former priest-professor crush–Schola. She shows the article to Mr McGinley, the lead attorney in the case. Mr McGinley is rather incurious. For such lonely and lame sympathies for his client won't bear on the eventual outcome of the trial.

Ms Stokes makes the decision of her life. She sends the article to Senator Conner. The Senator has already seen it but can't think of anything besides that a citizen's view happens to be sympathetic to his cause. But Ms Stokes convinces the Senator to bring Schola on his defense team. The Senator is amused. The Senator re-reads Schola's piece and his guts tells him that Schola is tied to his legal fate. Schola flies in from Fort Wayne to be acquainted with the team.

Now, the priest she falls in love with while in school and is still very much in love with lies on a bed directly below hers. He's no longer a priest. He's now an attorney like her. Now a man free to marry. And a brave man at that. Not afraid to swim against the strongest currents. The sort of man that Ms Stokes likes for a husband.

Never put the Lord your God to the test. Ms Stokes is very keen in seeing how God will prove her wrong. Tonight, like so many nights when she was a student and like every night after reading Schola's piece in the *Times*, she wishes she was sleeping on the same bed with Schola. Their faces facing, their breaths breathing in unison and their legs touching. Ms Stokes eventually falls asleep in tears and an unsatiable desire for Schola.

23

EXAMEN IN D.C.

ND THUS, SCHOLA FINISHES AN unusual day more confused than it starts. He doesn't know what to tell his parents. He sends this text:

"Met with Senator Conner and Mr MeGinley (a member of his legal team). I still have no idea why he invited me to Washington. Meets with them tomorrow morning and heads back ASAP. Miss you guys."

Schola is a man of routine – a habit formed from his astute formation as a Jesuit and years of the discipline of a priestly life as well as years of teaching at Harvard. Having departed both professions–in fact both callings–, Schola hasn't given up the quotidian routine his vocations inculcate in him. Each day is scheduled the night before and each minute of the next day executed exactly according to the schedule. No major deviations. A schedule helps to stay your course and attend to only that, which is important amid the competing minor distractions of modern life.

Schola starts today with a workout at the Farm gym at 5:00 am. Wash up follows the workout. Prayer. Then breakfast of coffee and an apple. He goes over the newspapers during breakfast. Most of the day these days is spent in the library reading and researching as well as on the farm sweating away. Dinner is with his parents. The Scholas value their evening meal together. It is a family tradition.

As a man of great faith and still a Jesuit at heart, Schola is faithful to the Jesuit practice of examination of conscience. Schola does the examen twice daily. The first examen is done in the quiet part of the family library at about noon and the last just before he sleeps.

The unexpected trip to D.C. intrudes into this sacred routine. Adds to the fact that Schola desists the noise of big cities, he can't wait for morning to arrive. He can't wait to leave D.C.

With three hours to midnight, his bedtime, he does three things. First, he turns on the news channels on the TV in his room. CNN, Fox News, and MSNBC. All covering the same topics but with different interpretations of the events. Sometimes with different facts from the same events. Amazing! It's as if Senator Daniel Patrick Moynikan of New York never existed or America never heard of Mohiyan's admonition that "everyone is entitled to his own opinion, but not his own facts." Schola can't stand the media partisanship.

Schola decides to read instead. When he travels, he packs more books than any other articles. Today is no exception. Schola comes with a couple of books — as always, he has the complete works of Plato by John Cooper (quite a volume), Killing England by Bill O'Reilly and Martin Dugard, and the Federalist Papers.

Which one does he read? He settles on the Federalist Papers.

All too soon, Schola is surprised it's almost midnight. He closes his book and before he closes his eyes for the day, he prays the examen.

St. Ignatius of Loyola requires the examen—twice daily—for every Jesuit and anybody really. It's a prayer that spans five to fifteen minutes. The examenee goes over the events of the day. Takes note of where he or she feels the presence of the Lord. It's not a mental catalogue of the events under review than as it's more of recognizing the presence of God at some point in the period under review. The examenee also takes note of where he or she might have drifted away from God, failing to cooperate with God's grace. Finally, the examenee ends in gratitude for God's love and grace.

Where was God in this day for Schola? Throughout the fifteen minutes prayer period, Schola struggles to suppress thinking about Ms Stokes. It is soothing thinking about Ms Stokes. It isn't her beautiful, long legs. Nor her radiant face. There's something about that young woman. His former student, she tells him. But Schola doesn't remember her.

Schola gives up putting out Ms Stokes from his mind. He allows his desires of Ms Stokes to color his examen. He fails to concentrate in prayer. Schola asks for God's grace not to be preoccupied with the thoughts of this beautiful woman. But is God listening? Or is that exactly what God wants of him?

A day that started very ordinary in Fort Wayne for Schola ends in a plush hotel in D.C. Schola is more comfortable with that which he plans. Schola is uncomfortable with this day; he didn't plan for it. But he accepts life as it unfolds, even with gratitude.

So Schola goes to bed very grateful for the day. But still thinking about the young woman. Schola doesn't realize how close she is to him—both physically and emotionally. If the ceiling just above Schola were to carve in, Ms Stokes will fall directly on Schola. But the ceiling separating the two will stay in place. For now.

24

MORNING IN DC

S CHOLA WAKES UP TWO HOURS before the 7:00 am breakfast. For the first time, he thinks he should've brought his physical workout outfit to D.C. But the suddenness of the summon compels a lighter than usual travel. There sure is a gym in the Hyatt. If only he had brought a workout suit. But Schola is ever committed to physical workout and doesn't miss a day. So he improvises.

Schola does some push-ups, sit-ups, and some imaginal skipping with an imaginal rope. Soon enough, forty-five minutes elapse with him panting from the brisk exercises. He baths. He meditates for a while and returns to his books. All this while, he wonders what he's doing in D.C.

At five minutes past seven, the ever radiant Ms Stokes summons Schola to breakfast. Schola's heart skips a beat upon seeing her. But Schola dismisses the feeling as a natural effect of Ms Stokes's natural beauty. The two walk down for breakfast in silence. But there's fire in the air when their eyes meet, which is more often than the two plan. Soon Schola joins the Senator and Mr McGinley.

The Senator looks tired and pale, Schola observes over breakfast. So he is less talkative—which is a good thing. But Schola knows what he's going through.

After the three men journey well into their elaborate breakfast of coffee, pancakes, scrambled eggs, fruits and much more, Mr McGinley breaks the silence. "As you're aware, Mr Conner has some legal challenges that my firm is working on." Mr McGinley takes some more bites of his scrambled eggs and continues. "My firm will like you to work with us on some of the issues. Given your relative youth at the bar and freshness since you are just out of law school, we expect you to scrutinize the details, raise questions, and provide legal solutions and strategies for the unexpected," Mr McGinley concludes. There's a long pause.

"I see," Schola finally breaks the awkward silence. Schola stops eating, takes a deep breath and looks far away. "I see," Schola says again. "Thanks a lot for the offer, but I'm not sure that I'll be of much use to the legal challenges given my relative youth at the bar as you mentioned and my general incuriosity of criminal law," Schola answers.

Senator Conner is incredulous. "I thought you are jobless?" The Senator asks in bafflement.

Mr McGinley cuts him short before he offers any more unhelpful opinion. "Sure Mr Schola," Mr McGinley clears his throat before continuing. "As I said, given your relative youth at the bar, we don't expect you to handle anything intimidating. Just some research and your opinion. You'll be the eye of the outsider. We really would like to have you. Please think it over again and get back to us. But as you know, we don't have time." There's another long pause. The Senator is doing well this morning, Mr. McGinley thinks. So far he is saying very little. So the silence continues.

"As you know," Mr McGinley continues, "the grand jury has paved the way for the prosecution to bring charges." Mr McGinley inhales loudly, "our checks reveal that the prosecution is ready to file formal charges anytime – even today." This surprises Schola, but he keeps quiet and listens. "So we must be ready. And we'll really like you to be part of this. We believe you'll make a vital contribution."

"It's preferred that you make up your mind before noon today," Mr McGinley gives the deadline. Schola is rattled a bit, for he is thinking of days or even weeks to decide.

The Senator is done being a morning monk all this while. "I'm going to pay you well." The Senator adds in the belief that he's aiding the cause of getting Schola to join his legal team with the offer of money. But Schola smiles pitifully at the rich Senator. Apparently, the Senator hasn't encountered people for whom money isn't a prime factor in making important decisions no matter how impoverished they're. And the rich Senator apparently doesn't know that Schola lives under the roof and protection of a man far richer than the Senator.

"*Carpe diem*," Schola murmurs and pushes his chair backwards. Take on the day, Schola repeats his Latin phrase in English. "Since I have a few hours to make up my mind, I better get started. I'll get back to you at noon," Schola informs them, already on his feet and on the move.

"We believe that you'll be of enormous contribution, Mr Schola. And the Senator likes you especially," Mr McGinley adds.

"Thanks a lot for breakfast gentlemen, I'll get back to you with my decision." Schola shakes their hands and leaves for his room.

25

CONSIDERING THE OFFER

BACK IN HIS LUXURIOUS HOTEL room, Schola paces up and down beside his bed, remakes his bed, rearranges the few books and articles on the table. He must make a consequential decision in a matter of hours. "Is representing Senator Conner, a man everyone despises, a wise thing to kick start one's legal career?" This question confronts Schola. An answer is needed before noon.

Schola's decision will affect others, too. As the College of Presidents argues, —and with fine points, too—an association of anyone with a link to the Schola Group with the fallen and disgraced Senator taints the Schola Group. The College is proud of its emphasis on morality that waves every thread of its business operations. Hence, the Schola Group or its members can't be seen to be aligned with a colossal moral failure, much less a criminal such as Senator Conner, if allegedly.

But the Governor doesn't care what Schola does as long as Schola is happy. The Governor gives Schola a carte blanch to operate. But Schola appreciates the practical judgment of the Dean of the College of Presidents stance on the matter. Schola is cautious.

It amazes Schola that Mr McGinley and his law firm hasn't discovered his link to the Schola Group and the Governor. Not yet. But Schola isn't altogether surprise at the same time because he never exploits his connection to the Schola Group or the Governor for any gains. For as the Dean of the College, Dr Devlin

Dingell, rightly notes, it won't be long before everybody knows that Schola lives under the protection of the Governor.

But for Schola as is the same for the Governor, this expected negative reaction isn't dispositive of Schola's engagements vis-a-vis Senator Conner.

The Jesuit that he ever is, Schola subjects the question – whether he should have any involvement in the unfolding scandal around Senator Conner–to discernment.

St. Ignatius of Loyola, the founder of the Jesuits, calls the process of coming to a major decision in life – marriage, career choices, – discernment. According to Ignatius, there are two types of discernments.

For the first kind, the path to follow is so clear that there is no need to decide otherwise. Every sign points in a particular direction, and the person is overwhelmingly so convinced that there is no need to further ponder an alternative course of action. Ignatius cites the conversion of Saul on his way to Damascus as typical of the first kind of discernment. After lightning strikes Saul, he gives up his old ways and becomes a new person, a Christian, now an ardent member of the group that he persecuted in his former life. Taking the new name Paul, he zealously preaches the gospel.

In the second type of discernment, however, there are so many competing and unclear options before a person. And it isn't immediately apparent to the person, which of the competing options is best. This second type of discernment often requires more time, more prayer, more consultation and more listening. It depends on the light and grace of God for resolution. Obviously, it requires more than a few hours to arrive at the best choice.

Schola faces this second kind of discernment. Unfortunately for him, he must come to a decision in a matter of few hours. Schola can't comprehensively consult anyone.

In any event, where the choice of a consequential decision isn't apparent, a person must consider the pros and cons of the decision very carefully. It is a balancing act that takes into consideration the totality of the circumstances. The cons of having a part in the legal representation of Mr Conner are palpable to any lawyer.

Everybody despises the man. The White House prevails on him to resign his position as majority leader and the GOP forces him to vacate his senate seat. Politicians whose campaigns Senator Conner funds regret publicly for ever accepting money from him. Some of them returns his donations. He earns some of the most horrible names in the media. Women groups protest and rally against him. The prosecution is in a hurry to lock him up. Even his wife, according to some reports, is filing for a divorce. This isn't a man to associate with, at least, not now, and perhaps, never.

Schola knows that there's a big difference between arguing for the constitutional rights of a citizen like Senator Conner, as Schola does in the *Times*, and representing him in court and defending his innocence. Schola thinks about the safety of innocent women. Sure, Senator Conner shouldn't be set free to pry upon harmless girls and women if indeed he's a pervert as widely believed.

And a further con against representing Mr Conner is competence. The model rules of professional conduct for lawyers require that a lawyer accepts to represent a client only if the lawyer deems himself competent to do so. Just out of law school, Schola doesn't have the competence to deal with such a high-profile criminal case with national, even international traction.

Competence is also implied where even though a lawyer is competent in skills and experience, the conduct of the client is "so repugnant to the lawyer as to be likely to impair the lawyer-client relationship or the lawyer's ability to represent the client." By all counts, like most people, Schola can't believe that Senator Conner did the things that over two hundred women are accusing him of. Senator Conner's conduct nauseates Scola, and not mildly.

These are the cons of accepting a role in Senator Conner's defense team. There are few pros, however. First, everyone is deserting the poor man. The sinner, no matter how horrible, is still a child of God. God hates the sin but loves the sinner is a phrase that then Father Schola used severally as a Jesuit priest. Even the worst of sinners must not be shunned simply because of the sins.

Second, accepting a role in Senator Conner's defense team gives Schola some experience in criminal defense. Luckily, the Governor houses and feeds Schola. The Governor is happy that he caters for Schola's needs. The Governor bears all the expenses of Schola's legal education. So while new lawyers are reeling under their student debts and loans, Schola's only debt is gratitude to the Governor, albeit a huge debt than any student debt. The Governor's one regret is that Schola is too frugal, like him. The Governor isn't too sure whether schola's frugality is out of sensitivity to his generosity. The wise doesn't abuse the generosity of the donor. But Schola could use some experience from being part of Senator Conner's defense. Schola is currently jobless, though he knows that he can get a position in any of the Governor's business outfits.

And finally, Senator Conner might be innocent. Many a widely believed guilty persons have been proven innocent. The case law is overwhelming on instances of wrongful convictions. The testimonies of the over two hundred accusers don't make this point any less probably. For "a multitude of suspicions put together" should not constitute searing proof.

So after an hour of pacing and pondering, Schola decides to join Senator Conner's legal team. Since his role is ministerial, merely research and nothing more, he accepts. After all, a lawyer isn't called to the bar to defend only the innocent. Now and then, an unpopular case falls on your desk, the professors of legal ethics teach in law school. These repugnant clients, too, must be represented with diligence and the utmost zeal. Schola thus decides to start his trial experience with an unpopular client.

But Schola attaches a condition to his acceptance. Schola doesn't communicate this condition to either the Senator or Mr McGinley. He will work on the case pro bono. But telling Mr Conner now won't help matters. Schola's condition would appear to be a further voice in the ongoing condemnation of the man. And it borders on self-righteousness, besides. But no money for Schola for this work for the Senator's defense.

26

SCHOLA JOINS DEFENSE TEAM

MR MCGINLEY WELCOMES SCHOLA TO the Senator's defense team. Mr McGinley briefs Schola on the nature and varieties of Senator Conner's legal hurdles. Until now, Schola thinks of the Senator's legal problem as one – the expected indictment of sexual harassment against him. No. Mr McGinley and the defense team are dealing with others. But the sexual harassment case is enormous, compare with the rest, and properly earns the name his legal problem. The stakes, here, are too high.

The Ms Larnage Pincus's case against the Senator, which is in the public, and of, which the prosecution thinks a conviction is a given, is the one the media and everyone is talking about. The prosecution convenes a grand jury whose conclusions reinforce the prosecution's firm conviction that a conviction is a sealed deal. But a date for the commencement of trial is yet to be set. Meantime, the prosecution names a litany of charges against the Senator including false imprisonment, assault, battery, concealing crimes, aggravated rape and other damnable crimes of the sexual family.

In addition to Ms Pincus's allegations are five other women parroting in the media, attributing various kinds of sexual harms to the Senator. It remains to be seen whether the prosecution will build a case on their stories against the Senator. First on the list is a Ms Raiser Forman who claims that Mr Conner, without her consent, tried undoing her pants on a flight. The two were apparently seated together in the said flight from New York to

D.C. This was over a decade ago. Ms Forman fails to report the case but is singing now because of the numerous outcries against the Senator. Ms Forman has family members and friends whom he confided in hours after the incident, and they are willing to corroborate her account.

The second is a former aid of the Senator, Ms Meldrum Leviero. She claims that while working for Mr Conner ten years ago, he directed depraving sexual conduct towards her. Mr Conner is also alleged to have groped her behind and front on numerous occasions. And on a few occasions, while others were gone home, he asked her to wait behind. She was invited to Mr Conner's office, with the door closed, he pinned her to the wall and had his way with her. All against her consent.

The third is a Ms Josefina Killian who sought employment at one of Mr Conner's company years ago. She couldn't get the job. During the job inquiry, Mr Conner invited her for a movie after which he drove her home. While she was about to get out of the car, Mr Conner attempted planting a kiss directly on her month which she repelled. After that incident, she was discouraged from moving forward with hopes of getting a job from Mr Conner's company.

The last two accusers are employees of an escort outfit. They both claim that on various occasions, Mr Conner requested and made use of their services. The claims are very similar: When Mr Conner is about to travel for business, he contacts them. They send their girl way in advance of the trip to check into a hotel. Mr Conner will join the girl in the hotel and take care of business both in the business world and in the hotel room, nailing, thus, two businesses with one stone. These two escorts are Ms Varina Tall and Ms Wapplier Vinson.

"Have these accusers contacted the DA office yet?" Schola asks.

"No," Mr McGinley replies. But all are threatening to cooperate with the prosecution.

"So why are they not cooperating yet?" Schola asks.

"Ahh…" Mr McGinley fumbles. "Because our client doesn't want any more stories in the public about him on this. The stories are really having a dramatic effect on him. So I have contacted them and we are talking settlement."

"I see," Schola replies, feigning agreement to the settlement.

The second biggest legal challenge is that the other two shareholders of Mr Conner's company want to buy him out. It's a closed corporation, and because of the negative name that the Senator now earns, it reflects badly on the company. So they want Mr Conner gone.

"How many shareholders are there?" Schola asks.

"Three. And the other two have teamed up against our client." Mr McGinley answers.

"Two against one, aah?" Schola whispers.

"Yes, they have a clear majority," Mr McGinley emphasizes the obvious.

"And the third thing that the Senator likes to see you particularly get involved is his divorce," Mr McGinley continues.

"Divorce!" Schola exclaims. "I thought the wife was giving him all the support?" Schola asks in confusion.

"Yes, but the continuous drib and drab has gotten into her skin, and now she wants out. She has already prepared a divorce petition and is asking for our client's signature," Mr McGinley says, pushing a big white envelope toward Schola.

Schola looks at the bulky envelope in amazement and chuckles: "I'm not the one she is divorcing, what do you want me to do with this?" Schola says laughing. But Mr McGinley doesn't share Schola's little amusement and remains stoic.

A divorce as Schola recalls from his Domestic Relations class in law school is a simple matter. Really. Once the once love birds are tired and parting ways, all they need is a court's signature. Nothing more.

"The divorce should be a straightforward case," Mr McGinley says. Schola shares his view. "After sixty days of filing the divorce petition, the judge certifies the papers and the marriage is over." Mr McGinley appears to conclude. But adds. "Yes, where there aren't issues of child custody, alimony, or division of the marital property, a divorce is simple," Mr McGinley explains. "In our client's case, the wife wants alimony and wants to set aside the premarital agreement." Mr McGinley inhales deeply and continues, "If she succeeds, this is a potential loss of a lot of money to our client."

"Besides, it's unfair if the pre-marital agreement is valid," Schola adds.

Schola immediately understands the enormity of the situation. If the court nullifies the premarital agreement the spouse will each take half of Mr Conner's entire property according to Indiana State law. Thus, given the Senator's net worth, the divorce is potentially more damming than the settlements with the five unknown accusers.

"I'll personally like you to go over the divorce papers and come out with a viable legal strategy." Mr McGinley tasks Scola. "We are scheduled to meet with her next week in Fort Wayne where she lives. Here are her lawyer's details," Mr McGinley says handing Schola a card. "Next week is preliminary talks, but I want a potent strategy when I walk into that meeting." Mr McGinley reiterates his demand of his new associate.

"My firm has offices in Indianapolis, Indiana, but none in Fort Wayne," Mr McGinley informs Schola. "We will open a temporary office in Fort Wayne for purposes of handling the divorce," Mr McGinley reveals. "You will be in charge of that office and will be able to hire a paralegal," Mr McGinley finishes.

The man with nothing to do yesterday suddenly has his hands full. And he must get out of D.C. and get to work!

27

TEMPORARY OFFICE

CHOLA IS BACK IN FORT Wayne from D.C. that very evening. Schola is already in his own office the following morning. The speed with which Mr McGinley acquires a temporary office in Fort Wayne impresses Schola. Money can sometimes work miracles. Schola's office sits on the fourteenth floor of the Lincoln Building adjacent the Allen County public library – right in the center of downtown. It's a two in one office room. The assistant's office leads into a much spacious room, Schola's office.

Schola steps into his office and walks to the widow and looks: first up, and then, down. The Lincoln Building is the tallest building in Fort Wayne. It houses many other businesses and entities. Schola looks down and sees people promenading the streets. Folks are enjoying the beautiful sunny summer, given the previous wild winter. Temperatures are steaming. Traffic is quite low, but quite a few cars are busy on the streets as are the human beings. Schola thinks to himself. This is about the highest floor that he maintains an office on. His Harvard office was on the second floor. It's a lofty feeling to be stationed almost above everybody. Schola feels on top. Momentarily.

Schola wanders out of his office into his assistance's –a table, with phone lines, a copy machine, fax, cabinets and all sorts of stationary are installed. Schola chuckles and wonders why he needs an assistant.

Life is sometimes unpredictable. Two days ago, he was jobless. Now, he has a job. And he has the power to hire someone.

Besides the feeling of not needing an assistant–and therefore not advertising and searching for one–, Schola wonders what kind of resumé qualifies a job seeker for his assistant's office he now stands. An assistant can wait. Now, Schola has a job to do for Mr McGinley: "Look over the divorce papers and recommend a potent legal strategy out of the divorce that is meritorious to our client."

Schola reenters his office, sits on his chair–for the first time– and brings out Mr Conner's divorce papers. "What? This guy is getting divorced for the third time?" Schola murmurs to himself. There is the divorce petition that Mr Conner's wife signs but which the Senator is yet to sign. Usually, in divorce proceedings in the State of Indiana, this is all the couple need to do—sign the divorce petition. After sixty days, a judge signs off on their petition and wishes the estranged persons well. Simple. The only reason required for a divorce in Indiana is the nebulous ground of irretrievable differences–whatever that means. And the family law courts don't appear to care what that means.

But a divorce proceeding becomes complex when there are contentions regarding custody of the children, division of the marital property, and of course, spousal maintenance or alimony. When these other sensitive issues are involved in a divorce, the hearing may be long, often leaving the couple with hefty legal fees. Schola knows this from his Domestic Relations course, which he took with keen interest in law school even though he has never married and currently has no reason to think that he would ever marry. The marriage institution has always fascinated Schola, though.

Schola puts aside the divorce petition and turns to the petition for spousal maintenance. Schola gives the petition a quick read and thinks to himself: It's likely to be denied if the Senator were a regular guy. But with what women have accused him of, are accusing him of, and probably would accuse him of, Schola won't be surprised if a judge awards alimony to Mrs Conner. After all, Mrs Conner is the unfortunate victim of the insatiable sexual appetite of a morally bankrupt husband.

Spousal maintenance—or alimony as other jurisdictions call it—is awarded on certain grounds. One is where a former spouse is physical or mentally handicapped and needs special care. Another ground is if a child born of the marriage is handicapped and the spouse seeking maintenance is the custodial parent, i.e., the child lives with this parent.

Apart from a handicapped spouse or child, a court may also ground vocational alimony. Here, at the time of the divorce a spouse is still in school or undergoing some vocational training. The court may allow spousal maintenance in such situation up to three years.

And the court will finally ground spousal maintenance where doing so is just and equitable given the circumstances of the parties.

None of these grounds exists in the case on Schola's desk. Ordinarily, Mr Conner's wife's motion should be thrown out. But Mr Conner isn't an ordinary party to a divorce petition. He is the symbol of male sexual perversity. Everybody hates this guy. The family law court won't be the exception.

Nonetheless, the law should treat all equally. So Schola recommends a motion for summary judgment on the issue of spousal maintenance. For no sane jury will grand maintenance, and the material issues against spousal maintenance are not at all in dispute.

Schola turns to the third, final, and potentially the most contentions of the claims—the motion to set aside the premarital agreement. The preamble ... But before Schola reads any further, the sound of the phone in his assistant's office rattles him. For a second, he doesn't know what to do. But eventually comes to his senses and goes in to answer.

"Hello," Schola speaks with a mild tone not sure who is on the other side.

"Hello, Mr Schola, I see you are already in your office," Mr McGinley begins.

"Yes, I came in this morning," Schola replies. "Beautiful office and nice view," Schola says gratefully.

"Thanks. We would give you anything you need. Just calling to make sure that you are okay out there. Mr Conner insisted on it," Mr McGinley says.

"Well, thanks," Schola says. Schola looks around and continues, "everything looks perfect in here."

"Happy to hear that Mr Schola. Please give me a call if you need anything," Mr McGinley says.

"Sure will," Schola replies. There's a brief silence and the line goes silent.

28

PRE-MARITAL AGREEMENT

SCHOLA HANGS UP THE PHONE and returns to his seat. He looks at his watch. About five minutes to eight in the morning. Schola wonders whether Mr McGinley is already in his office, too. In fact, Schola comes in earlier, leaving the Farm around 6:30 am, getting to the building about half an hour later. But the Lincoln Building is still locked when he gets there. He waits for close to an hour before he gets in. Schola isn't issued a card key to the building yet. Schola should be receiving a key card to the building by noon today according to security.

Schola looks at the legal documents in front of him. He retrieves the divorce petition, puts it under the motion for spousal maintenance and puts both away. Schola doesn't think that the Senator should sign the divorce petition now. Schola returns to the premarital agreement.

A premarital agreement is essentially a contract between two partners before marriage. A premarital agreement governs, largely, the division of property upon separation or divorce or death. A premarital agreement may cover any subject matter except child support and spousal maintenance.

A valid premarital agreement must be in writing, which both parties sign. Schola looks over the entire paper and sees that it's in writing. Schola scans the bottom pages and is happy to see the signature of both parties.

A crucial element of a premarital agreement is that it must be voluntary. No party must be coerced or forced into signing a premarital agreement. In assessing the voluntariness of a premarital agreement, courts look to a range of factors. One of them is whether a party, especially, the party seeking to set aside the agreement was unrepresented by counsel. Schola looks for who Mrs Conner's counsel was but sees none. Schola is agitated. The Senator was represented by Mr McGinley's firm. But Schola is surprised that the Senator (or the firm for that matter) didn't insist that Mrs Conner got a lawyer. This defect may deal a blow to a motion to decline to enforce the agreement.

Another vital thing, probably, the often-cited ground for nullifying premarital agreements, is that the parties must declare all their assets. Schola looks at the Senator's assets and isn't supposed to be surprised, but he is. The assets run into five pages divided into sections of real property, shares and stocks, holdings, businesses, cars, and annual income. Schola is surprised to discover that the Senator owns more than one Gulf Stream. This man is wealthy, Schola almost shouts to himself.

Schola puts down the agreement and ponders. But if the Senator intentionally or unintentionally left out as much as a single asset, the entire premarital agreement is off. It then occurs to Schola that he should consider the grounds for the motion to set aside the agreement.

It's in the third paragraph, a one-page motion – Mrs Conner wasn't aware of what she was signing, the motion claims. This most likely means that Mrs Conner is willing to argue that she should have had a lawyer. Schola almost rushes to the phone next room to ask Mr McGinley why the Senator's wife never had a lawyer. Schola gets up and decides to wait and finish the whole review first. At this point, the door rattles with a knock. Schola is compelled to answer the door. He probably needs an assistant, he murmurs.

Just a moment please, Schola says. Schola carefully picks up the papers, puts them inside his top drawer and goes to the door. Schola barely gets there when the security woman extends her hand. "I bring your key card to the building." The security woman says, handing what is Schola's picture on an ID. It opens the door at all times. You can come in at any time.

"I'm sorry, I don't have a key card for your assistant yet because I'm yet to get her particulars," the security woman apologizes.

"Or his particulars," Schola corrects, and the two laugh.

"I'm sorry about that. The assistants here are all females," the security woman explains.

"Good point, I'll make sure I get a female assistant also," Schola promises and the two laugh again.

The security woman further hands Schola two pairs of keys. One to the door of his assistant and the second to Schola's own office. "Please if you need anything that we can be of help, don't hesitant to contact the security office," the security woman advises. "I'll be sure to do so," Schola replies and with that he was back to finding a viable path to resolving the divorce petition in the Senator's favor.

Schola decides he won't be needing an assistant for various reasons. One, the job is temporary. Schola isn't sure how long it will last, but Mr McGinley is not thinking of maintaining a permanent office in Fort Wayne. So anybody hired will have to look for another job after the brief period. And two, what really will an assistant be doing? Schola wonders.

Another knock on the door, the second time this morning. Yes, Schola says looking up.

"I'm looking for the insurance company, the middle age woman explains," startling Schola. "Not here, I'm sorry," Schola replies.

"But do you know where I can locate them," the woman continues. "The security says they are up on this floor."

"I'm sorry," Schola says, "I just started today and barely know my way around." The woman leaves.

With these unwanted disruptions, Schola decides he might

need an assistant after all, if anything, to attend to lost people and answer the door. Schola has never hired anybody in his life—except recruiting candidates to the Jesuit priesthood. And a candidate to the Jesuit priesthood and a candidate for a paralegal job couldn't have been worlds apart.

For the first time, he realizes that even though he decides not to be paid, he hasn't discussed fees with Mr McGinley or the Senator. And if he were to hire someone, how much will he set the person's wages? Schola wonders.

These minute matters must wait for now. Schola intends to give Mr McGinley a viable legal strategy on the divorce case and its attendant issues. Schola gets back to work on getting the court to stay the premarital agreement.

29

PROSECUTOR LUCILLE KAST

EANTIME, AT THE STATE ATTORNEY'S office, Prosecutor Lucille Kast, the Chief Prosecutor of Allen County, is an exultant woman for several reasons. The first is the uproar in sexual accusations against high profile men. The sexual harassment claims have been growing and growing, each new allegation revealing almost the same pattern of sexual misconduct but a different high-placed man heading for the gallops. This means that Ms Kast is constantly in the media. A constant media present boosts her profile as a prosecutor, both locally and nationally.

Prosecutor Kast is especially happy because Senator Conner is by all counts the very face of sexual misconduct in Indiana. While the accusations against most men is attenuated and, therefore, likely to be thrown out before a jury deliberates, the case against Senator Conner is air-tight from different prosecutorial angles. Of the two hundred plus women accusing Senator Conner, Prosecutor Kast thinks that she has finally built a winning case against the Senator on one victim.

Ms Pincus is the perfect victim in the Prosecutor's eyes. She is a successful career woman and therefore has no financial interest in leveling any frivolous claims against the Senator. More important, Ms Pincus's case isn't statute bar. Most of the other allegations are too old, some over thirty years ago. Some are purely she says, he says. Lots of hearsays.

The prosecution office does a background check on Ms Pincus and finds no damaging behaviors that might kill her claims at trial, especially, if she is subjected to cross examination.

The other victims have made similar allegations against other men in the past. Few of them had their allegations sent to trial only to be crushed. Others have very questionable lives. A conservative state like Indiana looks less favorably, for example, on a woman who is divorced several times. Or a woman who has never married and has been living single all her life. Ms Pincus shares none of these defects. She has been married once.

In addition, Ms Pincus is stunningly beautiful. She is a traffic stopper. Most men stop to have at least a look. Thus many won't dispute that many a man may want to have a little bit of her. She is absolutely believable even in looks. She is a natural beauty.

Ms Kast is amused that looks play a crucial role in these sexual harassment trials. In Ms Kast's view, it shouldn't matter. After all, men are attracted to different women, sexually and otherwise, for a variety of reasons. But for most people, the less beautiful you are, the less likely that a man will sexually harass you. As one of the accused said: "Please look at me and look at that woman. Do you think I'll like to shake her hands?" The same reckless and brazenly fallacious argument can't be made against Ms Pincus. Yes, every man would like to hug her.

A further strength in Prosecutor Kast's case is that the Senator is guilty in the eyes of everyone even before trial. His wife says she is embarrassed and tired of the tireless accusations. She seeks a divorce. The Senator's business associates are disassociating themselves from him. Many news outlets have rejected adverting the Senator's businesses. There are unconfirmed reports that the long-time law firm of the Senator is threatening to cut ties with him given the harm and embarrassment that he has caused. The truth is that other clients of this firm vow to take their cases to other firms if the firm continues to represent the Senator. The

Senator is already guilty. The trial, in Ms Kast's view, is a mere formality.

To crown it all, the GOP majority in the Senate compels him to resign.

There is another reason that Ms Kast is excited. Elections are around the corner. A win in this case will surely warrant that she retains her office. And as far as politics goes, the top echelons are watching this case closely. A win will guarantee her moving up the ladder of her career: a converted judgeship or Solicitor-General of the United States.

The stakes are very high here. So Ms Kast assembles only the best in the prosecutor's office. Ms Kast keeps the file on the Senator under lock. She will be leading the trial. She heads the investigation, noting every detail. More crucial for her, nobody will be taking the credit for an eventual win. For this, she is the one doing all the TV announcements and appearances on the Senator's case.

And finally, the grand jury, quickly assembled a week ago, has indicted the Senator. How couldn't they? Sexually harassing women has been the long-time achievement of the Senator. It appears from the prevailing account that for the past thirty years, there has never been a day without the Senator pulling a woman from the street, pinning her to the wall, and having his way with her. The average person in the street believes that is what the Senator does. Prosecutor Kast intends to make the court and jury believe same. The Prosecutor's case couldn't have been simpler.

Like everybody, Prosecutor Kast believes that the Senator is a danger to society and must be put away. Also, with the growing number of cases, the public is longing for a form of retribution. Someone must pay to assuage the public anger. The Senator is the perfect scapegoat. Ms Kast looks at the evidence in front of her again. She is convinced that the Senator is going to jail. So convinced is she that she has ruled out any talks of settlement with the Senator. Mr McGinley the Senator's lead lawyer has been begging for settlements. Her answer – NO.

But more important for Ms Kast: This is a career improving case. Thanks to Senator Cornelius Conner Jr.!

30

PRESS CONFERENCES

SCHOLA WAKES UP TODAY EXPECTING a normal day in his ordinary involvement in the Senator's rather extraordinary legal spectacle. The hour of exercise—involving thirty minutes of running and thirty minutes of weight-lifting—follows another hour of silence – involving praying, reflecting, and meditating.

Schola looks up his schedule for the day upon reaching his office in the Lincoln Building. The major event is polishing up his legal strategy on the Senator's divorce case for Mr McGinley. But as the old saying goes: "We plan; God laughs."

The normal day takes an unexpected turn when Ms Harvanet calls and asks Schola to turn on his office TV. Schola fumbles with the TV remote for a while. This is after struggling to locate the TV. Schola remembers seeing the TV yesterday. Then, Schola concludes he'll never have a reason to ever turn it on.

After what seems like a century of punching the remote, Fox News, Schola's preferred channel, comes live on the screen. The Allen County Prosecutor is giving a press conference, one of many since the grand jury indicted Senator Corner. Prosecutor Kasts rumbles on and on. Her final pitch is that a trial date is scheduled, and the State is very convinced of convicting Senator Conner. The evidence against Senator Conner is overwhelmingly beyond reasonable doubt, Prosecutor Kasts informs the nation. The trial date is set for next Tuesday, a week from today.

The criminal case isn't really the remix of Schola. But the Senator is his client, sort of. So Schola dials Mr McGinley's number, much as to say good luck than to find out how ready the defense is for this rather speedy trial. Several dials to Mr McGinley's lines yield neither pick-ups nor returned calls. Schola figures his calls were unanswered on account of Prosecutor Kasts's press conference a moment ago.

Schola knows what's happening. The rules governing the professional conduct of a lawyer who's involved in the litigation of a case bars the lawyer from making "extrajudicial statement that the lawyer knows or reasonably should know will be disseminated by means of public communication and will have a substantial likelihood of materially prejudicing an adjudicative proceeding in the matter." Broadly interpreted, Prosecutor Kast's claim a moment ago that she has overwhelming evidence to convict could be interpreted as judging Senator Conner guilty even before the jury is empaneled.

When a lawyer makes extrajudicial statements as Prosecutor Kast does a moment ago on live TV, the same model rules of professional conduct allow the other side to "make a statement that a reasonable lawyer would believe is required to protect a client from the substantial undue prejudicial effect of recent publicity not initiated by the lawyer or the lawyer's client." No doubt, Mr McGinley is preparing a statement in response to the prosecutor's statement in response.

Schola can almost predict the content of Mr McGinley's statement. Something along the lines of "our constitution presumes an accused person – whoever, no matter how abhorrent the crimes he is accused of–innocent until a jury of his peers decides otherwise. As we speak, a jury is not empaneled. The defense intends to make some pre-trail motions. The court is yet to decide on these pre-trial motions. Yet Ms Kasts, for political gains, steps in front of the cameras to judge my client guilty. This is abominable. And the defense intends to drag Ms Kast before the disciplinary committee in due time," the statement should conclude. The only question on Schola's mind is how long before Mr McGinley emerges in front of the cameras.

Sure enough, Schola is about turning off the TV after listening to the opinions of legal pundits on the prosecutor's remarks when Fox News announces that defense lawyer for the Senator will be making a statement in a moment. Schola smiles.

And there's Mr McGinley, sweating and bespectacled, before the cameras in hardly five minutes after the prosecutor's remarks. Mr McGinley reads from a single paragraph of the one-page paper in front of him. His countenance is grave and his tone even graver, befitting the situation.

He clears his throat and begins. "My firm ceases to be Mr Conerlius Conner's legal counsel in the case of sexual misconduct and other alleged crimes against him." Shocked, Schola slips off the table he perches and nearly makes it to the floor. This can't be right, Schola says silently in disbelieve after getting himself back to the table. Almost in tears, and with deep pain, Mr McGinley continues: "We have over the decades represented Mr Conner in various capacities in various legal cases. We're grateful to have had the opportunity to serve him in those cases." Mr McGinley clears his throat again, takes off his spectacles, cleans his sweating face and puts them back on and finishes: "We think the time has come to part ways. We wish Mr Conner well."

Nobody expects this. It's a complete about face from the Senator's lawyers. None foresees it coming. Schola slumps into his chair and inhales deeply. The Senator's law firm just fires the Senator Conner. Though not uncommon, it is usually unlikely that a lawyer jettisons his client at high sea. A tenured client like Senator Conner is not easily thrown overboard. But the rules of professional conduct are unambiguous. Where a lawyer thinks that his client's case is so repugnant as to render him, in good conscience, incompetent of representing the client, the lawyer can terminate his services to the client. Schola recalls another provision of the rules of professional conduct governing lawyers.

The essence of Mr McGinley's statement is that Schola also ceases to represent the Senator's divorce matters. Schola begins to wonder whether he makes a mistake in being part of the case in the first place. Schola is back to his former state of joblessness. And even more than that, he is back to his former state of discerning what to do with his life both in the short and long term. Schola decides to call Mr McGinley. Schola needs to know what to do with the divorce file and the office. He picks up the phone but decides against it. He'll wait, for several reasons. For one, Mr McGinley is under serious stress now.

At this point, Schola must turn over every document in his care on the Senator's divorce case and his work product of the case to the client. In this case to Mr McGinley, who in turn, turns the files over to Senator Conner. Schola thus copies his written advice of how to proceed with the divorce case into a new pen drive. He puts the pen drive inside the single divorce folder. Schola is ready to hand over. What an unexpected end. Indeed: "We plan; God laughs."

31

SCHOLA FINISHES OPINION

SCHOLA FINISHES THE LEGAL ADVICE on the Senator's divorce case before the consequential press conferences of the prosecutor and Mr McGinley. Had Schola not finished, he would've stopped work on the divorce case. Since Schola works for Mr McGinley's firm, which no longer represents Senator Conner. But Schola's legal strategy for the divorce is ready.

Anytime today, Mr McGinley would call and guide Schola on what to do with the Senator's file. Schola is ready to hand over. Schola spends the afternoon waiting to hear from Mr. McGinley. By all accounts, it's a hell of a day for Mr McGinley. So Schola understands that Mr McGinley needs time to put things in order. Schola waits patiently. Schola is a patient man.

32

A KNOCK ON THE DOOR

A LOUD KNOCK ON THE DOOR startles Schola's silent wait. He's so unsettled that he doesn't know what to do. Then comes an even bigger and louder knock now. Springing to his feet, Schola dashes to the door. Standing with frown and mean faces are a security man and a lady.

"Yes, may I help you?" Schola asks still confused. The response is unequivocal and mean.

"I want you out of my building in the next minute," the woman demands. Schola isn't easily frightened and bullied.

"And may I see the eviction notion, please?" Schola requests. Perplexed, the woman steps back with a twisted face and asks: "What?"

Schola repeats his request in a firm and steady voice. "You have come to forcefully evict me; may I see the eviction notice from the court authorizing you to act as such?"

"I don't have a notice; I terminate my lease with Mr McGinley for representing a pervert. I want you guys gone as soon as you can get your perverse asses out of my building." She delivers her eviction notice in a shaky and angry voice and turns and walks away with her single security detail with her tail between her legs.

Schola closes the door and for the first time, locks the front door and walks back to his office. He is incensed. He is evicted – or is't an attempted eviction? He slumps into his chair and exhales deeply. The last time Schola was ordered out of a residence was three years ago. Schola was dismissed as a Jesuit, has all his faculties and privileges as a priest withdrawn and ordered out of any Jesuit residence as soon as was practical. The pain of those three years flushes through Schola's memory and manifests physically in his reddened cheeks.

Schola remembers that fateful day when Fr. Cantwell, SJ, then his provincial, said in his rather solemn and cold voice: "I have to ask you to ceased being a Jesuit and a priest." In concealed tears and total disgrace and confusion Schola packed only few of his belongings. He was so angry that he left most of the most valuable items of his life – books. Except for very few collections, he left decades of treasured collections behind. Over the years, Schola has often wondered what happened to his beloved books. On few occasions, he has been tempted to go for them. But a wiser voice asked him to forge ahead and leave the past behind.

Then, Schola owed, among other vows, obedience to his Jesuit leadership. And did everything they told him. Exactly. Cheerfully. Obediently. Totally.

But Schola doesn't own obedience to this landlady. Legally, a six-month lease can't be terminated just like that. And it can't be terminated for the stated reasons—no, not even for representing a perverse. A lawyer, per his professional ethics, is expected to give legal counsel to all manner of persons, both the perceived innocent and the rashly judged guilty, both popular and unpopular client, both powerful and pauper. It is wrong to penalize a lawyer for representing a certain client.

Anger doesn't help. It never does. Schola learnt this long ago. Staying any longer on the premises is an act of revenge. Schola wants to leave anyway. He has no use for the office again. Humility is a virtue. Let yourself be evicted, if unlawfully. Let yourself be disgrace, if wrongly. So Schola, ever the Jesuit, obeys the unlawful eviction notice.

But in this second sacking, there is nothing to pack. Just the single file for Mr McGinley. Thankfully, Schola never used any of the computers in the office—he does all his research and writing on his laptop. Lifting his brown bag, Schola is out of the office. And in this second sacking, a place to stay is not a problem. Not a problem at all.

Downstairs, at the security post, Schola hands over the keys and ID card to the man who a moment ago was at the door with the evicting woman. Schola thanks him. Schola walks out of the Lincoln Building. He turns around and looks at the imposing building and is sure that he's never returning to it. Schola smiles.

On his way home, he wonders again whether signing on to the Senator's criminal conundrum is a result of a faulty discernment, an uninformed judgment. He wonders.

33

FIRM DISCHARGES SENATOR

I N WASHINGTON D.C., IN MR McGinley's office, Senator Conner and Mr McGinley are exchanging angry words.

"I want all my files, every single one of them," the Senator shouts at the top of his voice. Mr McGinley fails in his attempts to convince the Senator that the managing partners of the firm voted only not to represent him in the criminal case. A compromise was made to still fight his non-criminal legal battles, Mr McGinley unsuccessfully explains.

"I say I want everything now," the Senator demands. Angry. Others turn and look in the direction of Mr McGinley's office. The Senator is an erupted volcano whose intense heat overflows Mr McGinley's office.

Mr McGinley's assistant, Ms Stokes, walks up to the Senator and puts her right hand on his shoulder and says, "Dad." This seems to cool the Senator off a bit. "Yes, you are entitled to your files, all of them," she starts. Next she puts her other hand on his other shoulder, establishing a physical proximity that was never between them, "but identify a lawyer or law firm where we can send all your files," she pleads, almost in tears.

At that point, the Senator realizes that he had neither lawyer nor law firm he's sure would take his case following the crisis of his life. Nobody likes him now. Everybody used to like him. Everybody, both males and women, especially, the women. He was so loved that he thought he had no enemies, save his business and political competitors. But he was mistaken. Now he knows his true friends. He has none. The Senator fights back tears.

"So here," Ms Stokes continues, "the prudent thing – though it is against any common sense – is to leave the files here." She breaths in deeply. "When you get a new attorney, that attorney will get in touch with us and get the files," she finishes. The Senator gently takes off Ms Stokes hands, though he wants them to remain. He walks out of Mr McGinley's office never to return. In his car, he directs his driver to the Hyatt Hotel.

34

HYATT EVICTS THE SENATOR

EVEN WORSE AWAITS THE SENATOR at the Hyatt Hotel. The receptionist refuses him the keys to his room. His luggage is packed. The hotel wants him out of their room. The Senator is dazed. He is homeless. His driver picks the bag and succeeds in preventing the Senator from arguing with the receptionist. On their way to the Senator's waiting limonesine, Ms Stokes intercepts them. Ms Stokes was told a moment ago that the Senator is evicted from the Hyatt.

"Please give me the bag," and follow my car with yours," Ms Stokes says, seizing the luggage from the Senator's driver. She puts the Senator's luggage in her car and drives to her new Washington home, which she hardly uses. Ms Stokes' home becomes the Senator's temporary place of abode. The Senator now recalls he owns five houses in D.C. but doesn't remember their exact locations.

At Ms Stokes' house, the Senator transfers his frustrations onto a bottle of gin and sleeps off. He wakes up five hours later with a pounding headache. He washes a dozen of capsules of painkillers down with another bout of gin and sleeps off again. He wakes up two hours later feeling a bit better. He orders dinner to his new home and decides to avoid another headache by drinking only water and juice.

The heavy pizza induces another round of sleep. When he wakes up the following morning, the problems still hang heavily around his neck, but he feels somewhat ready to face them. If only he has the legal help. Whilst waiting for breakfast that he ordered, he regrets not giving some of his legal assignment to a few law firms that continually asked him. Probably, those firms would have stood by him in these dire times. When Mr McGinley informs him that the firm was discontinuing their representation of the criminal case, the Senator calls those law firms that have been chasing him for work. None returns his call. None.

Everybody thinks him guilty. Worse still, everybody wants him locked away. The Senator has never even visited a prison. His only knowledge of prison is the movies. He wonders how he would fare behind bars. An inner voice tells him to stop thinking about prison and focus on getting a good lawyer. But who?

The Senator eats his breakfast absentmindly. He needs to talk to someone. But he hasn't spoken to any member of his family since this crisis started. In fact, his family appeared on TV and disowned him. He truly longs to talk to someone. Just to talk.

How flailing this life is. His one problem in life was how to avoid people. Now he can't even get a single person to keep company. It occurs to him that in all of this, an unknown individual writes an opinion in the *Times* cautioning people not to judge him guilty. The author of that kind piece argues that judging an accused guilty or otherwise is the duty of the jury. The Senator picks up that copy of the *Times* which he keeps. He reads it again. The author sounds not only sympathetic but a bit supportive. The author feels his pain. The Senator looks at the name again and smiles. When the author is summoned to visit, the Senator realizes that he likes him. Though he doesn't like his not drinking wine. And only God knows what else he doesn't do. Oh yes, he mentions that he used to be a catholic priest. But no longer a priest. A former Jesuit priest at least understands. That is enough for Senator Conner.

The Senator decides on his lawyer now. Schola is his lawyer. He would do everything to get him to represent him. Everything. What he needs in his defense is an angel. A former Jesuit priest who doesn't drink or sleep around is not too far off.

The Senator is beginning to feel a glimmer of hope.

35

THE SENATOR VISITS SCHOLA

WHEN SCHOLA IS AT THE Farm –that is, with his parents–he's an outdoors person, half of the time. The Farm offers him options on the field, in the stalls and in the woods to plough, dig and chop as well as wonder about. Schola glees in the outdoors – he feels closer to nature, and thus to God. It's in these very woods that Schola decides to go to law school out of the many options the Governor makes available to him three years ago.

Schola loves nature. Schola is at peace with nature. Schola is happy with nature. So when Schola is at the Farm he is mostly likely out in the woods and distastes being interrupted.

Mother comes looking for him after a few hours. She drags Schola in for either a meal or a snack. Out of security for Schola than the need for a snack. And mother doesn't leave until Schola follows her back into the house. And then Schola escapes again into nature, and mother appears in no time to get Schola back inside.

Schola feels like a prized jewel. The love is enormous. The love his new mother showers on him is special, second to none, equal only to the love of his biological mother. Now deceased.

Schola is surprised when mother appears just seconds after he comes to feed the cows. That's unusual, even for mother.

"Schola, you've got a visitor," mother says.

"What?" Schola retorts.

"You heard me; a guest is waiting for you indoors," mother says.

"Aah, they have finally come for the files." Schola thinks to himself. "Thanks mother, I'll be in, in a moment."

"Okay, it's bad to keep guests waiting." Mother admonishes.

Mr McGinley should have called him and have him mail the files, Schola thinks. Perhaps, given the sensitive nature of the files, it's probably better that Mr McGinley picks them up himself, Schola concludes. Or has someone pick them up.

It occurs to Schola that his guest could be the Senator's new lawyer, chasing down all the files. Schola is intrigue and wants to know who this new criminal defense messiah might be. As Schola walks towards the house he decides that he must attend the trial of the Senator. Though he isn't a fun of the trial courts, especially, the criminal courts, the Senator's case is different. And given his own minimal involvement, it makes sense that he attends and sees how the case goes.

At the front door, Schola is surprised to see what looks like a limousine and two other cars outside. The Senator is getting himself a big criminal defender. But what kind of lawyer goes about driving a limousine to a Farm in the outskirt of a small city? Schola pauses and wonders. The answer is inside.

When Schola gets inside, he is shocked to see the Senator himself seated, chatting with his parents over coffee and some mother-made cookies.

"There he comes," father says.

"It's bad manners to keep guests waiting," mother admonishes again.

"I just came in, the Senator intervenes. And it's a happy wait, if at all," the Senator says honestly.

"Senator, I must confess that I wasn't expecting to see you," Schola says, shaking the Senator's hand.

"Because I never thought that I would be visiting," the Senator replies. The room welcomes the Senator's reply with a laughter. The parents respectfully excuse the two men even before

Schola introduces the Senator. His parents stopped reading and watching scandals many years ago. So, it wasn't completely out of order that they won't know who the Senator is and why he won't be welcomed in any home in America. But again, his parents welcome anybody to their home. Anybody. Everybody. All.

Schola takes his unexpected guest to an adjoining room, now turned his study–sort of. The Senator looks around and gives a disapproving look, prompting Schola to apologize for the simplicity of his study. Or rather, the poverty of his study with its wooden chair and wooden table.

Now it's down to business. "I'll like you to represent me in the upcoming trial," the Senator starts. Schola laughs and regrets immediately that he does. Though the laugher doesn't offend the Senator. But the Senator is stone serious.

"As you know, Mr McGinley and his firm deposed of me, and nobody would take my case," the Senator explains. Schola is no longer amused. Schola wonders whether the Senator realizes what he's up against. The Senator continues, "I've been giving this case a lot of thought. And even if Cicero were on it now, I would love you to be the lead attorney."

Schola sits up straight. With hands clapped in a reverent posture. Schola looks through the window far into the woods and takes in the gravity of the Senator's request. He doesn't know what to say, and so keeps thinking.

The Senator dislikes silence. So he breaks the silence. "I'm sorry to be dumping this on you," the Senator apologizes sincerely. "But there's no time to even think it over. Please be my attorney," the Senator begs. Schola has never seen the Senator this beaten, humbled, and helpless. Pity for one of America's once most powerful politicians overwhelms Schola.

Schola is moved. Nobody has apologized to him for a long time. But he must consider this request very seriously and be sure that he's doing the right thing.

"Mr Conner, you see, I want the best lawyer for you. Because you need the very best given the gravity of the charges. I'm not that lawyer," Schola pleads. He looks at the Senator and realizes that there's no way to convince him to look elsewhere for another lawyer. The man's mind is made up.

"Please do this for me," the Senator begs again. The Senator stands up, taps Schola's shoulders and leaves. Leaving Schola with no choice in the matter.

36

DISCERNING ON TAKING
UP THE JOB

THERE'RE SEVERAL REASONS TO DECLINE the Senator's offer, Schola thinks. First is competence. The rules governing the conduct of lawyers forbids lawyers from representing a client involving a case that the lawyer lacks the requisite "legal knowledge, skill, thoroughness and preparation reasonably necessary for the representation."

Schola is ill-equipped to handle this case. He has never tried a case before. Not even a simple misdemeanor. He has never even sat in a court to watch proceedings. There're fewer cases with consequential outcomes than the Senator's case. Not to add the media dimension. Schola is a recluse and ill-suited to handle the media spotlight that the case attracts, which is a critical component for victory.

Also, there's the issue of material resources. He doesn't have an office. Schola still has access to LexisNexis and Westlaw, great resources for legal research, because his law school is yet to terminate its subscription for its alumni. These can be terminated at any point, however. Of course, the client can pay for these. But this case needs a standard legal office that is already up and running.

And of course, there is the stigma associated with representing an unpopular client such as the Senator. Generally, non-lawyers, and even some lawyers, think a lawyer who represents such allegedly repugnant clients is endorsing their conduct. Does Schola want to kick-start his legal career by advocating for the most unpopular client in the United States? Schola wonders what his Jesuits will think about him. The stain, Schola knows, would stay with him forever.

But again, a lawyer doesn't only offer his legal services to the innocent clients and the innocuous cases. The perceived guilty – especially, the allegedly repugnant and deplorable ones like Senator Conner – needs a lawyer, too.

And of course, the College of Presidents has registered its objection against Schola's involvement in the Senator's case from when Schola published that piece in the *Times* cautioning against finding the Senator guilty before a trial is had. Mr Post the editor of the *World* refuses to publish his sympathetic article on the Senator before Schola turns same over to the *Times*. The Governor sides with Schola. But the Governor has never disapproved of anything that Schola does. The College would be up in arms if Schola should be the lead-lawyer in the scheduled crucifixion of Senator Conner masked as a trial.

One good thing is that Schola doesn't have to explain to his parents who the Senator is. His parents don't seem to care what he does with his life. They only seek to ensure that he's a happy man. Truly, Schola is out in the open sea. As the Senator says, nobody will help him. This is the mission of the Jesuits—to attend to those left alone. But Schola is no longer a Jesuit, he tries reminding himself, always. He decides to sleep it off. But really, if the Senator insists, Schola must take up his nascent legal gloves and punch on the Senator's behalf with every strength in his being. And may God help Schola and save the Senator.

37

CLIENT'S FILE DELIVERED

THE NEXT MORNING, WHILE DRINKING coffee and quite convinced that the Senator should get a new lawyer, an SUV pulls up in the driveway of the Farm. "I've got this," mother says and goes out. She comes back and opens the door for a man and a woman with boxes. Without saying anything, the two return to the car and bring in two more boxes, and then a final one. In a plastic bag are labelled pen drives and various back-up devices.

One of the two bearers of the boxes, the woman, is Ms Ananda Stokes. Schola's heart limps upon seeing her. Schola spells his coffee. Upon seeing Schola, Ms Stokes nearly drops the file she was carrying. The mutual attraction surprises Schola. Mother knows love when she sees one. The chemistry between Schola and Ms Stokes fills the room. The room takes on an aura of consecrated love.

Mother takes Ms Stokes's hand and leads her to a chair. Seats her comfortably. Serves her coffee and some mother-made home pastry. Mother is sure that this is her daughter-in-law. Ms Stokes doesn't want to leave. She feels completely at home.

"These are all the files of Senator Cornelius Conner in the possession of the firm," the male visitor says. Turning to Ms Stokes, he says, "we must really be going." Ms Stokes is compelled to leave. But not until mother packs pastry for her. We must see you again, mother says. Ms Stokes just nobs in complete understanding, and the car drives away. Ms Stokes is surprised at the tears on her cheeks and wipes them off as the car picks up speed.

Schola stares. Schola is hired whether he likes it or not. Ordinarily, Schola would've returned the files. He dislikes being pushed. But the once powerful Senator is now a shadow of his former self. In fact, he could be in prison in a matter of weeks. The Senator is a leper. The process to ostracize him to the periphery of the proverbial village is on.

This is the sole reason Schola takes the case: nobody else would.

Schola puts the coffee away and takes a closer look at the boxes. They're well labeled. The first three are files on the three companies of the Senator's companies. The fourth box is on his holdings – his entire estate. And the final box, by far the smallest of all, is the criminal file. It contains a single folder.

One by one, Schola puts the other four boxes again. He has no use for them. Not now.

He takes the lone folder from the box labeled criminal defense. He inhales and exhales deeply and goes through the content. Complaint, affidavit of witnesses, and amended Complaint. And there's the defense's response to the complaint.

Schola knows that he can't do this alone. He needs help. And help must come very fast. He picks up his phone and calls someone he counseled three years ago.

38

HELP FROM MR CONKLING

PRIOR TO LAW SCHOOL, DURING his few months stay in Fort Wayne, Schola prays a lot at the St. Mary Mother of God Catholic Church. A troubled lawyer at the time, Mr Barfoot Conkling is a constant presence at the same church. Schola notices Mr Conkling and knows he carries a lot on his shoulders. The two strike a chord, build on trust.

At the time, Mr Conkling is suspended from legal practice pending investigation over various allegations. The charges against him are small and massive, ranging from misdemeanor to felonies: speeding tickets, failure in paying his attorney registration fees, delinquent CLEs, misappropriation of client fund, tax evasion, and domestic abuse of his then wife. Both the criminal trial and hearings pertaining to attorney misconduct were ongoing at the time.

Mr Conkling is a wreck. Schola helps the wreck stay sane. Mr Conkling comes across to Schola as an able and seasoned criminal defense attorney. Indeed, Mr Conkling was an able criminal defendant who failed to listen to his inner voice and never paid attention to his moral compass. This is the man Schola turns to for assistance with the Senator's case.

What Schola doesn't know is that Mr Conkling has been disbarred from law practice. Mr Conkling knew that the investigations were leading to only one thing – indefinite suspension at best. And because Conkling has no way of repaying the money involved, disbarment was inevitable. So Mr Conkling didn't even cooperate with the investigations to the end. He didn't show up for the disciplinary hearings. The final verdict from the

Indiana Supreme Court disciplinary hearing was an indefinite suspension, and subsequently, a disbarment.

Schola scrolls through his phone, hoping against hope to find Mr Conkling's contact–a functional phone number would be the ideal. Schola doesn't see Mr Conkling in his contacts and only realizes that he changed his cellphone over the years.

Schola puts down his cellphone and resigns in defeat. But then a thought occurs to him. Like all lawyers, Mr Conkling would have been a member of the local county bar association at some point. In Mr Conkling's case, the Allen County Bar Association (ACBA). The ACBA might be able to help.

Schola calls the ACBA administrative office. After hardly a wait, a voice answers. Schola doesn't know how to begin. "I would like the address of an attorney … ah … Mr Barfoot Conkling," Schola manages to say.

"May I know what for?" the receptionist inquires.

"Well, he represented me in a prior case. I've a new case and need his help," Schola lies.

"Let me see whether we have him in our data base," the warm receptionist says. Schola hears fingers typing away.

After a while, the voice reports its findings: "Mr Conkling was a member of the ACBA. He's no longer a member. In fact, he has been disbarred and cannot practice now," the voice concludes. Schola sights and asks for his details anyway.

The sweet voice gives Schola a phone number and an address. But the voice warns Schola that the details were five years ago.

Schola is hoping that since Mr Conkling was in practice for many years, he'll be able to guide him through some of the obvious things that rookie lawyers miss on their first trials. Even more important, Schola is hoping for the input of a seasoned criminal attorney. Schola recalls Mr Conkling telling him some of the notorious criminals that he freed in Indiana. But since Mr Conkling is disbarred, he's incapable of offering professional help.

Schola isn't giving up. At least, Mr Conkling can offer help as a paralegal. In any event, Schola is defending a perceived bad man. What harm could it possibly do to have another horrible man on the Senator's team. This's a team of the deplorables.

Schola dials the number. He gets no answer. Prompted to leave a message, Schola leaves one: "Mr Barfoot Conkling, this is an old friend, please give me a call. My phone number should register on your phone. It's very urgent."

Mr Conkling is having his second glass of whisky that morning when the surprised call comes in. Usually, his landlord calls to inquire of the late or unpaid rent and threatens yet another eviction. But this call isn't from his landlord. A complete strange voice. And Mr Conkling likes that voice—steady, erudite, and yet, full of humility. The kind of voice that's the signature of the most prominent lawyers and judges—except for the humility part—when he was in practice.

What puzzles Mr Conkling is the reference to friendship; "this's an old friend," the voice says. There're no more old friends. All of them have deserted him. They neither take his calls nor receive him in their offices. There're no more families. All of them were tired of carrying the load that has become a disgraced, prominent, former attorney. And all his friends have heard of his predicament. There're no friends anywhere whom he has not turned to. All of them turned him down.

For a while now, Mr Conkling has come to the considered conclusion that it was over for him. After he was disbarred, a friend offered him a job as a paralegal. Mr Conkling got fired after three weeks. Then he got a job at the community college as an adjunct professor of criminal justice and was fired as well. And so on and on and on. Mr Conkling couldn't hold a job. That's after he lost the one job he was best at—the practice of high profile criminal and corporate law.

Mr Conkling now lives as a destitute does. For food, he gets supplies from any soup kitchen. Money from his retirement has been competing between paying his rent and paying for his only companion—the bottles.

Mr Conkling could feel it in his body. His body is dying slowly. His spirit is gone. A staunch Catholic, he hasn't made the sign of the cross in a very long time. He is an empty man now. But Mr Conkling promises himself one thing, he wouldn't wait and fall sick and die slowly and painfully. He would exit from this world without the indecency of sickness.

For the purpose of exiting this world, Mr Conkling plans this week to meet with the funeral home and arrange his funeral. A fellow drunk tells him that it's done. The expenses paid in advance. He hasn't touched the last of his savings. He hopes to use this saving to start a firm, should he take up the practice of law one day. But there won't be another one day. That saving goes into his funeral expenses.

As part of the plan of exiting, he also gets his old phone number restored only last week. He wants to call his daughter and a few people before going. But for that restoration, this old friend won't have gotten him, at least, not on phone.

As usual, he starts his day with three rounds of libation of whisky. "An old friend" just interrupted his morning prayer of liquor. The gods liquor must be angry at the caller. But there was something new, vitalizing, about that voice mail. It sounds almost as if Mr Conkling is about to be handed another get at life. For the first time in four years, Mr Conkling pours his unfinished drink into the sink. He would somber up a bit before calling this unknown "old friend."

39

MR CONKLING RETURNS CALL

SCHOLA IS OUT IN THE woods again ruminating on a range of issues bordering on his role in the Senator's case. Nature is a great place for Schola to clear his mind. The fresh air helps. Besides praying and reflecting, the woods is where Schola resolves issues of greater importance and urgency. Here, in the midst of nature, urgent matters are put on the anvil of discernment and hammered out. Urgent matters like the one at hand: getting a fair trial for the Senator.

Schola is out in the solace of the woods for less than five minutes when mother calls. Usually, she comes after him after half an hour ostensibly for a snack break. Not less than five minutes. What's wrong, Schola wonders. He turns and walks towards his mother's voice.

"There you're," mother says in relieve after sighting him. "A call for you," she says.

"From whom?" Schola asks.

"I don't know, I didn't ask." Mother answers. "But I ask that they call back in five minutes. Come here, let's go inside," mother says, dragging him in, like a mother her toddler.

In recent times, mother's wish of not leaving him long in the woods is achieve with visits, now calls. Mother must be the happiest person in all of this. Indeed, she is. Her son now connects. People visit. People ask for his help. Tapping into his great, latent talent. Now people are calling. Good. Mother is happy as a mother should be.

Mother and son walk back to the room to wait. After ten minutes, Schola rises for the woods again, telling mother to ask the caller to leave a message. Schola's hand merely touches the door knot when the phone rings again. Schola picks the call on the third ring.

"Hello," Schola answers.

"Hello," follows an uncomfortable pause.

"Yes, hello," Schola repeats.

"Please this number called and left a message this morning," Mr Conkling finally says.

"Please is this Mr Barfoot Conkling?" Schola asks, not too sure.

"Yes, this is Barfoot here," Mr Conkling replies.

"Please who're you?" he asks. Immediately, Mr Conkling feels bad about his tone. He doesn't mean to be rude.

"I'm Schola, three years ago, I used to see you at St Mary's." Schola pauses for a while and continues. "You were navigating your divorce and job-related issues," Schola continues. "We met almost regularly for almost three months, on Saturdays, at about noon."

There's a very long pause, almost an eternity. The gin blurs Mr Conkling's memory and he takes a while to recall. But more because all of this doesn't make any sense. Besides, Schola is the last person Mr Conkling expects a call from. Mr Conkling recalls Schola. How couldn't he? The man was full of wise counsel. Mr Conkling takes the phone off his ear, looks at it again and then realizes that a response awaits him at the other end.

"Yes, I remember," Mr Conkling finally admits. "I must say I never expected to hear from you," Mr Conkling confesses earnestly. "It has been a long time."

"Yes," Schola replies. "But here we are again," Schola picks up the weird conversation. "I need some help with some important legal issues."

"I'm no longer in practice," Mr Conkling says. But Mr Conkling is surprised when Schola says that he knows that but still needs his help.

"It's a matter of the utmost urgency," Schola says, sounding desperate. "If you are willing to at least discuss it, I must see you as soon as practicable."

"I'm free the whole day," Mr Conkling says to Schola's relieve.

"I'm outside Fort Wayne. But I can come meet you wherever you are," Schola proposes. Mr Conkling looks around his dirty room and decides that it might offend God to have a former priest visit with him in the [obscenity] hole, especially, given that he would be dying soon and will be facing God for the judgment. Mr Conkling thinks of a different venue.

"How about the public library, main library downtown?" Mr Conkling proposes a different venue.

"Sure," Schola confirms. "Would 11:30 am work for you?"

"Sure, see you then," Mr Conkling confirms.

40

PREPARING TO MEET SCHOLA

FOR THE FIRST TIME IN years, Mr Conkling's day didn't go as planned or re-planned. He puts off his own pre-funeral arrangement. At least, not this morning. Probably, depending on how the meeting goes, till tomorrow.

For the first time in years, Mr Conkling worries about dressing well. He hasn't washed for weeks. And he must do something about his unkempt hair, too.

For the first time in years, Mr Conkling runs water over his body. Mr Conkling feels surprisely refreshed after the wash. He still looks awful, but he feels almost anew. He turns to his only way of telling the time – the TV. It's two hours before the meeting.

For the first time in years, Mr Conkling wonders what to wear. He settles on an old pants of jeans, a T shirt, and a coat. With a baseball cup over his hair, he heads to the soup kitchen for his weekly supplies. He returns to his apartment with supplies that were supposed to last a whole week. He takes out one of the two bottles of milk and washed it down his throat. Takes out the tuna sandwich and takes a bit. It tastes good and he finishes it off. The desire for a drop of some gin arises. And for the first time in three years, Mr Conkling overcomes his desire to take a drop of drink.

When he was in practice, Mr Conkling made it a point to always arrive before his clients for meetings. This ensures that he was never late for a meeting. Besides, his clients thought that he took them seriously. So Mr Conkling plans to arrive fifteen minutes earlier.

41

THE MEETING

BUT SCHOLA IS ALREADY WAITING. Mr Conkling is surprise to see Schola seated in the coffee shop in the library.

"Mr Conkling, thanks for meeting at such short notice," Schola says with an extended hand. Mr Conkling takes his hand, not sure what to say.

Schola digs in on the purpose of the meeting. "I'm an attorney now. I'm in charge of the Senator Conner's case, and needs some help with the representation. I believe that you can be a guiding hand given that I'm a freshman attorney."

Mr Conkling is nonplussed. Though not in practice, he keeps up with the legal world. The Senator's case is the case of the moment. Schola is a great listener and knows when to wait. And Mr Conkling takes his time to be sure that he isn't dreaming. When Mr Conkling appears awakened from his dream, Schola continues.

"I know that you can't act as an attorney. But I need an experienced criminal attorney. And I believe that you can offer immense help acting as a paralegal." Schola stresses the paralegal, and Mr Conkling sees his point.

"I live with my parents out in a Farm. It's best if we both work from there. Opening arguments are scheduled for tomorrow," Schola says.

"So there is no time to wait," Mr Conkling says slowly and rises to his feet, with Schola rising with him in unison.

With that, the hope of former Senator Cornelius Conner Jr. hinges on two unlikely pairs – a rockie lawyer and an alcoholic and disbarred lawyer. The weakest and worst defense team for an accused who needs a criminal defense messiah. May God help them.

42

OPENING ARGUMENTS
– COURT SCENE

CHOLA, SENATOR CONNER, AND MR Conkling, Schola's co-counsel disguised as his paralegal, arrive early in court, doing well to avoid the media. They arrive about thirty minutes before the start of proceedings. When Judge Avis Kaufman comes in thirty minutes later, she'll stride into the courtroom elegantly, perch on her higher throne, and look down on everybody in the packed room from her privileged perch.

Schola is inwardly nervous but does well to outwardly hide his inner uneasiness. His inner uncalmness is reminiscent of how he felt the first time he presided over Mass following his ordination eight years ago. It's the nervousness of his first day of teaching a class at Harvard eight years ago. But the intensity is more than doubled today. And the stakes much higher. The liberty of a citizen is at stake. The prosecution is asking for not less than fifty years in prison if the jury finds the Senator guilty. Worse yet, everyone, virtually everyone, is sure of the Senator's guilt. Fifty years behind bar means life imprisonment for the Senator, given his current age. The Senator will be over 100 years when he gets out, if he ever gets out. Essentially, the prosecution is asking for life imprisonment. The prosecution would've asked for the death sentence if the law allows it. The stakes couldn't have been higher. Schola's nervousness is at its highest ever.

It's the trial of the century. The trial that will take down one of the most powerful business mugols and promising politicians in American history. As the Senator sits in court, his political life is over. He resigns his senate seat, under duress. And his business empire is crumbling, and fast too. His life is over. Schola is tasked to save the one thing left of the Senator's miserable life – The Senator's physical liberty. Hence, Schola's discomfort. Schola fears that he might fail. Schola has never liked the humiliating taste of failure, though he has tested failure on many occasions and in different forms.

This isn't a regular trial: the unprecedented, packed room evinces that history is unfolding. More chairs are brought in. A seat meant for one person now seats two. Bodies are squeezed in every space available. The air-conditioner is at full blast. Yet the room is still hot and sweaty. Very hot. Mints should've been handed out at the door as people walk in, Schola thinks.

Journalists don't want to miss anything. Schola sees some scribing away on their note packs. Schola wonders what they are writing. Few are sketching portraits. Schola can tell from the pricking pencils.

The trial is of equal interest to the legal fraternity. Lawyers, both seasoned and young, despite their busy schedules—and some, despite conflicting schedules—are here. The attendees are observing every move, every cough, every sneeze. Seasoned attorneys note how they would have handled things differently. Young and inexperienced attorneys are picking up every trick that this trial offers.

Schola notices the muted commotion behind him and turns to look. Old acquittances are looking in Mr Conkling's direction. They either wonder what he's doing in court or mocking him or both. Schola does his best not to be sidetracked; he hopes Mr Conkling does same. The stakes are high.

Schola hears the one single and repeated question: "Who's this attorney?" The answer is always the same from different people: "never seen him before."

The answer is pleasing to Dr Devlin Dingell, the managing partner of the Schola Law Firm and the Dean of the College of Presidents. It's soothing that Hoosiers see no link between the man at the helm of the Senator's defense and the Schola Group. The integrity, purity, and polished political image of the Schola Group and the Governor are preserved. At the same time, Dr Dingell is beginning to like young Schola. He comes into the Governor's life only three years ago. It seems like yesterday when Schola sits in as guest in the meeting that proposes that the Governnor runs for the presidency of the United States of America. Schola brings the high-profile meeting to an end when he suggests that the Governor be allowed to pray about running for president. That newcomer of three years ago is the lawyer of the moment. It's a plus for the Schola Group. One of theirs is in the spotlight. But his identity should be shielded. For now.

Schola's demeanor diminishes Dean Dingell's concerns. Schola does his best not to make this trial his. He understands his role very well. His role is to offer effective assistance to the Senator. Nothing more. This isn't an opportunity for Schola to play to the media and the public and the legal world and ride on the momentum of the trial to prominence. So far, Schola turns down all media requests for comments and statements. It helps that Schola never liked the public glare. That's way he chose a priestly life earlier. It offered a life of sufficient seclusion for Schola.

43

SIMILARITIES CHURCH AND COURT

TALKING OF PRIESTHOOD. SCHOLA COULDN'T help but notice the similarity between a courtroom and a church. The silence. The decorum. The professional dress. The formality. The measured language. How you walk and sit. A courtroom has a lot in common with a church–a Catholic church especially.

Even more in common is the art in the room. Of course, there's no crucifix or the statue of the Blessed Virgin Mary– the patroness of the Jesuits and Schola's own patroness—in this courtroom. But there's the Blind Lady Justice. Schola isn't happy that Lady Justice is rendered blind in order to render impartial judgments.

It's Schola's considered view that justice be administered with the principle of difference, not indifference. Sometimes, exceptions should be made to the rules. But only when these exceptions favor the poor and less privilege of society. Lady Justice can't implement the difference principle if she is blind. It's a view that the American political philosophy, John Rawls, advances in his book – A theory of Justice.

A good judge in Schola's view should know the parties before him. Their stories. Their strengths. Their limitations. What forced them to do what they did. Sympathizes with them when appropriate. A distance isn't appropriate. Both eyes of a judge must be opened. Sometimes spectacles should aid a judge who can't see well. The judge must not miss anything.

Hopefully, Judge Kaufman is not blind. Schola almost laughs at the thought. And she shouldn't be blind-folded as she hears this case.

Apart from Lady Justice, there were other magnificent art work in the solemn room. To Schola's right on the far top corner is a scene of a trial. The judge seems very angry. With a sword in his hand, he is swearing at one of the parties. The poor woman is on her knees crying. The other party is smiling. In the hands of the smiling party are gifts of sorts for the judge. Gold in bags, it appears.

Schola cynically wishes he were appearing before this judge. The Senator still has lots of money. Schola believes that despite his business troubles the Senator can still outbid the prosecutor. The trial would have been over and the Senator declared innocent.

But then, Schola's attention shifts to the far-left corner of the room. This judge is very recollected. Sits calmly. Hand to his cheek. Listens very carefully. Very somber. His counselors are equally calm and attentive as the judge. None of the parties is bearing gifts. Both parties seem confident in this impartial judge.

Schola especially focuses on the composure of the poor party in this case. Her face is peaceful. She senses no danger because of her social status. Schola wonders what the point of the paintings was in locating them in a place where the presiding judge can't see them. The trial scenes on the wall of the courtroom should have been situated in front of the judge.

44

OLD TRIALS

CHOLA'S THOUGHT SHIFTS TO HOW far trials have come. From the stone age to the medieval period to the dark era, trials have evolved. In the medieval age, for example, parties to a dispute hired wrestlers to represent them. The claimant whose wrestler won the fight was deemed innocent. And the claimant whose wrestler lost was expected to accept that his claim was in the wrong.

Wrestlers were paid to fight. The rich hired the best wrestlers. So justice was always for the folks of means. Sitting back with a modern eye, this seems a barbaric manner of getting justice. But for the medieval mind, this was their way of vindicating the innocent. Justice has come a long way, indeed.

But in deeper thought, the situation isn't any different today. Criminals that hire the best law firms – the most expensive ones – have a better chance of never seeing the inside of a prison. Money gets you the justice you want. Law firms with resources ensure that.

The poor defendant whose best hope is the public defender, if lucky to get one, is almost certain to go to prison. That explains in large part why our prisons are full of poor people. The rich commit worse crimes. But bigger law firms and great lawyers see to it that they stay clear of prisons.

That's why the Senator's decision to retain Schola as his defense attorney is insane, probably, stupid. The Senator hires an untried wrestler to face a life-long wrestler with state resources energizing her punches.

There were even more absurd forms of adjudications in earlier times. In some instances, parties to a dispute were made to put their hands in burning fire. According to this legal system, the hands of the innocent party were unharmed. The guilty party's hand burned. This is incredulous, Schola thinks. Fire will surely burn anybody's hand. But coming from a tradition where hungry lions refused to eat up Daniel, Schola believes.

Suddenly, the front door opens, closing Schola's thoughts. Two law clerks walk in. Smartly dressed. The clock slightly to Schola's left indicates that it's five minutes to the start of trial.

And five minutes later, Schola doesn't notice Judge Kaufman walk in and up to her exalted seat. He sees people standing up and for a moment he wonders what was going on. Mr Conkling taps his shoulders and whispers in Schola's ears – stand up.

The Senator now begins to wonder whether his instincts haven't failed him in settling on Schola as his attorney.

45

PROSECUTOR'S OPENING

JUDGE AVIS KAUFMAN ASSUMES HER seat and politely requests same of her rather large audience. The largest since she started presiding over cases in Room 13 of the Allen County Court Complex. "Please if there are no preliminary motions, can we go straight to the opening arguments," Judge Kaufman says. Prosecutor Kast stands up. "Your honor, my name is Lucille Kast for the state. The prosecution is ready," and she looks in the direction of Schola and resumes her seat.

Following her lead, Schola rises: "Your honor, the defense is ready. I'm Priestley Plusbriuschola for the defense, your honor."

At the mention of the month-full and never-heard of name in local legal circles, the room goes up in murmurs. "Who's he?" "What does he say his name is?"

Judge Kaufman brings the room to the solemnity befitting of the occasion with a raise of her robed hand.

"Okay, prosecution may proceed then," the judge directs. Prosecutor Kast walks up to the jury, pauses and begins. It seems to Schola that Prosecutor Kast was born for this moment.

"Your honor, ladies and gentlemen of the jury, humanity has come a very long way." She waits for effect. "Civilized nations like ours have come a very long way from a very barbaric past."

This time, the room appears to be thinking with her. Different minds go to different human pasts. True, some of the past was horrible, some minds conclude.

"And from this regrettable past, evolved a refined and civilized mind, which deems certain acts and behaviors, well, deplorable," she pauses again. "The actors of such deplorable behavior are seen as less human; the perpetrators of such vile acts are grouped among beasts and, hence, unfit to leave among cultivated men and women."

Schola is fully attentive to the statements of the prosecution as well as how others were receiving those statements. The hostile manner that one of the clerks, Mr Blix Pritish, looks at the presiding judge troubles Schola. Whatever rift that exists between judge and her male clerk is obvious to the keen observer. What could be so pressing as to divert the attention of a law clerk from the case of the century? Schola wonders.

Judge Kaufman is the senior judge of the criminal division. She has two law clerks to herself. For a long time now, Judge Kaufman hasn't hired any female clerks. Nobody knows why, except of course for the law clerks. And these clerks will never share the reason.

Judge Kaufman hires from her pool of highly competent applicants, very active, athletic, young lawyers. Of course, they must graduate top of their classes with impeccable academic records as well as be meticulous and hard working. Judge Kaufman doesn't compromise on these basic standards. But in addition, to be hired, these male candidates must be willing to play ball. Judge Kaufman makes this clear from the beginning.

Indeed, the interviews are either conducted at her home or over dinners. In the case of Mr Pritish, Judge Kaufman makes it very clear after the five minutes of preliminary questioning that the extra-judicial aspect of the work is equally important.

While Judge Kaufman isn't astonishingly beautiful, she is so sexy as well as seductive without intending. She is irresistible to the man of even below average sexual appetite. And it doesn't help that Mr Pritish walks into her home and meets her in her workout outfit. Things get out of hand when Judge Kaufman welcomes Mr Pritish with a tight hug. She takes him by hand to the couch and tells him to be at ease. She freshens up and gets the interview going. Mr Pritish arrives a full hour before the interview.

She soon emerges from freshening up, professionally dressed but not any less appealing than before. She sets opposite him and begins the questioning. Mr Pritish doesn't know what pulls him to her side. She doesn't resist either, and they're at it. The interview is in full session, sooner than Judge Kaufman hopes for this rather reserved applicant. And it's over as it started. No force, no threats. The power of attraction won.

You passed your interview; she whispers in his ears as he buttons up. Judge Kaufman is honest and out front about it. She is divorced and needs a bit of action from time to time. She hopes to rely on trusted aids and confidants like Mr Pritish anything she is lonely. And if Mr Pritish doen't like this aspect of the job he doesn't have to do anything.

But her demands for clerking on bed as well as in court become a burden for Mr Pritish. His wife notices something out of place and is complaining. Mr Pritish loves his wife. He wants to save his marriage. When Mr Pritish tells Judge Kaufman about his wife's complaints, Judge Kaufman says she understands

Mr Pritish is deeply hurt when Judge Kaufman informs him that she is thinking of replacing him after this tenure. She appreciates his time. She will help him get a job. Even a job that pays more. But she needs a new face. To keep his job, Mr Pritish makes a visit last night to his boss's home. After the home clerkship, Mr Pritish says to her in tears that he wants to keep his current job. Judge Kaufman replies that she doesn't want to interfere with his marriage. If he can keep his job and his marriage, she has no problem.

Mr Pritish is angry that the sexual harassment thing is viewed virtually one way – men abusing women. This explains why Mr Pritish is menacingly looking at his boss. Of course, Schola doesn't know any of this, and Mr Pritish would never tell anyone. But if Mr Pritish were on the jury, he's freeing the Senator.

Schola's full attention reverts to the prosecutor who was still giving her opening address. "Unwanted and brutal sexual advances of any kind are some of the barbaric acts unfitting of civilized beings." She turns and looks the Senator in the face, maintains the gaze and continues. "Mr Conner seated here, has proven himself a beast. He punches on unwilling and helpless women for his sole sexual satisfaction. He claws them like a lion would a rabbit. Devours them completely. And throws them away with no regard for how they feel."

Schola notices moisture in the Senator's eyes. The Senator's head is beginning to quiver. And his blood rises. His temper is in the reds. Schola whispers in the Senator's ears; "Don't mind her, she is describing her first boyfriend." The Senator looks at the ex-priest lawyer in disbelief. The Senator doesn't' know that the ex-Jesuit priest could be dismissive, if consoling. But there's a lot the Senator doesn't know about this ex-Jesuit priest, ex-Harvard professor.

Prosecutor Kast continues: "Because of his money, power, influence, and privilege, he gets whatever he wants including any woman that catches his fancy." Prosecutor Kast stops, ostensible to fight back tears. Her mourning voice evidenced a truly sad woman. "Mr Conner doesn't care whether his victims like him or not. Mr Conner gets what he wants. When he wants. Where he wants. How he wants. Women are objects for his voracious sexual appetite."

Schola shifts his attention to the jury. Jury number three, Jane Sisson, is visibly in tears. Ms Sisson washes bowls in a restaurant for ten dollars an hour. She is a single mother with two young children. Ms Sisson has a duty to keep her children alive. The dish-washing is one of the three minor jobs she jostles to put bread on table and avoid eviction.

Every day her supervisor walks behind her and grabs her behind. The supervisor alienates the dish washing area for this perverse purpose. Ms Sisson is very helpless. In the beginning, she drops and breaks a bowl in retaliation anytime she is grabbed. The beast begins subtracting the damaged bowls and plates from her paycheck, reducing her meagre earnings. So she learns to cope with the situation. She does her best to be still when groped. But now that she is still, the hands come up front and all over her body.

Ms Sisson is ready to shoot the Senator. Incarcerating the Senator isn't enough for her.

Schola sees in Ms Sisson a hostile juror. Schola wonders how he might change her heart to see things differently. Schola decides that to win, he must convert Ms Sisson. It's impossible for a privileged white male like Schola to make a single black mother in her late twenties see things differently. But how many times hasn't Schola changed students to embrace an opposite ideology than the one they come to the course with. Schola's task in this trial is cut: speak to jury number three to see things differently.

The prosecution's damning opening renders the court room dead silent. It isn't only Ms Sisson who is angry and almost in tears. The Senator's head is down. Schola prompts the Senator to keep his head up and his shoulders steady. "Please don't look guilty," Mr Conkling censors in a whisper. "Shamed and bowed heads won't help," Schola admonishes the Senator.

The prosecutor comes to the tail of her long opening: "We have long decided that men like Mr Conner who demote themselves from full humanity don't deserve to live among us. They belong to the prisons. God knows that Mr Conner should have been in prison decades ago. We've collectively failed as a people to ensure that. Today, you members of the jury have the duty to correct this error." Prosecutor Kast finishes her colorful opening and takes her seat. She looks at her team behind her and they beam with pride and approval.

46

SCHOLA'S OPENING

EVERYBODY APPEARS TO HAVE FINISHED chewing on the provoking words of Prosecutor Kast. Not so Schola. Schola remains in profound thought after Prosecutor Kast resumes her seat. Schola's silence becomes uncomfortable. Judge Kaufman keeps looking at Schola's direction. Schola's gaze and thoughts are far from the crowded court room. Ms Kast's opening drama carries Schola ago. Prosecutor Kast hits on some true chords. Schola decides to deviate from his prepared opening statement that sits in front of him in a notepad. Schola sees Mr Conkling's hand reaching out gently to touch his shoulder, and without looking back, Schola gently pushes it away, prompting a stifled laughter in the courtroom.

Again, the Senator wonders whether his instincts hasn't misled him on his choice of Schola as counsel. This ex-Jesuit priest is out of the ordinary.

Judge Kaufman is uneasy and clears her throat to get Schola's attention. And because this attorney has never appeared before her, she has to look up her files to dig up his name. A rather long name for that matter – Mr Priestley Plusbriuschola.

"And Mr Plusbriuschola, do you have opening words for the jury and the court?" the judge asks cynically. Schola remains seated and motionless for a while and then rises and walks up to the jury.

"I completely agree with the prosecution, ladies and gentlemen of the jury," Schola begins and pauses. This unexpected beginning jolts both the Senator and Mr Conkling as it did the rest of the room. The prosecutor's team look surprise.

"Civilized and evolved and refined and educated minds and societies have come a very long way from their barbaric and regrettable past of ignorance and abominable mistakes," another brief pause. "Mistakes of convicting people for crimes that they didn't commit. Mistakes of selecting individuals as scapegoats for our collective crimes and wrongs," Schola says and looks around him.

He has the attention of the room. Not least, the complete attention of the jury. Nobody is now mistaken as to whose side he is on and where he is going.

"There's widespread sexual assault in this country and beyond. What must we do? Let's get a scapegoat and make an example of him. The most powerful, influential, and high-placed the scapegoat, the more placating our sacrifice," Schola says and turns and looks at the Senator.

At the sound of "wide spread sexual assault," Mr Pritish looks at Judge Kaufman's direction for a while and their eyes meet. The clerk quickly takes his gaze away. Judge Kaufman looks away, too. The Judge recoils into her private thoughts. She's convinced that her thing with her clerks is consensual. They love it; or so she thinks. But few like Mr Pritish backdown alone the way. In that case, she allows them to go.

"My client isn't a saint. He would make a lousy candidate for sainthood." Schola's saintly statement is received with a laughter and even a few claps of the hands. The light laughter awakes the Judge from her private thoughts. She wonders whether she should gavel for order. But the laughter dies as fast as it comes, negating the use of a gavel.

"Perhaps, perhaps, and only perhaps, he is a better candidate for the prisons than the office of holiness," Schola continues, prompting even more laughter. The Senator even appears to be enjoying this himself.

"Can Mr, .. ah" Judge Kaufman stumbles to remember the name. "Mr Schola, your honor," Schola helps the Judge with the short and common usage of his name. "Yes, Mr. Schola, can you get to your point. This court does not canonize people, and I'm no Pope," the Judge finishes to much laughter.

At this, Mr Pritish thinks to himself. "Thank God, you are no Pope." In the Judge's mind, her remark is meant for his clerk. So she looks in his direction and their eyes meet again. This time Mr Pritish looks at her with pity and understanding.

"I'm sorry your honor, Schola sincerely apologizes," and continues. "Sexual harassment is endemic both in our dear country and the world. It's a big problem. And it is against the law. And must be punished by all means," Schola pauses.

"For this, I agree with the prosecution. I also agree with the prosecution that we have come a long way as a nation. In the past, when there is a crisis, a massive crisis such as we have in our hands currently, there was the tendency to identify a scapegoat. We punish the scapegoat to massage our troubled conscious."

Schola stops, finds his throat dry, swallows saliva to smoothen it a bit and continues. "To prevent innocent people from being sacrificed for our collective guilt and crimes, the founding fathers of our nation, our civilized nation, set the bar for the prosecution to prove its case."

Schola's widening of the trial to unidentified culprits of sexual abuse didn't trouble only the judge. The females in position of power in the room are experiencing inner turbulence. On such person is Prosecutor Kast herself. Just yesterday, she was so tense because of the enormity of this trial that she needed a channel to release the tension. The usual channel – sex.

For a while now, she has had a crush on one of the new attorneys. This new attorney, Mr Ball Dundas, is due for promotion to the felony division. Deputy Prosecutor Dunda is surprised when Prosecutor Kast summons him to her office to talk about his promotion. There're many others in line. Persons he even deems more qualified than he.

"You ask to see me," Mr Dundas announces as he enters her office."

"Yes, it is about your promotion and I wonder how badly you need it, if at all," Prosecutor Kast says, turns around to show her back side and re-turns to face him with a wink and a warm smile.

Deputy Dundas is confused at this sudden proposal but gets the drift. "I'll do anything for the promotion," he fumbles.

"Happy to hear that," Prosecutor Kast replies in a sexually charged tone. Both know what should happen next. The unsolved issue is the time and place.

The place is proving a problem. Prosecutor Kast's daughter is back from college and is at home most of the time. The last time her daughter sees a man – an applicant to the prosecutor's office – emerge from the bedroom with her, daughter and mother communicate less. And daughter's trust in mother enervates. Mother is still trying to get back that trust. So her home is out of the question.

On his part, home is out of the question, though Deputy Dundas' wife isn't expected to be at home now.

"I'll be in the evidence room, and the single washroom beside it has no cameras directed at it," Prosecutor Kast suggests. And that is how it goes down.

And for understanding, Deputy Dundas gets assigned to be part of this high-profile team for this trial at the last minute. He now sits on the prosecution side of the room. Prosecutor Kast regrets that she brings him on the team. She has moral quims now.

But like Judge Kaufman, she consoles herself with the thought that it's consensual. They're both adults. There's no coercion. But this is false. Her inner being knows it's false. So she feels guilty for prosecuting a man of a crime that has become her pastime.

Schola's voice resonates in the courtroom, drawing Prosecutor Kast from her moral remorse. After five minutes of a preamble that diverts from his prepared remarks, Schola feels he is driving the opening in the right direction and his confident voice and posture reflect it.

"The state must prove beyond reasonable doubt that the defendant is guilty of the specific crimes charged. The state must prove every ingredient of these charges beyond every reasonable doubt," Schola pauses.

"I didn't hear the prosecution point to any evidence. None at all. Instead, the prosecution demonizes my client as a beast. A monster. An evil doer." Schola must work on his throat again. It's dry. He wonders for the first time whether he can drink water in the courtroom. It's not allowed at Mass. And there's no water on his desk, anyways. The saliva, which is increasingly in short supply, is his only way out.

"The laws of our state, those civilized laws that the prosecution references so referentially, don't allow us to send people like my client to jail because they are very bad people. The law does allow us to jail because a person has committed a specific crime or crimes. The law does allow us to jail or even kill (sometimes) because the government has proven beyond reasonable doubt that the defendant has committed a specific crime or specific crimes," Schola builds his point.

Schola still has more meat to add to the skeleton he sketches. But decides that given his dry throat, it is better to end. "You members of the jury are not angels either. Some people might think you beast or monsters," Schola looks at their faces.

Jury number four, Mr John Tarde is currently banging his babysitter. The poor girl is an illegal immigrant. She doesn't talk much when babysitting. Though she doesn't protest when Mr Tarde does her, Mr Tarde knows very well that she doesn't like it. He knows very well that she allows him because she has limited options for work. Also, and more important, she is afraid of deportation. And so the harassment goes on, will never be reported and will never be punished. But guilt is powerful. Mr

Tarde's head bows at the mention that "some people might think you a beast."

"Yes, my client, as I said at the beginning is no candidate for the sainthood. To be sure, he might even be a better candidate for hell than heaven. I don't know for sure. And I don't care about that now. As I don't care what your personal moral loads are. And we all have personal moral loads, some heavier than others. We all do," Schola says and looks around the silent room.

"But when one of us is charged with specific crimes as my client is, such charges should be backed with proof that is beyond reasonable doubt."

Schola turns, walks to the defense table and sits down.

The room remains silent. Judge Kaufman is miles away in thought. And so is everyone. Most people in that room are guilty to some degree, some more than others.

The silence breaks finally. "We recess for fifteen minutes. We'll take the first witness when we return." With that, Judge Kaufman disappears into her chambers less elegantly than she walks in this morning.

47

RECESS/FIRST WITNESS— DIRECT EXAM

"**G**OOD OPENING FOR A FIRST day in court," Mr Conkling whispers to Schola during the recess. Schola isn't sure whether the praise is to cheer him up or it's really an okay opening. Schola has no way of telling. After all, this is his first trial and his first day in court. All of that is unimportant. Focus on what is next, Schola tells himself.

The fatigue-looking Senator sits quietly throughout the fifteen minutes recess with his chin on his folded hands, his emotions hard to read.

All too soon, recess is over.

Judge Kaufman walks in quickly and takes her imposing seat. Before the murmurs end, she directs: "let's have the first witness."

"Prosecution calls Ms Renick Laniel to the witness box," Prosecutor Kast announces. The rear door of the court room opens to a woman in her sixties. She is decently dressed and looks mature and believable. But a deeper look reveals an aging woman unwilling to let go of her youth and the transient things of a young life. She is the party type from her dress. Couple of divorces maybe, judging from her ringless left figure. Probably widowed. But her waning strength won't allow her to do the things she once did in her youth. Schola could sense from her, a regret of the good, old days. Days never to return. She's unhappy. Her shallowness reveals in even her up to date fashion dress, revealing bits of her flesh here and there.

"Please state your name and address for the records," Prosecutor Kast begins.

"My name is Renick Laniel. I'm Ms Larnage Pincus's mother," she says, looking at the victim. "And I live with the victim at 1232 Maumee Ave." The prosecution looks at her notes, there're few preliminaries to go – work, community involvement and others. But she skips these and gets to the meat. Because the judge looks impatient.

"Please do you remember the night of 22 nd December 2016?

"Yes I do," Ms Pincus says after a pause and what seems like a period of trying to recollect. The prosecution waits for her answer, but she isn't forthcoming. So Ms Kast prompts.

"Please tell the jury what happened on that unfortunate night."

"I'd gone to work that morning. And around five o'clock, I decided to go to the gym for some workout. For some yoga classes actually. I'm a yoga fun. After yoga, I went home and fix some dinner for Larnage and myself. She didn't show up after eight o'clock, so I decided to eat alone."

She clears her throat, takes out a handkerchief and wipes tears that Schola doesn't see. Prompting Schola to look around for someone who might have seen her tears. None.

"I barely touched my food when she, my daughter called. Her voice was shaky. She could barely speak. I sense that she was crying. I couldn't eat. I asked whether she was fine. But the line went dead."

She clears her throat again, and this time, the tears wiped appear real but not genuine. And the jury isn't unanimous on the sincerity of her tears. Juror number twelve smiles ironically.

"I'm sorry, you have to relive this again," Prosecutor Kast consoles her. Schola thinks of objecting. But he couldn't think of any grounds.

"I tried calling her. But her phone was dead. I didn't know what to do. I thought of calling the police but didn't know what to tell them. I didn't know where she was, I would have driven to her. But I didn't know where she was. So I waited in pain."

"I'm sorry," Prosecutor Kast says again.

"After about thirty minutes, she drove up and came in. She was a complete wretch."

"By she you mean the victim, right?" Prosecutor Kast asks.

"Yes, my daughter, the victim. She was shattered emotionally. I even wandered how she drove home."

The witness performs the ritual of tears wiping again.

"Finally, she spoke up. She told me that Senator Conner drugged and raped her."

"Objection your honor," Schola says. The room goes silent for a while. Nobody expects an objection. The story is about captivating the room.

"On what grounds, Mr. aah, Mr ..." the judge searches for Schola's name again.

My name is Schola, your honor. "Yes, Mr. Schola on what grounds?"

"Hearsay your honor," Schola states. "What the victim told this witness is an out of court statement offered here, in court, for the truth of the matter at issue in this trial," Schola explains. And your honor, hearsays are inadmissible evidence.

"Yes, Mr. Schola, generally, hearsays are inadmissible except there's an exception," the judge adds.

"Ms Kast do you have any ground for an exception to this hearsay?" Judge Kaufman asks. Prosecutor Kast expects this objection and is prepared.

"Yes, your honor." "It falls under the excited utterance exception to hearsay."

Schola is on his feet again. "Your honor, this hearsay can't take cover under the excited utterance exception. From the witness's own admission, her granddaughter came home about 30 minutes after initially calling her. About 30 minutes your honor. She isn't sure. It could be more than 30 minutes, hours, days, weeks, or even years before she decided to call grandmother." Schola argues, but regrets going overboard.

The room chuckles a bit. And the judge is thinking about what to do with Schola's mixture of solid reasoning and exaggeration.

"Your honor, the victim at the time, as now, lived with the witness. On the night in questions, she called her immediately she was raped."

"Your honor, Ms Kast is testifying," Schola objects. "Your honor, she is also prejudicing the jury by saying that the victim was raped. She can't rule that" Schola objects.

The judge agrees with Schola. "Ms Kast stop testifying to what you don't have personal experience of."

"Folks, let's move on." The judge directs.

"Ms Laniel, the events in question happened five years ago. Why didn't you report to the police?" That was the prosecutor's last question.

"I was afraid of further harassment and retaliation from the Senator. He's such a powerful man and can do anything he wants with his money, power and influence."

The Senator shakes his head in disbelieve. She in fact called him after the incident to plead with him. Said her daughter over reacted. Said she had mood swings. Said she would make it up to him. In fact, days after, she asked for financial assistance to pay their rent. The Senator was quite a kind man. He didn't want to see people suffer. So he wrote a check to cover rent for that month. In exchange, both mother and daughter said they wanted to give him a free massage.

Apparently, these subsequent events have escaped their minds. They pestered him. He didn't go after them.

"I understand," Prosecutor Kast says cynically. "So if you were afraid of him then, why are you now speaking up?" Prosecutor Kast anticipates the defense's question and smiles cynically at Schola as she puts it to the witness.

"Because so many others started speaking up. Dozens recounted similar conduct by The Senator. Hundreds other victims were unafraid and so we spoke up too."

Prosecutor Kast interrupts her: "So because many others are speaking up, that gives you the courage to also speak up?"

"Yes," the witness answers.

Schola feels like objecting, rose halfway but changes his mind. He'll have a chance to cross. Thanks to the Sixth Amendment and its associated case law.

"The prosecution rest for now your honor," Ms Kast takes her seat.

48

CROSS OF MOTHER

THE PROSECUTOR'S DIRECT EXAMINATION OF the first witness is a coherent, albeit rehearsed pretestimonial statements. It worries Schola that the tears aren't genuine. Ms Renick is acting. And she is a terrible actress. She never would have landed a job with Hollywood.

Schola wonders whether it's because of the lapsed time. The alleged crimes happened years ago. Probably, they lived through it and had gotten over it. Or probably, they simply decide to be part of the mounting allegations against Senator Conner. Lots of probables.

In any event, trials are supposed to aim at unearthing the truth of the matter. The court (the jury in this case) should be interested in knowing the truth. Then the sword of justice falls where it ought.

But all too often, neither party cares about the truth – largely. The prosecution is interested in winning the case, some prosecutors, sadly, at all cost. Prosecutors want to tally up their conviction numbers. The defense isn't any less guilty of this. The defense aims to get his client off the hook—at all cost. The defendant's guilt or the lack thereof doesn't matter. Neither party appears to be a friend of the truth.

Thanks to the greatest legal inventions—Cross examination. Cross examinations are crucial in this truth gathering process. The examining lawyer points out inconsistencies and hammer out the truth. The truth is cooked in the crucible of cross-examination. The rules of cross examination allow lawyers to be ruthless.

Before now, Schola was really conflicted as to what to do with this old woman who does her best to appear young. Schola had initially decided to be gentle with her. She is like Schola's own mothers—one if she were alive and the other still living. Though Schola's mothers won't put up a show for a trial of all things. Schola's mothers will never lie for the world. Schola has a duty and he goes for it politely but strategically and strongly.

"Good morning Ms Laniel," Schola begins with a friendly tone." But Ms Laneil declines to respond. This gives Schola a reason to cut off the niceties.

"According to you, in the morning in question, you went to work?" Schola pauses, allowing the question register. "You went to work, and from work, you went to the gym," Schola pauses again.

"Yes, I went to my yoga class in the evening," she finally says.

"Yes, you went to the gym for your yoga thing," Schola affirms.

"But let's stay in the morning and the afternoon for now," Schola suggests. You said that you went to work until 5 pm, is that right?" Schola asks.

After an unsettling silence she says yes.

"Great, that is what I thought you said when the state led you in testimony," Schola remarks.

"Objection your honor; is there a question?" Prosecutor Kast is on her feet.

"Yes, Mr Schola stay with the questions and not what you recall hearing," the judge intervenes.

"I'm sorry," Schola apologizes.

"Ms Laniel, who was your employer?" There is an even longer silence.

"Objection your honor! Relevance," Prosecutor Kast interjects again.

"Credibility your honor," Schola replies before the judge could say anything.

"Please the witness should answer the question," the judge directs.

"Where did you work that morning and during that period?" Schola repeats his question.

"I didn't work for anybody, I didn't work for a company," she answers truthfully.

Schola and his team anticipate this and are very surprise when she says that she went to work. For most of her life, Ms Laniel couldn't work for any employer for more than a year continuously. She has been fired from one job after another. Mr McGinley did some nice research on this witness.

"Thanks for clarifying. But you did go to work that morning. The jury might want to know where you worked that morning if you didn't work for some employer." It's both a question and a suggestion.

"Objection your honor. Call for what he thinks the jury might want to know," Prosecutor Kast is sensing that his witness is going down.

"Please, let's make some progress I believe the jury would like to know where she worked that morning and whether she even worked at all," the judge throws out the objection.

The prosecution team wonders whose idea it was that she should talk about her work.

"I was working for myself," she answers.

"Okay, I got y'all," Schola is almost teasing. "What work did you do?"

The tears this time are genuine. The daughter joined her. And they both reached for their handkerchiefs to clean the drops. But the judge, the jury, and the room are very confused. Schola sympathizes. But he has a job to do.

There're murmurs in the room. "Quiet everybody," Judge Kaufman calls the room to order. The Judge looks in Schola's direction, indicating that he should take control of his cross.

Schola's voice cracks out of pity. "What was this job?"

Even the jury realizes that Schola shares the witness's discomfort. The jury likes this sympathetic lawyer. A lawyer who wouldn't exploit a vulnerable situation to his advantage. But the Senator and Mr Conkling are very angry. This's the time to crash her. This's the time to take her down. Schola is playing the priest instead of the attorney.

"I gave massages," the witness finally says. The room says what, almost in unison. Even the judge is wondering what she says.

"Please can you repeat that, I doubt the jury heard you," Schola requests.

"I gave massages," she repeats. Louder this time.

"By massages, you mean body massages?" Schola seeks for clarity.

"Yes, body massages," she confirms.

Many in the room wonder why she is reluctant to admit that she is a masseur. There's nothing criminal about that. Apart from the deeply pious, many people get a massage every now and then. Prosecutor Kast is happy that the worse is over. She has no idea.

"Were you a licensed masseur at the time, Ms Laniel?" Schola knows the answer. But the question surprises the prosecution.

So an objection is badly needed. "Objection your honor! Relevance."

The judge doesn't know how to rule. The judge is yet to decide, but the witness speaks out. "I don't remember, it was a long time ago."

Schola chuckles with the rest of the court. "But she remembers what her daughter told her that evening," Schola says cynically.

"Objection your honor!" Prosecutor Kast objects.

"Yes, Mr. Schola, you are out of order," the judge says.

"The prosecution requests for a brief recess your honor," Prosecutor Kast decides she needs to talk to her client. The request is granted.

49

CROSS CONTINUES

WITNESS LANIEL LOOKS COMPOSED WHEN Judge Kaufman takes her seat after the recess. Ms Laniel appears steady and ready for the questions, and Schola goes after it.

"You testify that fear prevented you from reporting Senator Corner to the police: fear of intimidation, of retaliation. Did I hear you correctly?" Schola asks, maintaining an unflinching gaze with the witness.

"Yes."

During the break the prosecution coaches the witness not to elaborate on her answers.

"I see. The Senator is big. He's physically imposing. He's wealthy. He's powerful. And he's influential. Yes, the Senator might be able to intimidate you."

"Your honor, please, is there a question," the prosecution objects.

"In what form could the retaliation take?" Schola rephrases.

"I don't know. But I was very afraid," the witness answers.

"Exactly my problem. You don't work for him, so he couldn't have fired you. Or demoted you. So he was in no position to intimate you?" Schola struggles to put a clear question because its varied articulations are calls for speculation.

"I was afraid," she repeats her answer.

Schola realizes he was heading nowhere with this line of enquiry and so changes tactics.

"So until now, you have never threatened to report or actually report a man of the status of the Senator to law enforcement?" Schola poses while looking in a document different from his note pad.

The witness is confused. She doesn't know what's in that document. She stretches her neck in the document's direction in vain. Because beside massage, her most lucrative job over the years is blackmailing her clients and creaming them of all the money she could get. So she has made so many complaints to the police. So many complaints against people like the Senator. But she thinks that nobody knows of these complaints because this was so many years ago. And because the issues were largely settled in private, they weren't in the public domain.

Realizing her discomfort, Schola re-focuses on the document, takes out a pen and begins marking and underlining.

Even the prosecutor is rattled. This new lawyer is proving unpredictable. She turns and looks at her team to her right then to her left and behind her. All six of them shake their heads. How didn't they dig this up. This witness is crumbling before Prosecutor Kast's very eyes. Prosecutor Kast regrets in the background check lapses and makes a note to change her entire investigative unit.

The room realizes the commotion and is interested in the answer to the defense's question. And Schola doubles down on this promising line of inquiry.

"Have you in the past reported similar charges against persons similarly situated as my client – rich, powerful, influential – to the police?" Schola's voice vibrates with confidence.

Ms Laniel looks at her daughter in search of a clue in reply. And Ms Pincus looks at the prosecution; Ms Kast is guideless. In fact, Ms Pincus, the victim, doesn't want to be part of this trial. She's talked into coming. Her past isn't exemplary. And she doen't want to put her past out in the open.

Schola looks happily confused but cautionary as is Mr Conkling. Senator Conner's memory of this family comes into clearer focus. In fact, he wrote them a big check, saying the check makes up for any wrongs. He has since closed his account at that bank. That might be why it never occurred to him. And wait a minute, a year later, didn't he pay for her medical procedure. He believes that he did.

In truth, Ms Laniel buys her first house with settlement money from two clients: a former congressman and a mayor.

The congressman in question requests and pays for a massage. Back massage. She arrives with her equipment. Collects cash in advance. And gets to work. She is pretty good at it. Her fingers do wonders. As she works on this congressman, things get out of hand. The congressman might have been starved of sex for long. He grabs her hands first. She mildly asks that he let go of her hand while praying that he doesn't. For it means more money. "Please, let me hold you small," her client pleads. "No," we agreed on only a massage. The congressman doesn't feel from this language that she really objects. Planning on paying more, he grabs her and kisses her and gets on top of her. Her "no, no, no" were faint and fake. But after the act, she alleges raped, threatens to go public. That money contributes to her first house.

The mayor's is similar. And there are many other victims of her scheme. The recalcitrant ones, those who refuse to settle, she reports to the police. Virtually all of them settle after the police contacts them. When monies are paid, she refuses to cooperate in investigations and the cases are dropped.

Given this litany of blackmail, extortion, faking, defrauding, and cheating, she doesn't want to take any chances.

Schola's confidence goes off the roof. "Why do you report those powerful people to the police but afraid of reporting this other powerful person here, the Senator, my client?" Schola's gaze still fixes on a notepad.

The witness is quiet and ashamed. And in tears again. And answers aren't forthcoming.

Another merciful tactical recess saves the prosecution the ongoing embarrassment.

50

SECOND RECESS

DURING RECESS, BOTH THE SENATOR and Mr Conkling are deeply crossed with Schola's mild cross. The two are mad at Schola. Schola knows that he is soft on Ms Laniel. But the high level of discontent of the Senator and Mr Conkling suggests that it might be more than the mild cross examination.

The Senator speaks first: "Tell me why you left her off the hook?" Schola stares at him and pretends not to hear him. "We have the fish in our hook, completely secured for the meal, you remove it off the hook and throw it back into the lake," the Senator laments. "Please I will like to know why," the Senator demands. Schola just stares at the ground.

Mr Conkling is angry as he is amused. The witness comes to the edge of breaking, a little pressure would have done it. Mr Conkling knows Schola is soft on the witness not because of his inexperience. This might be his first case, but the man isn't naïve.

But Mr Conkling doesn't want to escalate the situation that the Senator's flared tempers is generating. So Mr Conkling comes up with a reason that might placate their client – the Senator. "We've a grand plan. We are mild now to be harder next time." But the Senator isn't buying Mr Conkling's explanation.

"Good job," Mr Schola says Conkling. Both the Senator and Schola look at him with incredulity. And Mr Conkling is even more ashamed of his pretense. He bows his head in shame. This group of defense team doesn't have patient for fake praise singers, Mr Conkling just learns that.

Still, Schola is lost in his thoughts. The history of wars over the years has evinced the power of mercy. A forgiven enemy is likely to be a loyal friend. One could almost flip such a former enemy. Of course, there're those exceptions that mercy shown, turns out to be a grave miscalculation. A completely wrong move. The beneficiary after gaining advantage makes an about turn and inflicts the greatest of harm on the merciful. But in most cases, mercy wins over the most hateful of hearts.

Recess is as over as it was quickly requested. Heading back inside, Schola is determined to show even more mercy to this mother and her daughter. Schola will show them love.

51

CROSS CONTINUES

"WOULD MR. SCHOLA PLEASE RESUME his cross," Judge Kaufman invites, rather impatiently upon sitting. Schola rises to his feet and strolls towards the witness: "thank you your honor," Schola says as he wraps up his cross of the first witness.

The witness is expecting the worse now. She lies that she didn't call the police because she fears retaliation. She is afraid that this lawyer has the list of men that she has reported to the police over the decades, blackmailing and extorting money from them.

During the break, the prosecution examines the list, obtained from the police data, and found it very unsettling. It's a long list. It would appear to others that almost every man that encounters Ms Laniel harasses her, and she reports him.

And of course, besides the official reports, there were the numerous men that she blackmailed and extorted monies. This second list is extensive as well.

The prosecution sees its case crumbling. What troubles Prosecutor Kast most is why opposing lawyer decides not to move for the kill when he had the chance. Schola could have refused her request for another recess. But Schola didn't. In her experience, an opponent delays a win to further a bigger win. Or an opponent – rarely – delays a win because he's stupid. Prosecutor Kast hopes for the latter. Schola is stupid. But this unknown new lawyer doesn't at all come across as a fool.

"Again, thanks for the time to assist the court in ascertaining the truth in these matters so that justice might be done," Schola begins. "I've very few questions, in fact, only two."

"Did you ask my client for a date after he allegedly sexually assaulted your daughter?"

The truth is that the Senator was one of her high-profile clients in her massage business. She didn't want to lose him. While in fact, she didn't ask him for a date, she did try to arrange dates for him. Her hope was that their friendship would continue.

The truth is that the Senator was nice to her daughter. Extremely caring towards her. Besides the money, the Senator was sort of in love with her. And she felt that she was in love with him, too. The two love birds took trips together. Beautiful pictures were taken during those trips. But after six months of no proposal from the Senator, the girl decided to move on with her life. The Senator willingly obliged. The Senator had always thought that she was too young for him.

"Did you ask my client for a date, or even try to arrange a date for him after these alleged sexual assaults?" Schola repeats the question, breaking the awkward silence.

Even the Senator is surprised at this line of questioning. The Senator recalls that if he wasn't marriage at the time, he would probably have married the victim. But what even amuses the Senator is how Schola gets all this information. The Senator had forgotten most of the details. He wonders what else Schola knows about his own amorous life that he doesn't remember. The Senator feels very stupid.

With no answers forthcoming, Schola continues. "That's fine. After many years it's hard to remember," Schola genuinely consoles the witness. Mr Conkling is very angry. You bring the court to a standstill until the lying witness confesses in tears. Or die. The jury must see the witness weep and beg for forgiveness. The problem with inexperience, Mr Conkling concludes.

"Okay, my last question," Schola says to the relief of the witness and the prosecution team. "You stated that ..." Schola leaves his question midway. He sees that the witnesses head is shaking in an unusual way. Schola knows from his pastoral experience as a Jesuit priest, symptoms of this sickness. Schola turns and looks at the daughter; she is in tears, too. Her grandmother needs her meds. The judge realizes the situation but wants the cross examination done with.

"Your honor, I'm not feeling too well. I could use a five minutes recess," Schola pleads. The judge looks at Schola with amazement. The judge begins to wonder whose side this rockie lawyer is on.

"As you please, Mr. Schola," the judge says cynically and leaves for her chambers.

52

RECESS AND CROSS

THE WITNESS, MS LANIEL, HEADS straight to the washroom. Ms Pinkus, the victim, follows her inside the washroom. Both are very angry but don't know whom to blast. Both are very ashamed but don't know whom to blame for their shame. Ms Laniel realizes that her old game is catching up with her; the bill is becoming due. She feels that her public embarrassment is a result of years of dubbing men. She regrets talking her daughter into this mess.

But for Ms Renick Laniel, it's all about the money. She sees this trial as an opportunity to earn more money. But this scheme is proving far too difficult. With everybody now doubting her and her story and some even repulsive at what she has been doing in the name of massage, she now doubts whether the Senator would ever be convicted as the prosecution claims from day one.

Daughter puts the blame mainly on the prosecution. The police and the prosecutor go about visiting victims of alleged sexual assault. One of these alleged victims tells the police that mother says that daughter was also sexually assaulted. So the prosecution visits them to hear this new accusation. Ms Laniel so embellishes her story that the prosecution thinks that hers is the perfect case.

And once the criminal trial is over, they could take the Senator on in a civil trial for damages, the prosecution tells them. The man is worth billions. And we are talking about hundreds of millions in damages. At the mention of millions, Ms Laniel's spirit lifts. And against daughter's reservations, she is willing to testify.

She is doing it alone even if daughter refuses to get involved. In fact, health wise, she starts feeling better. The millions were enough to cover the expenses for the expensive operation that she needs badly.

But then, this lawyer catches Ms Laniel lying. Lying under oath. Lying in court. And lying to the public. She has always lied. But lying in court and lying in public and lying under oath is a different kind of lying. It's perjury.

But this lawyer has a friendly face. Who is he, she wonders? Obviously, the lawyer doesn't need a break. He realizes that Ms Laniel needs a break and requests one.

"Mother, do you know the lawyer?" Ms Pinkus asks. Mother is surprised at the question. Ms Laniel, too, has been trying to recall if she knows him somewhere. But no, their paths have never crossed until now.

"No, I have never seen him prior to the trial," mother answered truly.

"So why is he very nice to you?" Ms Pincus probes.

"I've no idea. I guess some people are just nice and considerate," mother says, gulping more water to push down her meds.

53

JUDGE KAUFMAN ON RECESS

JUDGE KAUFMAN WAS VERY SURE that this jury would convict Senator Conner. And she relished, then, at the prospects of the news of associating her name as the judge who presided over the conviction of the famous sexual pervert. Even more important for the judge, she had hoped for a judicial promotion that a likely conviction would have facilitated. She would have had few years on the bench before retiring, ensuring that she eventually retires on an income that will provide a life of relative comfort.

But this soothing hope is evaporating before her very eyes. This rockie lawyer is proving up to the task than she had imagined. This new lawyer is turning a very bad case into an exercise of victimizing the accused. Schola shows the first witness, Ms Laniel, lying on several occasions, thus destroying, completely, her credibility. She wonders who this new lawyer is. And she wonders why the handsome lawyer isn't clerking for her.

"John who is the new guy?" the judge inquires of Schola from his other law clerk. In fact, Mr John McAdoo has been digging into the new guy without much success. He isn't on Facebook. No tweeter accounts. No Instagram. Nothing out in the public glare of his life. And he went to law school out of state – The Georgetown Law Center in D.C.?, but nobody is too sure about that, too. So no local classmates to feed them with gossip. Of course, his name shows up on the Rolls of Attorneys of the State of Indiana. That's about it.

Judge Kaufman is tempted to call Schola in for a conversation. Though asking of his background won't be extra judicial communication, her long years on the bench has taught her to stop talking to any of the counsels of a party alone until the case is over. After the case, she will have the occasion, probably, to grab coffee with him.

54

DEFENSE ON RECESS

I F THE WORLD OF THE witnesses and the judge are largely in wonder of who Schola is, the universe of the defense isn't amused at all. The Senator and Mr Conkling are both infuriated and confused in equal measure.

"Tell me, whose side are you on?" The Senator asks Schola with a raised and angry tone. "Do you realize that I go to prison if the jury convicts me?" It's a lament than a reprimand or even a question. Mr Conkling intervenes to cool things down. Mr Conkling calls the Senator aside and speaks to him. Schola wonders what he's telling him.

But that's the least on Schola's mind. A lot is flushing through Schola's mind. Schola can't wait to escape to the lonely and lovely forest of the Farm to think through these matters.

Schola is still deep in thought when Mr Conkling taps him on his shoulders. "It's time to go, your meaningless recess is over." The Senator looks at him menacingly as the three men walk back into the court room for Schola's last question of the first witness.

55

CROSS CONTINUES

"**I**S MR SCHOLA NOW WELL and able to continue with the cross," Judge Kaufman says sarcastically with an inviting smile.

"Thanks for our prayers, your honor, I'm sure I'm feeling far better now and ready to continue," Schola says appreciatively while casting a look at Ms Laniel.

"Okay then, let's have it," the judge says.

"Ms Laniel, you testify that you came forward only after many, many accusers, came forward with their stories against the Senator?"

Schola waits for the witness to affirm or deny the question. But the witness is mute. So Schola rephrases the question.

"Wasn't it the prosecution that, in fact, first contacts you and incentivizes you to speak about your experiences with the Senator?"

Ms Laniel looks at Prosecutor Kast, who turns his face away. There's no answer. But everybody knows the answer.

"Defense is grateful for the chance to ask the witness some questions, your honor," Schola says and takes his seat. And with that, the court adjourns for the first day.

56

DIRECT OF DAUGHTER

JUDGE KAUFMAN HURRIES IN AND sits just when the clock strikes 9:00 am. "Is the prosecution ready with another witness?" It's more of a directive than a question.

Prosecutor Kast rises and calls Ms Larnage Pincus, the victim, and the prosecutor's star witness, to the witness box.

"Please state your name and address for the records," Prosecutor Kast invites Ms Pincus to get her testify started. Ms Pincus is an arresting-looking woman. Tall. She radiates the beauty of the goddesses. Prosecutor Kast relishes in how the men descend on her with their eyes as she makes her way to the witness box. The male jurors are impressed.

"My name is Larnage Pincus and I live at 1232 Maumee Ave with my mother," Ms Pincus provides her name and address in a mild voice.

"Ms Pincus, what's your occupation?" Prosecutor Kast asks to complete the preliminaries.

Schola sits listening with utmost detachment and complete indifference. Mr Conkling is worried. Schola should be taking notes. All inconsistencies and contradictions should be noted. A direct examination might take a while. An opposing counsel who fails to take down contemporaneous memos while the witness is testifying might forget crucial points. But again, this ex-Jesuit priest, former Harvard professor is different. He does his things against the known norms without violating the common conventions. Still, Mr Conkling sees his role as a "paralegal" to help however way he can.

Tapping Schola on the shoulder from behind, he asks, "are you taking any notes?" Schola turns around and smiles with the reply: "notes from the prosecutor or the witness? None of them is my professor. And there's no exam." Senator Conner overhears the comments and all three men stifle a laughter, causing the room to look momentarily in the direction of the defense team.

Judge Kaufman hears the happy noises from the defense table and silently wonders what the defense is happy about. But the noise disappears as it starts, rendering a bench reprimand needless.

"I've been a college volleyball coach much of my life," Ms Pincus answers. But the event in question has nothing to do with volleyball or college. Prosecutor Kast is impatient and wants the witness to get to the essentials.

"What else do you do apart from coaching college girls volleyball? Are you for example a physical therapist?" Prosecutor Kast asks.

"Objection your honor!" Schola shouts mildly. "Leading the witness your honor," Schola gives the ground for his objection and sits down.

"Yeah, yeah, yeah, objection sustained. Ms Kast please stop leading the witness," Judge Kaufman rules.

"I'm sorry your honor, I'll rephrase," Ms Kast says. But before she rephrases, the witness answers.

"Coaching besides, I also provide physical therapy on demand. I sometimes work with Ms Laniel, my mother."

"Do you know the defendant, Mr Conner?" Prosecutor Kast asks looking at Senator Conner. The answer is obvious.

Ms Pincus nobs her head in affirmation.

"Have you ever provided physical therapy for the defendant?" This's a much better question. Schola thinks.

"Yes, on a dozen of occasions," the witness answers and steers her gaze away when it meets Mr Conner's.

Schola leans towards Senator Conner and poses: "Is she good?" Mr Conner is taken aback. It's incredulous that his attorney should be cracking jokes when it matters most. This guy is out of the ordinary. He has a weird sense of humor, and it comes at the wrong time. He doesn't crack jokes in a relaxed atmosphere. He does it during high tension moments.

"I don't remember; it was so long ago, and they were so many of them," Mr Conner replies Schola.

Schola chuckles and says: "That's a great answer. Maybe I should get you in the witness box. I believe you will do better than the two testifying women." Mr Conkling also overhears the comments and the three men do their best, again, to stifle the laughter.

The jury and the audience as well as the judge note the lightness from the defense side and baffle at their lack of seriousness.

"Do you remember a visit to the home of the defendant on December 22, 2016?" The prosecutor poses.

"Yes, I do," the witness answers, again turning her gaze towards the defense table.

"Please tell this court what happened on that day?" Prosecutor Kast invites the longest narrative of the witness and the main point of the entire direct examination.

"Mr Conner requests for my expertise with a back problem. Mr Conner is eating when I get to the house. He invites me to join him for the meal first before the massage. I do. And after diner, I start working on his back. I barely get far when I felt very weak and tired. I think that I'm sick. I pass out. I wake up naked, my privacy violated," she says most regrettably.

"You mean you wake up and realize that you have been raped?" Prosecutor Kast seeks clarity.

"Yes," the witness answers.

Senator Conner tries again to remember the day and event in question with lots of difficulties because of several reasons.

One, it happens years ago. Though his memory isn't failing him, he turns not to remember events of mere pleasure. Two, he has no problems with the witness over their six months of what he considers courtship. He takes her on trips, and they vacation together. Hardly did they ever fight. As he recalls, but for his marriage at the time, he might have married her. He loves her at the time. And he thinks she, too, loves him at the time. It's a shame his weird lawyer says he should forget about testifying.

"So what did you do after you realized that you were raped?" Prosecutor Kast presses on.

"I was confused and lost. I was weak and could barely walk," she answers in shame.

"Did you call anybody or tell anybody about the rape?" Prosecutor Kast poses again.

"Objection your honor," Schola shouts. But before the judge rules, Prosecutor Kast rephrases her question: "did you tell anybody what happened?"

"Yes, I called Laniel, the first witness, and told her about my ordeal. I was very ashamed."

"Who else did you tell?" Prosecutor Kast builds up her list of corroborating witnesses.

"A close friend too, Ms Calein Wilkens. This was a day after the ordeal. She suggests that I go for a medical examination. But because I was feeling better, I decide against seeing a doctor," the witness answers.

"Why didn't you go to the police?" Prosecutor Kast asks her final question, more of an attempt to preempt the defense's cross.

The witness hesitates in saying that she was afraid as she is coached to say. But she must answer, and so she says, "because I was afraid and ashamed." Her tone betrays her insincerity.

57

EXPOSÉ ON DAUGHTER

AN UNKNOWN INFORMANT – SCHOLA prefers to call this informant an opposition research assistant – is mailing exposés of the characters who matter in the Senator Conner's criminal debacle to Schola. The informant leaves the exposés by Schola's door. The package is never there before Schola goes to bed – at about midnight; but the white envelope tacks nicely by his bedroom door when he opens the door to run or when he returns from a run.

So over the weeks, Schola receives dirt on the witnesses. Schola also receives the financial record, family life, professional life, and the reckless romantic life of his client – Senator Conner, a reckless life that is partly to blame for his current legal conundrum.

And just when he thinks that the unsolicited deliveries of the unedited, personal lives of these characters are over, Schola receives another dose of the personal failures of Ms Pincus in the same size white envelope by his door hours before Ms Larnage Pincus is scheduled to testify. If Ms Pincus is sexually harassed, it appears that she goes around looking for the harassment as suggestive from the dossier dumped at Schola's door.

At age 21, Ms Pincus marries, has a child, a girl – who is now an adult. She divorces a year later. For reasons absent in the memo, sole custody of the child is given to the father instead. It doesn't appear from accounts that Ms Pincus is in touch with her daughter.

Thereafter, Ms Pincus goes on to three other failed marriages. The records don't reflect a child in these later failed marriages. None of these marriages lasts for more than a year.

Ms Pincus's professional life is as much a failure as her personal live. She plays volleyball in college. She appears really created for the game of volleyball. Beautiful and tall, she doesn't need to jump that high in the court below blasting a ball over to the other side.

But she "resigns" from all four colleges of the State of Indiana where she coaches volleyball. The longest of such coaching engagement until her final employment at a college was three years.

Her last coaching job lasts for a while, running into almost a decade. Under her charge, the school's volleyball team wins lots of championship titles. On dozens of occasions, she is either nominated or wins the coach of the year of the college. Pictures of Ms Pincus from this period see her smiling most of the time. She appears a happy woman. And indeed, she was a happy woman. Then.

But then she gets fired from this job, too. She is asked to proceed on leave, an investigation ensues, and she is eventually fired. The charges upon, which she is sacked concerns Ms Pincus's adventures with a student, the captain of the college basketball team. Apparently, the two were in love. The athletic tall boy visits her at night, sleeps over and leaves at dawn for the gym. Obviously, it violates the ethics rules of an educational institute for a teacher to be seeing a student.

But for a while, nobody really cares. The boy isn't forced, and it's largely unknown. Things, however, get out of hand when Ms Pincus asks him to join her any time she goes on game trips with her volleyball team. He doesn't travel with the team; but he drives and checks into the same hotel as Ms Pincus's team. At night, he goes to Ms Pincus room or she comes to his for the private party. Schola gives them credit. They do well to keep it discrete. Almost.

A player of the volleyball team has a crush on the same guy. They also start an affair on the side. The girl suspects nothing until, on a trip, she accidently goes into the coach's room – thinking it to be a student's – and sees the two of them at it. The poor girl is badly hurt. Packs her bag, leaves the games, and quits college. But not without lots of noise about her coach and her student boyfriend.

School authorities get wind of the drama. Or better still, popular opinion forces school authorities to act. And with the scandal upon scandal on college campuses involving coaches, the college is on a face-saving mission. Ms Pincus is first put on leave. An investigation ensues. Findings find her in breach of several ethical rules. Probably, some criminal laws, too, given the boy's age. So Ms Pincus is fired and the president of the college ensures that a public announcement accompanies her sacking to save the face of the college.

Without a job, and not employable, she expands her expertise of physical therapy. Her mother is already into massage. The two team up, expanding their "clients" base. She needs the money badly. At first, it is pure body massage. Specific parts of the body hands, legs, back, and neck. And Ms Pincus is good at it. With time, it goes into full body massage. And at times, when the client asks for it and she likes the client, the two work it all out to a happy end. The money is good.

Senator Conner has always had a terrible back pain. Massages help ease the pain considerably. But daily massages are needed to keep the pain at bay. Massage and sex are far better distractions for dealing with the pain. And a newer therapist allows for the Senator to experiment with different people. The new encounters are also better at dealing with the pain than old faces. And so the Senator hardly has a masseur returned a third time.

The number of masseurs isn't unlimited, especially in Fort Wayne when the Senator visits from Washington. So Ms Pincus gets her chance. On their first day, Ms Pincus gives the Senator a real professional massage. Ms Pincus realizes something unusual about Senator Conner's back. The Senator is surprise when Ms Pincus asks him whether he experiences severe back pain. She insists that they bike before the massage. At first, the duo will cycle around the Senator's spacious mansion. As the Senator's interest in cycling becomes voracious, they begin pedaling long distances. The Senator's back gets better. In addition, the Senator believes that he feels something for Ms Pincus. The two ride into love. Until …

58

CROSS OF DAUGHTER

MS PINCUS IS THOUGHTFULLY DRESSED for her testimony – conservatively and carefully. Her heavily hidden beauty still radiates. Schola observes that the male jurors are taken by her beauty. The female jurors take note of her choice of clothes and make-up. Prosecutor Kast is happy for her choice of the fashioner who recreates Ms Pincus for the testimony. Ms Laniel's testimony didn't go so well. This's it or nothing for the prosecution.

No reasonable person doubts that Pincus's inviting beauty might make her a target of ravenous men who can't control their libidos. A target for men like Senator Conner. True enough, Conner feels her heart pulsating at the sight of Ms Pincus, even in these circumstances. And his blood pressure goes into the reds when Pincus' eyes lock with his for a moment. The jury didn't miss the moment as is Schola. Schola smiles at what love can do.

It's the job of Schola to set aside the prosecution's portray of Ms Pincus and set before the jury an alternative Ms Pincus. That other Ms Pincus isn't as innocent as she claims and looks now. And that other Ms Pincus isn't as beautiful as she portrays and looks now.

Cross examinations are typically brutal. The rules allow for the brutality visited on the witness. Every dirty linen of the witness is washed right there before the interested audience. All the dirt is squashed out so much so that often all others see in a person after a good cross are her dirt.

That's exactly why Schola isn't putting Senator Conner on the stand. Senator Conner has more than dirt. He has all sorts of skeletons. If Senator Conner were to take the stand, the prosecution would bring out one skeleton after another until he passes for a mass murderer. The jury will like to hang him themselves. In fact, even now, some women want to shoot him. And not a few men understand the hatred these women have for the Senator

For even the saint has a dark side. All the saints had reason to go for confession. Daily. As a former catholic priest of five of years, Schola knows this very well.

But attorney Schola brings to cross examination a different attitude. To love the witness and show mercy where the witness is most vulnerable. Never disgrace a witness on the stand. Never tear witnesses into pieces for the sake of embarrassing them. Touch only those sensitive nerves that are indispensably relevant to the search for truth. Show them love. Show them mercy. Love triumphs over all else. Love always wins. Always.

Already, Schola has secured a special place in Pincus's heart for not going hard on Ms Laniel, her mother. But Ms Pincus still has a reason not to trust Schola. Because Schola is out to defend the man she's helping to hang. So it doesn't make sense that Schola is kind to them.

"Good morning Ms Pincus," Schola greets the witness with a genuine smile. Ms Pincus could feel the kindness of the man in front of her. The prosecutor tells her that Schola would come very hard at her. But here he's with a smile. Daughter returns Schola's smile with a shy smile of her own.

"Would you say that my client, Senator Conner, was in love with you?" Schola asks. The question is completely unexpected. So Ms Pincus is out of script. Prosecutor Kast shifts in her seat uncomfortably. She, too, is out of her scheme. Ms Pincus looks at her for direction; she has none. Prosecutor Kast feels like objecting but finds no ground.

"He has never told me that he loves me," the witness replies.

"Hmmm," Schola breaths in. "Never?" Schola queries.

"Well I don't recall him telling me that he loves me," she clarifies.

"That might as well be true, Ms Pincus," Schola affirms her answer. "But from his actions (and omissions), did you think that Senator Conner deeply loved you?" Schola stresses the deeply.

There's a longer pause. Ms Pincus memory is full of the past. All those trips. All those gifts. All those monies he gave her. The man was very kind to her. Never hurt her. Except for that once …

Senator Conner considers the question also. He loved her. He would have married her but for his age and the fact that he was nominally married at the time. On occasions, he was thinking of divorcing his wife and marrying Ms Pincus. But he has many failed marriages under his belt. He wasn't sure how a marriage with Pincus would turn out. And the divorces come with significant cost to his business. The first divorce, in fact, nearly destroyed his then incipient business empire. The division of the marital property per the court's order saw his wife taking half of his entire business and wealth in accordance with the law of Indiana. The women bring nothing to the marriage and go out of it very rich.

The only consolation was that he had a daughter with her. A beautiful daughter who doesn't want to see him now because of all these allegations.

Senator Conner gets wiser. So in subsequent marriages, he gets them to sign pre-marital agreements. Even with that, during divorce, they would want to set aside those agreements they so willingly and knowingly signed. Thanks to his team of good lawyers who argued for respecting the agreement. The women even at that give up the fight after a compromise in million of dollars.

"Did the Senator by his conduct toward you suggest that he loved you?" Schola repeats his question, jolting both Ms Pincus and Senator Conner from their romantic reminisces of yore.

"Yes, I believe Con loved me," Ms Pincus eventually admits. Schola pretends to be confused by the name Con.

"Who is Con," Schola seeks clarity.

"I'm sorry. I used to call Mr Conner, Con," Ms Pincus explains.

"I didn't know that. You see, Mr Conner trusts you more than he trusts his own lawyer," Schola says to a chuckling room.

"I don't want to know what Con calls you in return," Schola says to a rapturous room.

"Objection your honor," Prosecutor Kast is on her feet.

"Yes, Mr Schola, please the jury doesn't care what you don't want to know," the judge says to even more chuckling.

Prosecutor Kast sits down in resignation. Her witness is falling for the warmness of opposing counsel. Not good.

At this point, the next question would have been whether she loved him. During the rehearsal she was told to deny it. But now, she remembers writing cards and letters with I love you on them. As Schola heads back to pick a pack of papers, Ms Pincus has no doubt that those are hers. So denying that she loved him would be disastrous.

Schola in fact retrieves a pack of cards. Schola shaffles through them. Ms Pincus recognizes the love cards that she purchases and hand-writes to the Senator. Ms Pincus's blood pressure climbs the summit of Mt Everest. Schola sees her checks redden and decides to show mercy. Schola returns the cards to where he picks them. Schola looks at her with those pointed priestly eyes of his – a stare that speaks a lot. The gaze of mercy.

"Why do you think Mr Conner loves you when he never proposes to you? And as you say, he never says that he loves you?" Ms Pincus breathes in relieve.

"Objection your honor, call for speculation," Prosecutor Kast objects.

"Objection sustained," the judge rules.

"Okay let's talk about the night in question," Schola suggests. "Has Mr Conner ever assaulted you in anyway or even remotely shown signs of such assault until the night in question?"

Ms Pincus doesn't have to think. "No, that was the first time he hurt me." She answers truthfully.

"Thus for the six months that you have been providing him physical therapy, he has never manhandled you?" Schola probes.

"No, he has never," Ms Pincus replies.

"Let's recap the events in question in detail," Schola suggests again.

"You arrived at his house in the evening?"

"Your honor, the prosecution would like to have a word with the witness," Prosecutor Kast requests of the court.

The judge looks disappointed but allows the requests. "Okay, five minutes."

59

CROSS CONTINUES AFTER RECESS

REALIZING THAT SCHOLA'S HUMANE APPROACH to cross examination is shrewdly penetrating the tender heart of the star witness, the prosecution asks for a recess to refocus Ms Pincus. Schola scatters the credibility of prosecutor's first witness. Prosecutor Kast knows that the word of the first witness holds no value for the jury. The prosecution's entire case now hinges on the account of their star witness. So far, she is taking Schola's bait, a bait that is shrouded in kindness. She must be refocused.

"You are doing very well," Prosecutor Kast lies to Ms Pincus. Now I want you to focus. We're almost there. After this case, remember we'll help you bring a civil suit against him worth millions. So stay focus. Just say you do not remember. You woke up disoriented and naked and defiled and violated and every bad thing. You had no idea what was in your drink. A drink that Senator Conner gave you."

But Pincus is merely present and only half listening to the rumbling of Prosecutor Kast. She's far off in her own world. Though Conner was wealthy, Ms Pincus loved him not because of his money. She truly loved the man. And even now, she can feel that she loves him. So she wonders what she should say if asked whether she loves him. Prosecutor Kast is thinking along those lines.

"And remember if asked whether you love him, say it was long ago and you don't remember the feelings you had for him."

Ms Pincus looks at her in disbelieve. And Prosecutor Kast looks away.

The camp of the defense is more relaxed. Schola is surprised that nobody chides him for going soft on the witness. Schola wonders why that is so. And takes to pulling the legs of the Senator and Mr Conkling.

"I see, for you guys, a sauce for the goose isn't a sauce for the gander."

"Why would you say something like that?" Both men chant almost in unison.

"Because nobody is reprimanding me for going soft on the daughter as you both did in the case of the mother," Schola explains.

"Would it change anything? We would be wasting our time again," it is the Senator who speaks unconvincingly. And they all remain silent.

Schola is in very deep thoughts. Just last night, just before he goes to sleep, he thinks that he hears some footsteps. He opens the door and sees another envelope, this time, a smaller one. It has a pen drive. Schola decides it's too late to be offered as evidence even if supportive of the defense's case. So he goes to sleep.

But after more than an hour, he can't sleep. So he switches on the computer in his room and opens the drive. There is only a single file on it. He opens it and checks the day of recording. The evening of the alleged episode in question. It's revealing.

Since last night, Schola has been debating within himself whether to put it in evidence.

60

CROSS CONTINUES

"WELCOME BACK," JUDGE KAUFMAN ANNOUNCES herself while plunging into her seat. "Mr Schola, please get on with it," she directs.

"Ms Pincus, your recollection of events that night would help the jury find the truth and serve justice. So please do well to recall if you are able," Schola entreats her earnestly.

"At about what time did you arrive at the house on the day in question?"

"I don't remember the exact time, but sometime in the late afternoon."

"Why did you visit?"

"Please I don't understand your question," Ms Pincus replies.

"Did Mr Conner ask you to come or you went on your own volition?"

The question startles Ms Pincus. Because the therapy sessions seamed into a date of sorts, the dynamics changed. Initially, she follows the timetable. But then she starts taking initiatives of her own. Sometimes visiting unannounced. She was almost certainly the first person to visit when the Senator returns from D.C. or a trip.

"I provide physical therapy, so the purpose of the visit was to …" Ms Pincus didn't know how to finish the sentence.

Schola breaks the uncomfortable pause. "Yes, how were the sessions arranged? Does he call you when he needs therapy?

Was there an agreed upon timetable on when you should attend to him?"

"I don't remember the exact arrangement, but the purpose was for physical therapy," she dodges the question again.

"I want to be clear in my mind of the events of that evening," Schola continues. "Did Senator Conner call you for a therapy or you thought he needed therapy, so went over?"

"As I keep saying, I don't remember."

"So it's possible that you went uninvited or invited yourself?"

"The reason I go to his house is because he needs physical therapy," Ms Pincus struggles again.

"In fact, he does, doesn't he? He even needs more of such therapies especially these days." The room laughs. Schola waits for the laugher to recede. "Yet you have not visited in a long while; don't you think he has been wondering why?"

Amidst the laughter, the prosecutor shouts "objection your honor."

"Mr Schola, please watch it," the judge warns.

"I'm sorry your honor," Schola apologizes.

Walking back to the defense table, Schola says, "I received a pen drive with a video of the events of the evening in question last night. I've looked at it. And it answers all the questions I have. I had wanted to ask the court's permission to have it entered as evidence. But after Mr Conner looked at it, and after seeing how you are portrayed in it, he decides against it. And as a good lawyer, I take the orders of my client."

"Objection, your honor," Ms Kast is on her feet.

The gavel hammers away amidst the chaos in the room. The room is livid. Tongues wrangle. The gavel has a hard time maintaining order.

Ms Pincus is as pale as a mediaeval ghost. Ms Laniel looks paler. Even Senator Conner is utterly surprised. Mr Conkling wonders what's going on. The earth is suddenly derailed from its axis in this courtroom.

"I want both counsels in my chambers now," the judge orders and walks out, visibly infuriated.

61

JUDGE'S CHAMBERS

IN THE JUDGE'S CHAMBERS, SCHOLA realizes how sexy judge Kaufman looks out of her judicial robes. The judge notices and likes the admiration, even invites it. But Schola does his best to avoid looking at her delicate features. It's admiring such beauty that is the cause of all this furor.

"Mr Schola when did you receive this video," Judge Kaufman asks.

"Last night your honor, at about midnight just before I went to bed." The judge is intrigued. Her face shows it.

"It was brought to your house?" the judge asks.

"Yes, your honor," Schola answers.

"By whom? the judge asks.

"Your honor, I wish I know the deliverer. I have no idea." Schola registers his frustration with his inability to find out the identity of his unsolicited opposition party research assistant.

There's a knock on the door. Mr John McAdoo, Judge Kaufman's second clerk, comes in and whispers in the ears of her honor. Sadness engulfs her. Ms Kast and Schola wait to hear what could be more important than the present mystery of the pen drive.

"I'm told that the most senior judge just died a moment ago."

"Sorry your honor," the prosecutor says.

"My condolences your honor," Schola says.

"So this in-camera hearing is adjourned till tomorrow morning at 9 am in my chambers," the judge concludes.

62

JUDGE KAUFMAN RECALLS LATE JUDGE

THE PARTIES RECONVENE FOR THE in-camera hearing, which the announcement of the death of senior Judge Chotiner Vavala cuts short yesterday. Judge Vavala has been a judge for over fifty years and a member of the judiciary for over sixty-five years. It is proper that the courts, especially the courts in Allen County, Fort Wayne, observe a holiday as a mark of respect for his many years of dedicated service to Hoosiers.

Judge Kaufman is especially grateful to Judge Vavala, the late senior judge. Forty years ago, Ms Kaufman is out of law school, passes the bar exam and is freshly sworn-in as an attorney. But no job. Then attorney Kaufman remains jobless for over six months.

One day, she goes for a reception for a retiring judge at the Court House in Fort Wayne. During the cocktail following the ceremony, she says high to Judge Vavala.

"Good evening your honor, my name is Avis Kaufman," the young attorney introduces herself to the middle age judge.

"Hello, how're you?" Judge Vavala responds.

"I'm fine," Ms Kaufman replies.

"It's a beautiful evening," Judge Vavala looks around and says. "I'll miss Judge Walsh Wisner dearly. He has been a mentor and a friend. He talked me into becoming a judge. A decision I don't regret. And he was my springboard for most of the issues I needed thinking through." Judge Vavala delivers a short laudatio for the retiring judge to the then quiet and timid Ms Kaufman.

"I'm sorry, you're of which law firm again?" Judge Vavala asks Ms Kaufman. Of course, Ms Kaufman is jobless at the time. On learning that Ms Kaufman has no job and no interviews pending, Judge Vavala invites her for an interview the following Monday morning.

"Please tell me, where did you go to law school?"

"Indiana University Law School, your honor," she answers.

"And would you like the job of a law clerk to a judge in the criminal division?"

"Of course, I would your honor," she answers.

And with that she is hired. Ms Kaufman clerks for him for three years. Then later works for a law firm. But she comes back to clerk for him for two more years. And later gets the position of a circuit judge.

But there is a dark side to the late Judge Vavala. Former clerks accused him of sexual harassment of all sorts. Judge Kaufman knows that those allegations are true. Because the judge makes similar advances at her when she clerks for him. But she won't say the judge forces himself on her. She's never retaliated against for refusing his advances. The senior judge wasn't a revengeful fellow. But after several refusals to Judge Vavala's advances, Judge Kaufman decides to give in out of pity for the man. The two carry on for a while. And when it begins taking a toil on her marriage, Ms Kaufman leaves to work for a law firm. Among a lot of other things, she is unfulfilled working for this law firm. And so she returns to the chambers of Judge Vavala.

Clerking and romance go hand in hand. But it isn't her affair with the senior judge that eventually ends her marriage. She just doesn't have time for her then husband, a college professor. And as their marriage wanes, so does her love for him. But her husband, now ex-husband, is a good man. The best man she has ever met. He was a good father. She misses him these days. And wishes she could tell him that.

But the irony isn't lost on Judge Kaufman: A man she knows have deep weaknesses for women, the fulfilment of which sometimes border on the criminal, dies just when she is hearing the sexual harassment case of her life.

63

IN CAMERA HEARING

THE KNOCK ON HER DOOR sees her law clerk usher in the two counsel – Prosecutor Kast and Schola.

"Good morning your honor," they both say almost together.

"Good morning counsel. Sorry I had to postpone yesterday's hearing. Senior Judge Vavala was my mentor. In fact, I first worked for him as a lawyer," she explains.

"Now, let's talk about this video in your possession, Mr Schola," the judge says.

"You got it few nights ago?"

"Yes, your honor."

"And you have seen it?"

"Yes, your honor."

"Your honor, it can't be the subject of cross examination until the court admits it as evidence," Prosecutor Kast interjects.

"Please I haven't invited your opinion yet," Judge Kaufman reproaches Ms Kast angrily.

"Your honor, she is partially wrong. While evidence may not be admitted, it may be referred to for purposes of questioning without asking that it be admitted," Schola counters the prosecutor's argument.

"Now the two of you, listen well. I didn't invite you to my chambers to play lawyers."

"Mr Schola, where's this video?"

"But your honor ..."

"No buts, where is the video?

"Right here in my pocket your honor."

"Give it to me." Schola hands a red pen drive to the judge.

"Thank you very much," Judge Kaufman says sarcastically.

"I'll review the video myself and have you both back." The two lawyers are confused.

"Your honor, can I please join you. It isn't fair. He has seen it. You'll be seeing it. I'm the only one in the dark," Ms Kast protests.

"I have thought about that. After reviewing it, if it's fair for you to see it before we proceed, I'll allow you to satisfy your inquisitive eyes, counsel. Now please leave me alone."

With the door closed, the judge takes out her laptop and plugs it in a socket behind her and turns the laptop on. It then occurs to her that she should have asked how long the video is. She has no idea that it is a two-hour recording of a drinking party whose revelers didn't know they were recorded.

After the two hours, Judge Kaufman invites counsel back in her office.

"This video won't be admitted. It implicates third parties who aren't persons of interest in the current trial," the judge rules. "Therefore, Mr Schola is to refrain from making any reference to it," she stops and looks at their disappointed faces.

"And finally, the video remains with me as long as the trial last," she rules again, ending the in-camera hearing.

64

MS PINCUS IS AFRAID

WARENESS OF THE EXISTENCE OF a recording of the evening in question deeply disturbs Ms Pincus. Least of her worries is that she might be caught lying. More troubling is that she might be breaking the law herself. She truly wonders how long the video has been in the custody of Senator Conner and his strange lawyer.

Ms Pincus learns physical therapy from the college therapist who worked on her volleyball players. By watching the therapist work on the girls, she learns and masters the art. And by performing little massages on the players sometimes, she becomes better at it over time. She was thus never licensed as a physical therapist. She isn't an attorney. But she knows that she needs a license to practice physical therapy, especially commercial therapy. She remembers few practitioners get into trouble because their licenses expired. These therapists were licensed but fail to renew their license. Yet they're in trouble.

She wonders why Senator Conner's attorney isn't even asking for her license, or would he ask later?

As well, after a while, the physical therapy seams into sexual acts. This is how it goes down. For new clients, she starts with mere physicals. The neck pain, the back pain, the knee, etc. And since most of these men are lonely, they need more than a touch. With practice she becomes good at luring them into sex, which pay additionally. And for regular customers, she asks them up front: whether they need more than a massage.

The issue is even very complicated in the case of Senator Conner. They're dating in fact. Though they never officially articulate their relationship that way. The cycling that she introduces to him helps with his back pain. The massages become relaxers. And after a while, there're no lines between the massages and their sex life.

The monies that Senator Conner gives her aren't presented as payment for her services. Senator Conner is a very generous man. He opens an account for her. Tells her not to allow it dip below a certain figure. He keeps topping it up generously. She, in turn, gives him happiness. And she in turn finds meaning in him.

She hopes that the Senator would marry her. The Senator would have married her. But with dozens of failed marriages, and with a marriage only in name at the time, Senator Conner all but gave up on the old institution of marriage.

And suddenly, here's a video. Ms Pincus is truly troubled. She wonders what's in the video.

65

CROSS CONTINUES

"OKAY, LET'S SEE WHETHER WE can wrap up the witnesses today," Judge Kaufman says as she sits, leaving no doubt that she's in a hurry.

With the ruling that the video is out of evidence and that no reference is to be made to it whatsoever, Schola is at a lost as to how else to cross-examine Ms Pincus. Plus, pursuant to Schola's humane cross examination principle, issues of whether she has a license as a therapist, whether she sleeps with a man for money, whether she even pays taxes for her work are completely out of the question. Schola has no further arrows in his quiver.

Schola looks at his legal pad. There're no questions left but for the three ungoable areas— license, sleeping with men for money, and taxes. But cross examination must be done, and now.

"Ms Pincus let's revisit the events of the day at issue," Schola invites the witness. Schola pauses and doesn't know where to go next.

"Or better still, let's revisit the early part of the day before you went to the Senator's house," Schola changes his strategy.

"Did you visit with anybody before visiting the Senator on that day?"

"Objection your honor," Prosecutor Kast leaps to her feet, "Relevance your honor."

"Yes, I wonder what the relevance is," the judge agrees with the prosecutor. "But let's see where Mr Schola goes," the judge rules.

"Well, in the morning I went to the wellness center and worked out," Ms Pincus begins.

It's such a long time ago. But that's her typically day in those days. She tries to remember what next.

"Yes, after the workout I went home and had breakfast. Then I met my girlfriend and her new boyfriend at the Main Library Coffee shop for coffee before heading to Conner's house," Ms Pincus concludes.

Schola does his best to suppress his surprise and delight. Stoic as ever. A new door of possibilities opens for Schola.

"So you had coffee with your girlfriend and her new boyfriend before proceeding to Mr Conner's?" Schola repeats Ms Pincus's previous response with no indicia of interest while looking at his notepad.

"Yes, I had coffee with them," Ms Pincus affirms.

In questioning, or building up a big point, the path to the critical point must appear innocuous to the other discussants. If possible, the questioner must appear very ignorant. The answerers must think of themselves as sophisticated and enlightening their audience. The answerers must not know that the questioner is goading them towards a position they can't defend. Otherwise, they would realize that their answers would lead them to admissions that they don't like. Socrates employed this method very well. He would often call himself slow-witted while praising his opponent. The answerers get very complacent and tangle themselves with positions that they can't defend.

"You have a very sharp mind," Schola flatters Ms Pincus. "This was long ago, and you still remember."

Ms Pincus doesn't know what to make of the praise. She looks at the handsome, tall lawyer in front of her and is genuinely shy.

"I know it was long ago, but do you remember the kind of coffee you had, or whether you had some other drink besides the coffee?" Schola asks.

It now dawns on the prosecutor where this has led to. But it's too, too late. There's no going back.

"Objection your honor, relevance" Prosecutor Kast shouts in a defeated voice.

It's the last cry of the black swan.

"I don't drink coffee, so they might have offered me something else, a soda," Ms Pincus innocently explains.

"Let's be clear, you didn't get the drink yourself, your girlfriend got it for you?" Schola asks.

"No, her new boyfriend got us the drinks," Ms Pincus explains.

"In cans?"

"No, they were mixtures of different things."

"Did you see him order the drink?" Schola asks, smiling respectfully.

"No," she answers, realizing what she has just done.

In fact, the new boyfriend in question, Mr Bea Quill, intends the first drink for his new girlfriend, Ms Calein Wilkens. He puts pills that would render Ms Wilkens useless after about an hour. But when he gets to the table, there is a stranger. He gives the drink to Ms Calein Wilkens, his girlfriend. And goes back to get another for Ms Pincus. Mr Quill arrives with the second drink and sees Ms Pincus sipping away at what is meant for his girlfriend, Ms Wilkens. The harm is done.

To Mr Quill's credit, he ends the coffee meeting immediately. Makes sure Ms Pincus gets into her car and drives to her next destination before he falls unconscious on the wheels. Mr Quill follows her until she packs at the Senator's driveway.

"Did you even see him buy the drink from the shop?" Schola pushes his luck.

Ms Pincus's silence is long and eternal.

"Ms Pincus, can you say beyond reasonable doubt that this new boyfriend didn't put anything in your drink?"

"No," Ms Pincus says in tears.

66

RE-DIRECT

JUDGE KAUFMAN LOOKS DOWN AT her notes and shakes her head. It's amazing how often this happens. When she is, and when every reasonable person is sure that a case would go one way, it ends up in an unexpected way. Just when she thinks that the jury will decide the *State of Indiana v. Cornelius Conner* in favor of the State, the weight of evidence is pointing in the opposite direction almost beyond reasonable belief.

Judge Kaufman's interest in the outcome is very much to seal her judicial legacy as the female judge who presides over the case that puts a powerful political pervert away. But except something is done drastically, and now, she might as well forget about her dream legacy as well as the promotion she envisages coming with it as well.

"Does the State wish to re-direct," Judge Kaufman invites Ms Kast to cure Schola's damage. Ms Kast is surprise that the judge will invite a re-direct when she hasn't solicited one.

"Yes, your honor," Prosecutor Kast rises to do some damage control, and if possible, sway the odds in favor of the State. This's by far the test of her professional life as the chief prosecutor in Fort Wayne.

"Did you fall asleep after drinking the mixture that your friend's boyfriend gave you?"

Ms Pincus doesn't know how to answer the question. But she sees the lead and follows it. "No," she answers.

"You didn't fall asleep in the coffee shop?"

"No."

"In fact, you were able to drive your car for miles after the stranger gave you the drink?"

"Yes, I drove for a distance of about five miles," Ms Pincus answers, feeling guilty for lying.

"You only passed out after you had a drink in the Senator's house?"

"Yes."

"The Senator offered you the drink?"

"Yes."

"And this was after many hours of leaving the coffee shop and saying goodbye to your friend?"

"Yes."

"Thank you, your honor, that'll be all," Ms Kast says, sitting down.

Ms Pincus couldn't wait to get out of that little box. She knows that she's lying. The kind of lie that only the liar knows. The lie that others can't prove.

But how could she be so stupid. Because a week after the incident, her girlfriend, Ms Wilkens, calls to say that she has broken up with her new boyfriend. At the time, she's still battling with the trauma from her own experience of passing out and waking up naked and violated at the Senator's home. And breakups are very normal for most of her friends. Even divorces are the norm rather than the exception.

So she doesn't see the need to ask what causes their split. She now remembers Ms Wilkens telling her that the guy drugs her on several occasions. On one occasion, Ms Wilkens has to be treated at the hospital. And there, while recovering at the hospital, she ends it.

Besides, she feels dizzy while driving to Con's that day. She wonders what's happening to her. But quickly attributes it to the morning workout at the gym. Plus advancing age, she thinks.

She looks at Senator Conner and realizes that he's staring at her, so she turns her gaze away. She recalls the Senator repeatedly asking her that day whether she's okay.

"Please take me to bed, I want to sleep," she now recalls her last words before she wakes up naked and apparently defiled.

67

CROSS OF RE-DIRECT

AND WITH THE PROSECUTOR'S LAST question, and without knowledge of what is going on in Ms Pincus's mind, the effect of Schola's cross is sufficiently neutralized. So Judge Kaufman wants things to remain this way.

"I'll schedule closing arguments for tomorrow," Judge Kaufman rules.

"Your honor," Schola is on his feet.

"Yes, Mr Schola," Judge Kaufman turns to him.

"The defense would like to exercise its constitutional right to cross-examine the defense's re-direct." Judge Kaufman wants to avoid this. But this rockie lawyer isn't naïve after all.

"Yes, but be fast about it," Judge Kaufman reluctantly agrees.

"Thank you, your honor," Schola says while approaching the witness.

"Have you ever met this guy – the boyfriend of your girlfriend – before?"

"No."

"So he has never offered you a drink of any sort before your meeting with him on the day in question?"

"No."

"Would you say you fell asleep less than an hour after you had a drink from this guy?" The answer is very long in coming. But the room, including Schola waits with measured patience.

"Yes."

"So you didn't fall asleep after many hours of leaving the coffee shop as Ms Kast would rather want us to believe?" Ms Pincus is drying her watery eyes.

"No," she concedes. The next question is unexpected. And even Schola is surprised by his own question. And he is even surprised that he takes the risk to ask it.

"Has your girlfriend ever complained to you that this guy ever drugged her?"

"Yes," the answer is hardly audible

"I'm sure the jury will like to hear you?" Schola says without sarcasm.

"Yes." The witness says in a regrettable voice.

"In fact, they – your girlfriend and this guy – broke up not so long after they met?"

"Yes," the answer is weak.

"For the records she says yes," Schola repeats her answer.

"How long did their relationship last?"

"A week."

"But your relationship, no, your friendship, or better still your getting to know Mr Conner lasted six months, that is, half of a year?"

"Yes."

"Has he ever drugged you before that day?"

"No."

"Can you think of anything that will motivate him to want to drug you?"

"Objection, your honor, call for speculation."

"Objection sustained," Judge Kaufman rules.

"That'll be all, your honor," Schola says and takes his seat.

If there is any doubt that the defense establishes doubt in the minds of any Thomases that doubt vanishes now. Even a staunch Thomas accepts that there is reasonable doubt about the prosecution's case. Schola does his job well. He knows it. Senator

Conner knows it. Mr Conkling is proof that this lawyer might be saving more than a single life – his and Mr Conner's.

But this case isn't even about convicting a guilty person. The parties know this very well. It's about scapegoating anybody for the sexual decadences that has enveloped the world, our nation included. The stain of sexual abuse needs cleaning. The blood of anybody would do the job. Often the blood of the innocent is best. And so is the blood of the most powerful. Schola, the ex-priest— and an astute disciple of the American social anthropologist, Rene Gerard—knows this very well.

68

A SECOND RE-DIRECT

THE JUDGE THINKS THAT SHE didn't hear her well. "Your honor, I'll like another redirect," Prosecutor Kast requests.

"But you already re-directed after the initial cross," the judge observes, almost in surprise.

"Yes, your honor. But I request another re-direct," the Prosecutor pleads.

"Do you realize that after your second re-direct, the defense would surely like a cross of the re-direct?" The judge asks, wondering when these lawyers would stop lawyering.

"I'll be very brief, your honor," Prosecutor Kast pleads again.

"You better be," the judge reluctantly allows the prosecutor's request.

"Before you passed out at the Senator's house, did you give him the consent to have sex with you?"

"No."

"And after you passed out, you were incapable of giving such a consent?"

"No."

There's a glimmer of hope for the prosecution. These two questions breathe a life into the prosecutor's dying case. The jury looks pleased. But that was until Schola rises to his full length of six-nine feet.

"Your honor, may I ask the witness a few questions?"

"I wish I could say no Mr Schola," the judge admits sincerely.

"Your candor is appreciated your honor. Please may the jury learn from our honorable judge and do what the law says and what the facts prove and not how they feel," Schola says smilely.

"Move it Mr Schola, and stop stretching your luck," the judge reprimands him.

"Ms Pincus, have you ever slept with Mr Conner before the … well before that debacle that evening?"

Ms Pincus incredulously looks at Schola. But sees no malice or sarcasm in his demeanor. And immediately regrets the demeaning look she casts at him.

"Of course."

"Please, of course, what?"

"Of course, I have slept with him."

"Thanks."

"How were consents given before the act?"

"Hmmm … I don't understand the question."

"Well, you consented to his sleeping with you, right?"

"Except for the night in question," Ms Pincus corrects Schola.

"Indeed. I predicated my questioning on encounters before your last encounter with him."

"In the previous ones that you had the act, how did you give consent."

"I didn't resist, and we just did it."

"In fact, have you ever resisted a request of Mr Conner's to have you since you started sleeping with him?"

"I'm not sure, it was long ago."

One final question; "You did tell him to take you to bed just before you passed out?"

"Yes, because I was feeling sleepy."

"I understand you were feeling sleepy. But you felt into his arms asking him to take you to bed?"

"Yes."

"You couldn't have uttered those words if you had passed out before falling into his arms?"

"No."

"Thank you very much. That would be all your honor."

"Would the prosecution like another go at a re-direct," the judge says sarcastically. Her question wasn't even answered.

"Very well then, closing arguments are set for tomorrow." Judge Avis Kaufman adjourns the famous case of the *State of Indiana v. Cornelius Conner Jr.*

69

PROSECUTOR'S CLOSING

"**L**ADIES AND GENTLEMEN OF THE jury:" Ms Kast greets the jury in the opening address of her closing argument.

"Our great Constitution provides that nobody—including even a powerful, influential, well-resourced, man—is above the law," Prosecutor Kast pre-stages the closing argument of her life.

"But for some time now, some powerful men deem themselves way above the law. But for some time now, some influential men deem themselves law onto themselves. But for some time now, some well-resourced men deem themselves law onto themselves. Men like Senator Cornelius Conner hold themselves well above and beyond our laws. These demo-gods get whatever they want. Whenever they want it. Wherever they want it. However they want it. From whomever they want it. Their desire is the law and must be fulfilled." Prosecutor Kast looks at Mr Conner and appears to believe everything that she is saying.

"These demi-gods don't care how their fragile victims feel. They don't care how their poor pry feels. They don't care that their object of desire is married. She has kids. She has a happy family. She'll like to save that family. The rest of us are sacrificial lambs on the alters of their most primitive inklings." Ms Kast blasts away.

Mr Conner wonders sincerely whether that is how he lives his life. He looks uncomfortably at Schola. Schola taps his hand and whimpers: "relax, please."

"Woe betides you if you dare refuse them what they demand. Woe betides you if try to expose them. They hunt you down. They end your career. They make your life miserable. They crash you." Ms Kast is on fire. The jury appears to be with her.

"And so for a very long time, for far too long, we cow in passivity while they run amok satisfying their insatiable barbaric desires, devouring one victim after another. Victims are afraid to come forward. For these demi-gods have all the money to hire the best of lawyers to bury the case."

Schola chuckles at the mention of best lawyers as both Mr Conner and Mr Conkling sight in disbelieve. Schola at the time of his hiring was at best an unknown lawyer. Prosecutor Kast realizes her gaffe and so quickly moves on.

"Mr Conner is such a demi-god. They're several allegations of rape, battery, unwanted touches, and sexual assault of all varieties and degrees against him. Hundreds of accusations against just one single man. These hundreds of cases can't all be false. Some of, which he has settled with large sums of money. I don't know how many cases and how much money in settlements. Cases he decides not to settle, he frightens the hell out of the victims." Ms Kast team nods in approval.

"But today, we have a very brave woman. Who against all odds decides to tell her story. The facts are not in dispute. Ms Larnage Pincus goes to the house of Senator Conner. She's his physical therapist at the time. Mr Conner has a terrible back pain. Ms Pincus's eases his back pain with her expertise." Ms Kast narrates the facts as they favor the prosecution's side.

"What happens next is despicable. Senator Conner drugs her. He waits until she passes out. He takes her to his bedroom. And does with her as he pleases. Ms Pincus is unconscious through it all. So she is unaware what Senator Conner is doing to her. But she wakes up naked. She wakes up defiled. She wakes up in deep pain, physically and psychologically. This's a man she has come to trust completely." Ms Kast turns and looks at the prosecution table who knot in agreement.

"In any event, the law is clear in this matter. And the facts are even clearer. Senator Conner assaults, batters, harasses and rapes Ms Pincus. The facts support all these charges. Ms Pincus is unconscious while Senator Conner ravenously ravages her. So she couldn't have granted consent."

"This jury has the duty, a sacred duty, to send a message not only to Senator Conner and his deplorable likes, but a message to the whole world that abominable behaviors such as Mr Conner demonstrates are frown upon in our civilized nation. The greatest survival republic on earth at present, our nation, has the heavy duty of exemplifying decency, humaneness, civility, and above all, the rule of law."

Ms Kast takes her seat, leaving the fate of her case in the hands of the jury. But not before Schola addresses the jury in his closing.

70

SCHOLA'S CLOSING

"**W**E HAVE A BIG PROBLEM. We have a massive crisis. In fact, we have a disaster. It is an pandemic, which, the incarceration of my innocent client, Mr Cornelius Conner wouldn't cure. Things have gotten out of hand, many say. And we must do something. Or we must be seen doing something. Find a scapegoat. Sacrifice him. And wash our hands." Schola begins his closing argument."

"The problem with this proposed solution is that the problem still rages. Because its root cause isn't properly diagnosed:"

"Look around you. Look in our streets when you take a walk or drive. The sight of almost naked women can't escape the eye. Their dresses – if the transparent garments on them can be so called – are too revealing and inviting. Sadly, it's a sign of their liberation and a mark of our advanced society. Our civilized society – the prosecution calls it."

"This evening you may watch the news. Watch out for the advertisements. Virtually all have one thing in common – sex. Ads of commodities that have no bearing on sex are marketed with naked women. Even the news is conveyed alongside relentless sexualized materials."

"Look at the movies coming out of Hollywood and other sources – sex. It is difficult to differentiate some of those films from pornography. Yet this is the civilized world we are so proud of and must save."

"Look at our taste of fashion. The less the clothing on the body the better. Dresses of women are designed and put on to reveal those spots that are supposed to be hidden. Apparently, a mark of women's freedom. A mark of the woman's ability to express herself. Freely."

"And tell a woman that she is beautiful when she wears one of those scanty things, and you've made her day. She returns the next day with an even scantier one for another round of senseless compliment. This's what gives our women pleasure, satisfaction."

"The picture even gets more disturbing beyond the world of dress. The sole ground for licit sexual activity is mutuality. Our civilized world of freedom allows any people or group of people to have sex with whomever as long as there is mutual consent and mutual satisfaction."

"It doesn't matter that the parties are married, even less so if they are already courting someone. It doesn't matter that they are in school and should concentrate more on their books, even less so if they work at the same place. In fact, we are reminded: why else do we go to college if not to have sex."

"Life is short, have an affair, is the mantra. The culture promotes it. The workplace promotes it. The schools promote it. Even the church might be promoting it."

"Divorces are at their highest, yet. And still climbing. The family law attorney is the busiest. The family law attorney has more work than the prosecutor. The more partners you change the better. The more marriages, the better."

"Yet we appear appalled when a stranger that we, by our dressing and conduct, invite to have a go at us, grabs us."

"Indeed, our civilization is under siege, more by our sexual decay than by ISIS. And yes, we must do something."

"The prosecutor tights before you members of the jury a scapegoat. A sacrificial lamb. The prosecution is asking for permission to sacrifice this scapegoat on the throne of justice to cleanse our collective failures, shame, sin, and, probably, crimes."

"Members of the jury. The proposed solution itself, sacrificing my innocent client, has two problems. One, my client is not some savior like Jesus Christ. There's no justification in making a superficial example of his excesses to serve as an example for the rest of a continuing decayed society."

"The second problem with the proposed solution is the reason my client has hired me. Our Justice System – when it works – sets the standard for the conviction of any accused person. We don't convict a man because the public has passed the severest of judgments on him. We don't convict a man because he is accused of the most repugnant of crimes. We don't convict a man because we need to appease an outrage. The founding generation of this nation know better. They certainly know better than us."

"By all means, we may, and we have at times convicted people. But we convict when the prosecutor diligently proves the guilt of the accused beyond reasonable doubt. The prosecutor fails this standard of proof, here, miserably. She fails to prove that my client commits the crimes he is charged with. As well, she fails to prove her imagined charges against my client beyond reasonable doubt."

"Members of the jury, you are all too familiar with the facts of this case. The true facts. My client has back pain. He searches for and secures the professional expertise of Ms Larnage Pincus, the supposed victim. Their therapist-patient relationship seams into a de facto wife-husband relationship. Ms Pincus does more than ease the pain of Mr Conner. Easing pain besides, she brings happiness to her client. Mr Conner loves her. She probably loves him too. They take trips. They vocation at exotic places. They hold hands. They Kiss. And much more. Everything you can think of. Except, make a baby. All in full consent and mutual satisfaction.

"One day, on her way to see Mr Conner, Ms Pincus decides to visit with a girlfriend and meet her new boyfriend. An innocuous gesture. This new friend whom she has never met offers her a drink. She doesn't remember the drink. She doesn't know what was in the drink. By the grace of God, she drives safely to Mr Conner's after gulping the drugged drink. On her way and at Mr Conner's house, Ms Pincus feels that something is wrong with her. She feels weird. Dizzy. Sleepy.

"True, she drinks some more at the Senator's house. They chat a bit. But Mr Conner realizes that something is wrong with Ms Pincus. He keeps asking her: "are you okay, dear?" "I don't know," she replies, "I feel kind of weird."

"A short while after arriving, she falls into Mr Conner's loving hands. Tells him to take her to bed. And to bed they go. Remember he has taken her to bed several times. And she has never objected to her being taken to bed. And until that night she has never regretted her being taken to bed."

"She wakes up naked. Naked under the sheets. Also, she doesn't feel well. She realizes that someone put something in her drink."

"In the moment of dizziness and heavy headedness, the only person she can count as a possible suspect is Mr Conner. In that moment of confusion, she forgets, and quite understandably, that she had, less than an hour ago a drink from an unknown new boyfriend of her girlfriend. She can't remember."

"But this trial prompts her memory and pricks her conscious as it should yours, members of the jury. She now remembers a lot of things on that fateful day. For example, less than a week after they met, her girlfriend broke up with the new guy. Reason. 'He kept drugging me, she told Ms Pincus.'"

"As we speak, this guy is the guest of the the Federal Correctional Complex in Terre Haute, Indiana. He's yet to serve close to half of his fifty-year prison sentence.

"And what's Mr Bea Quill, the former boyfriend of the victim's girlfriend, serving time for? Many things, we discovered. One of these is drugging a girl. To this charge even arises manslaughter. Because the dose killed this unlucky girl. Yes, Mr Quill is doing time for manslaughter."

"Come to think of it, ladies and gentlemen of the jury: Mr Conner has never drugged Ms Pincus during their six months togetherness. Mr Conner has so many dark sides. As I said in my opening statement, he might even be a great candidate for hell. Surely, he's a lousy candidate for sainthood. But drugging people isn't one of them, has never been. As the prosecutor says, he is a powerful man. He needs not drug a woman before she asks him to take her to bed. This's way out of his character."

"If only the prosecutor and her team had done due diligence, they wouldn't have wasted your time, ladies and gentlemen of the jury, petering away the limited resources that you and I, the taxpayers, have provided them in a case with no merit."

"But no, they need a scapegoat. The country is angry. The women are fed up. Any jury would convict anything. And so they come after Mr Conner. They are sure that you would suspend your reasoning to convict any man to appease the anger of the nation."

"But this trial is not altogether a waste of time. We should take the chance to ponder. To reconsider our sexual culture. We have taken it to an unhealthy level, an insane level, even for a nation where freedom in personal taste is almost unlimited."

"Probably, our women should start putting some clothes on their bodies. They should stop allowing their nakedness to be used in ads that have nothing to do with human bodies."

"And as for the men, we should learn to look away. St. Ignatius of Loyola calls this the custody of the senses. Of course, we will be mocked for looking away. This is the modern era. And you can do whatever you want. But given where these excesses of our freedoms have landed us and are still heading us, we should take counsel from this medieval religious figure. Please look away."

"Until we take notice of how our bodies response to various invitations in our civilized world. Until we take notice of why our desires are aroused. Until we take notice of who is stirring our desires. Until we notice what our inner motives are – Gregory the Great calls them "inward motions," our efforts will be in vain. #MeToo will fail."

"As for convicting Mr Conner, that is unjust. For he didn't commit the crimes he's here charged with."

Schola takes his seat, leaving the jury thinking. And thinking hard.

71

JURY DELIBERATES

TWO WEEKS PASS SINCE THE parties make their final submissions, and the jury retires into seclusion for deliberation. The jury is yet to produce a verdict. Word from the jury room is that members of the jury can't reach a consensual decision; the jury is hopelessly hung.

Mr Conkling tells Schola that if the jury returns after two days, it's very likely that the outcome will favor the defense. But there're several two days in two weeks. Schola is beginning to think that they should be a timeline for trials and jury deliberations. Timeline ensures that a jury deliberation doesn't go on ad infinitum. As it is, some trials last for a whole year, others, years.

In the first week, the parties linger around the court premises when the jury is in session, hoping to be called in for news, hopefully, good news. For the prosecution, good news means convicting Mr Conner; for the defense, good news means acquitting him. Believe it, both sides pray to God. Schola wonders whether God isn't often confused in situations like this. Which side does God side with?

This wait is reminiscent of a similar wait four years ago. Professor cum Father Schola, then a university professor is accused of sexual impropriety. An investigation duly constituted is ongoing for three months. All that while, Schola waits in the Holy Mountain, a Jesuit spiritual center in Rochester, NY. The committee snails on and on for three excruciating months of wait.

Schola is an active person. He fills his day with all kinds of things from dawn till dusk up to midnight. So he would often repair to his room from the daily activities, collapsing on his bed. Until this period of waiting, Schola has no idea what insomnia is. Yes, he keeps busy during the day – reading a lot. Still, he could hardly sleep at night. The much he could sleep is two hours at any given time. And he often wakes up with a nightmare.

Schola wakes up many a night with sweat and headaches during the wait four years ago. Schola experiences the dark night of his soul during this period in the phrasing and spirituality of John of the Cross.

This present wait brings back those painful memories of yore. So Schola knows what his client might be undergoing. One of the things that keeps Schola going during the dark night of his soul is lots of physical exercise. In fact, it is Fr Mentor, the director of the Holy Mountain, who encourages these bouts of physical exercises beyond the normal.

So Schola runs the ten miles trail around the Holy Mountain every morning before Holy Mass and breakfast. In the afternoon, he does the same ten miles, but this time, he walks. And in the evening, he does the same ten miles, half run and half walk. Sometimes, he stops in the middle of the tracks and reflects and thinks and meditates and prays.

Fr Mentor is always waiting upon his return. With a bottle of water in hand, the two priests talk about the walk or run or walk cum run. Schola relates his experiences and feelings and insights to the older priest. The conversations last at first for about five minutes, then fifteen, and later more.

So Schola gets to know Fr Mentor more and loves him even more. Fr Mentor loves him as a father would his son. Fr Mentor is well on in years at this point. But exercise, an excruciating timetable, and a long life of hard work keep him very young. As well, he eats well: a cup of coffee and either a banana or apple in the morning; for lunch, a peanut sandwich of two slices of bread. Fr Mentor eats much more for dinner. Even at that, it's a much smaller portion. Schola takes notice and tries to eat that way as well. But it's a struggle at first.

It's during one of these routine exercises that the idea of studying law first occurs to Schola. Schola has mastery of jurisprudence – the philosophical underpinnings of the law, especially, the jurisprudence of Aquinas, Augustine, and the consequential philosophers—Plato, Aristotle, Kant, Jeremy Bentham, Hart, Kwame Anthony Appiah, and many more. Yet, he must admit that he has very little knowledge of secular law and its ways. Of course, he's a canonist, an expert of canon law—having studied it under some of the best canon lawyers in Rome, obtaining a PhD in ethics and canon law, the third doctorate that Mr. McGinley fails to mention during their first meeting in Washington this year.

Upon one of his returns from his ten-mile exercise, Schola intimates to the ever-keen Fr Mentor of this new emerging desire that possesses him.

"Tell me more, Fr Schola, are you now thinking of going to the moon?" Fr. Mentor teases. The two men laugh.

"No, Fr Mentor, the idea of law and its practice is pre-occupying my mind for some time now. Well, that committee is investigating me. I look at the list of the committee members—lawyers, mainly. I wonder what secular lawyers and judges do."

A long and serious frown comes over the older priest. Fr Mentor recalls his old friend—now Governor Sparkman Schola. They join the Jesuit novitiate together. Bond tightly. Study philosophy together. While Fr Mentor pursues advance studies in philosophy, Sparkman studies Classics. They both finish their studies and return to Regis High School in New York City and teach. Sparkman Schola will decide to leave the Jesuits years later, study law, go into business, make money, lots of it, then, go into politics and leave a legacy of service.

Fr Mentor is lost in thoughts of his old friend. Fr Mentor keeps in touch with the Governor – sending him cards on his birthdays. Calling him on Easter day, Christmas day, and on the feast of St. Ignatius, the Governor's patron saint.

When Sparkman Schola leaves the Jesuits eventually, he goes on to become a lawyer. It occurs to Fr Mentor that today is the birthday of Sparkman Schola. He wonders whether he won't have forgotten had Fr Schola not mentioned studying law. Fr Mentor wonders whether he isn't getting too old

"Fr Mentor, please what's wrong?"

"Forgive me Fr Schola. Nothing. I'm lost in thoughts of years ago. Please forgive me.".

"Please Fr Schola is saying?"

"Never mind, it isn't that important, Fr Mentor. I'll wash for dinner. See you in a while. Schola says and leaves the ponderous Fr Mentor."

Schola's idea of becoming a lawyer isn't an important thought at the time. But it becomes a reality. And old and wise Fr Mentor has a hand in this reality.

Word comes out that the jury finishes its second week of deliberation without a verdict. Schola wonders what will become of this new long wait.

72

THE HOLY MOUNTAIN

WISE FR MENTOR HAS BEEN director of the Jesuit Spiritual Center, also known as the Holy Mountain, for ten years now. Prior to his becoming director of America's most coveted spiritual center, old Fr Mentor has worked there as a widely-sought-after spiritual director for fifteen years. The Holy Mountain serves a variety of spiritual purposes. And so are the variety of people who go there to seek God's face or meaning in life.

For example, the Holy Mountain houses a tertian program for Jesuits. Tertianship is a six-month program for Jesuits preparing for their final incorporation into the Jesuit Order. It's a sort of second novitiate. Tertains re-examine the Constitution of the Jesuits, the history of the Jesuits, and, of course, why they're Jesuits. And more important, whether and why they want to continue being Jesuits. But the capstone course and experience of Tertianship is the thirty-days retreat. At the end of the thirty days of silent retreat and prayer, the Jesuits return to their provinces and take their final vows of consecrated chastity, evangelical poverty, and religious obedience. Fr Mentor has been tertian director for ten years before assuming the role of director of the Holy Mountain. Fr Mentor is a spiritual guru of almost unmatched experience.

The Holy Mountain, of course, runs routine retreats. People from all walks of life, but mainly, priests, nuns, religious – and not infrequently, cardinals and bishops – would leave their busy schedules in their dioceses, parishes, schools, hospitals, soup kitchens, care homes and others for a spiritual rejuvenation at the Holy Mountain. The duration and intensity of each retreat depends on the person, the purpose, and on a practical note, the available rooms and retreat directors. Personal retreats are tailored on these contingencies to fit purpose.

Thus, the Holy Mountain is also home to, for want of a better phrase, troubled people. These're folks thinking of making a major transition in their lives. Priests seeking to leave the priesthood/ or being asked to consider leaving the priesthood. Candidates for priesthood who think the priesthood is no longer their calling. Sisters thinking of packing out of the nunnery.

Thus also, the Holy Mountain is also home to folks thinking of making a major decision in life. People thinking of marrying or joining the priesthood or the convert or even deciding what major to study in college. And of course, bishops considering resigning from their office. The latter became quite common when the Church became riven by the child abuse scandals.

So the seventy-bedroom spiritual facility is host to all sorts of guests. Fr Mentor has seen it all. And he has been journeying with all sorts of people. Most people find solace during their stay at the Mountain, and it's ever the hope of the Mountain and Fr Mentor that the new found peace would guide them in the rest of their life.

Fr Mentor's role as director of the Center means that he engages in very minimal spiritual direction of attendees. In any event, there're dozen Jesuit priest helping out who are equally good, though not as renowned as Fr Mentor. In addition, the Mountain welcomes renowned Spiritual guides from other religious orders such as the Franciscans, Dominicans, Benedictines and many others including known spiritual leaders of other faiths such as the Dalai Lima.

So Fr Mentor's main task is supervising and coordinating the various components of the program. A task that often leaves him with very little time for spiritual direction of others. The last time he directed a guest was about a year ago. The directee was a Republican presidential candidate who had just lost the national presidential election and had come to discern God's new purpose in his life.

Hence, Fr Mentor is utterly surprised when the Provincial, Fr. Cantwell, SJ, specifically asks that he directs the young Harvard priest professor who is on his way to the Holy Mountain for an unplanned sabbatical. The young priest professor has been ordained five years ago. He has been teaching philosophy and ethics at Harvard since his ordination. The Provincial is very emphatic, Fr Mentor should direct him. No other person.

The email doesn't specify for how long Fr. Priestley Plubriuschola was to stay at the Mountain. So the ever meticulous Fr Mentor writes to the Provincial asking for the duration of this unusual guest. The reply comes. "Well, there's an investigation ongoing. Keep him safe there until the investigation is over." Indefinite is his stay.

Fr Mentor is eager to meet this peculiar priest professor who is under investigation. In all of his years working at the Mountain, his bosses have never specifically assigned a priest to him. Even less so as director. He deals with the high-profile visitors. And other retreatants don't know of some of the guests there. For example, Cardinal Andrew Johnson is a guest for a day before he went to Rome for the conclave that elects him Pope Marinus III after the demise of Pope Paschal III. It's expected that Fr Mentor directs Cardinal Johnson. And the whole affair was tightly kept a secret. And Fr Mentor could feel the aura of call to higher spiritual office around Cardinal Johnson.

Now, a priest of only five years earns the same status as Cardinal Johnson, now, Pope Paschal III. There is something around this Fr. Priestley Plubruischola guy, Fr. Mentor thinks to himself.

So on the rainy morning of October 29, 2017, Fr Mentor expectantly waits for the arrival of Fr Schola. Sure enough,

Schola arrives. Fr Schola makes a permanent first impression on Fr Mentor without intending to. Since he teaches at Harvard, Fr Mentor concludes that he's smart. As well, he's good looking and well built. God might have spent a few minutes creating Fr Schola, Fr Mentor imagines.

And there's a calmness about him. A perfect peace. Usually, people in transition or hoping to make a transition carry worried and unhappy faces about the Mountain. At least, when they first arrive. Schola is different. Fr Mentor senses that he's carrying a big load. But he has it well-balanced on his broad shoulders. A mark of a great men.

In the words of Roosevelt, Fr Schola might have made mistakes and is coming up short again and again. But Fr Schola appears to be the fighter in the arena. A fighter who knows the taste of defeat. And probably on occasions, relishes the glorious feeling of victory. But defeat largely marks his station in life. Defeat regardless, he doesn't give up. At every fall, he gets up and stays the course. Fighting with every fire left in his being. Such a person, according to Roosevelt, is the one who matters. Not the arm-chair critic who neither knows the taste of defeat nor those few glorious moments of victory. Fr Schola is the man in the arena in the initial appraisal of wise Fr Mentor. Schola is a man to be admired. Not pitied.

"Fr Mentor, I guess," Fr Schola says, extending his cold and wet hands.

"Yes, I'm Fr Mentor," Fr Mentor says, extending his holy dry hand. "And you must be Fr Schola," Fr Mentor extends the courtesies.

"For now, yes," Fr Schola says with a sincere laughter. "We never know what the wise guy upstairs has in store for us," Fr Schola says again.

"You are quite right, Fr Schola," Fr Mentor says. "As the saying goes: Man proposes; God laughs," Fr Mentor says.

Both men laugh at the joke. But quickly realize that this is the Holy Mountain and the noise must be below the sound of the drop of a needle.

The two priest, one old, old enough to be the father, perhaps the grandfather of the other, walk to the west side of the building where the younger priest, young enough to be the son or the grandson of the other is shown his room. For how long, they don't know. At that point, nobody knows much.

Fr Mentor becomes very fond of this collected, young priest with a day of reckoning coming for him. And that day could change his life forever. So young Fr Schola has all the reasons to be a sad and moody man. People are very depressed during this period from Fr Mentor's experience. But not this guy. He keeps at it. He keeps hopes alive. A mark of a great man.

Of course, there're low moments for Fr Schola. Times when he's down. Quiet. Withdrawn. Sad. Disappointed. During those times, Fr Mentor offers words of encouragement.

Besides his lovely demeanor, Fr Schola is by far the person who exercises the most on the Mountain. More than anybody that visited the Mountain that Fr Mentor recalls. Those trails. He runs them three times a day. Fr Schola's discipline is unparalleled.

And Fr Schola devours books like a hungry lion its prey. And real books. Three in two days. Schola is a ravenous intellectual.

Even more, Fr Mentor loves Schola when Schola begins sharing his recent sad life. Fr Schola loses his entire family recently. And Fr Schola shares with Fr Mentor the current allegations against him. Such forthrightness. Fr Schola tells him every detail of the incident that is now the subject matter of a committee's investigation.

True, it isn't often infrequently that two people share the same surname. But it isn't often the case that two unrelated people share the same surname and almost the same personality with no biological ties. Fr Schola keeps reminding Fr Mentor of Sparkman

Schola, the now retired governor of Indiana. Fr Mentor's closest friend before the Governor left the Jesuit Order and pursued a life of public service in politics while amassing so much wealth in business.

73

THE SOUP KITCHEN

SCHOLA WOULD HAVE FOUND THE weeks of waiting for the verdict unbearable if he were idle and just waited. But Schola learns to always find a purpose and something meaningful doing no matter what. Hence, Schola is never idle.

This sense of purpose and direction is re-enforced during his sojourn at the Holy Mountain three years ago. Schola doesn't know when the committee's findings would end and give him a respite from months of pain and anxiety. Fr Mentor doesn't know, either. But the two men agree that Schola should find something to fill his open schedule.

Of course, there's about three hours of exercise a day. Fr Mentor suggests an hour of exercise initially. But Schola loves the trails and outdoors that he runs and walks them three times a day – morning, afternoon, and evening. As a scholar, reading was an expected pastime. He devours several books of ethics and philosophy and the classics and history and spirituality during this period.

Fr Mentor has always been a man of the poor. Born in a family of relative means, it's probably curious that Schola fights the cause of the poor. Fr Mentor helps set up a soup kitchen in the inner city of Rochester. The soup kitchen serves over five hundred soups every day. Out of curiosity at first, Schola volunteers to go with Fr Mentor to serve soups on Fridays. So, on Fridays they go downtown. Cook, package, and serve. After which, they wash.

It's an eye-opener for Schola. He doesn't know that so many people are this hungry in America. Whole families are relying on the charity of the soup kitchen to survive. So Schola goes down on Mondays, Wednesdays, and with Fr. Mentor on Fridays. Fr. Mentor realizes that this young priest who has so far been locked up in academia loves ordinary people. The young priest loves the poor. A love that bonds the two priests.

And so, when the jury closes its second day of deliberation without a report to conclude the trial, Schola decides he won't be waiting around all day. But he can't be far away from the courts and from the city for that matter. He thinks about doing something new and different while waiting. And so literally looks around him and sees a man in shattered clothes holding food.

"I know what that is and where you get it from?" Schola says to himself, very excited.

"Mr Conkling, where's the soup kitchen from which that man gets his supplies?"

"From St. Mary's Soup Kitchen," replies Mr Conkling.

"Why?"

"I'll like to check the Soup Kitchen out."

"They close in about thirty minutes," Mr Conkling tries to dissuade Schola from going to the soup kitchen.

Without another exchange, the two men head to the soup kitchen. Patrons often stop showing up for pickups about an hour to the time for closing. So it wasn't unusual for volunteers to start locking up before time is up. Schola and Mr Conkling arrive just before the soup kitchen closes.

"Please, we'll like to see the director," Schola announces their mission.

"She isn't in today," the volunteer replies. "But how can we help you?" she inquires.

"We'll like to volunteer," Schola answers.

The woman is quite surprised. Two men in suits wanting to volunteer for the Soup Kitchen. The papers are filled and Schola's volunteer times set up. So it happens that Schola spends the entire morning cutting onions, potatoes, tomatoes, meat, and others at the soup kitchen.

Mr Conkling is ordered to stay put at the court and keep an eye on the jury. Mr Conkling is to summon Schola to the court if something comes up. And for almost two weeks now, nothing of note comes up. Hence, Schola isn't called to the court's premises. And so he busies away at the soup kitchen.

Again, Schola finds something doing while waiting. Schola's major concern is the Senator. He's haggard. He looks pale, tired, and spent. You can't blame the poor man. Senator Conner has lost some of his businesses and is in the process of losing it all. He lost his wife a short while ago. Though they were about divorcing, Schola knows the Senator is grieving. And any minute now, he could lose his freedom as well.

When Schola suggests to the Senator that they both volunteer at the soup kitchen, the Senator almost vomits.

"Like for real?"

"Sure," Schola replies.

"I can write a check for them," the Senator compromises and thinks he's offering a better alternative.

"You're right. They probably need the money. But the volunteering isn't to help them but to help you," Schola says.

The Senator is surprised. But his lawyer has always been a strange fellow. He doesn't drink. No women. No cigars. No social life. Not even social media life. So the Senator learns to tolerate him. And the Senator knows Schola has so far been right about everything. But not this idea of a soup kitchen.

The Senator initially plans to work at the soup kitchen for a day. Write a check the next, that's, if the jury hasn't concluded yet. And say bye to the soup kitchen. On the first day, Schola disguises him, and ensures that he's at the window, unnoticed, giving out the supplies.

The procedure is quite simple.

"How many soups today?"

"One, two, or three, the poor fellow responds."

"Any bread?"

About half of the patrons would decline the bread.

Everyone served always says thanks. And their gratitude is sincere. For months now, no one ever says thanks to the Senator. Later, the Senator joins Schola and the rest in washing and drying up the cooking pants.

And for a while, the soup kitchen is the one thing that gets the Senator out of bed. He looks forward to it. It gives him a purpose for the day. More important, it makes a very positive difference in the lives of the hungry beneficiaries.

And the Senator overhears the conversations of patrons while they wait to pick their food. Real life shattering experiences.

"I'm completely screwed. My landlord just kicked me out," he hears a patron complains.

"What're you going to do?" The concerned listener inquires.

"I've no idea. I've no idea where I'll sleep with the kids today."

This and other similar stories get into the Senator's once aloft skin.

But there's this one story the Senator can't get out of his mind. And decides that he needs to do something about it.

74

THE HANDYMAN

VOLUNTEERS AT THE SOUP KITCHEN hear a lot about the world of the poor. While waiting for their turn to collect their sustenance for the day, patrons, most of which know one another, give outdates of their lives. How the sick baby is doing. How the eviction has been resolved and on and on.

Senator Conner hands out soups and hears his fair share of these stories. One of such stories concerns a handyman. According to this handyman, who appears to be in his mid–thirties, he works for this guy and "hasn't been paid right." He says that he's a good worker. He hasn't been paid all his hours. Besides, the owner of the house which he renovates cuts down the hourly rate from ten to five dollars.

Senator Conner wonders how any person paid less than five hundred dollars an hour can survive. But five dollars an hour? And he isn't even paid all the hours that he works for. Senator Conner wishes he could do something for this poor guy.

The cheating hurts Mr Handyman badly. For a week now, he keeps relating the experience to anybody with ears and willing to listen. Senator Conner listens closely and gets the exact hours and amounts. So far, he did a total of 25 hours. And the initial agreed amount of $10 per hour gives Mr Handyman a total of $250.

As is usually the case, Schola and the Senator are two of the three last persons to leave the soup kitchen. The third person locks up. At Senator Conner's direction, Mr Handyman waits for him. Senator Conner rounds everything up to $ 2,500 in cash for the man. He hands the sack of money in $100 bills to the confused man. The man opens the envelope and nearly collapses. He has never received up to that amount in his life.

"What's that about?" Schola asks.

"Some home owner refuses to pay the poor man after the guy works hours for him."

"I see. What're you now? Mother Theresa?" Schola teases.

"No, Pope Francis," the Senator replies. The two men laugh.

"By the way, you haven't paid a dime for attorney fees. And you're giving out free monies," Schola protests.

"My understanding from the beginning is that you are doing this pro bono publico," the Senator replies.

"I didn't know that you liked Latin," Schola teases back. Their laughter is uncontained. Onlookers think they are two insane men in the street of Fort Wayne.

75

THE TRANSCRIPTS

THERE'S THE STORY OF ANOTHER patron of the soup kitchen, a young woman, Senator Conner can't keep her out of his mind also. The Senator so far fails to come out with a solution to her problem as he does for the handyman. According to her, related only twice, she wants to transfer from her current community college to a different one.

In the past year alone, twelve deaths occur at her present school. And in the past month alone, they have been five different shooting incidents on campus two of which resulted in the dead of two students. Deaths besides, these shootings leave severe and lasting injuries on victims, both physical and psychological. Students don't feel safe anymore. These deaths and shootings and injuries have cast a pall over the school in recent times. A multitude of students have left and are leaving. Workers have left in their numbers and the remaining ones have updated their resumes, looking at other employers.

This single mother seems to be in her early twenties. The school won't release her transcript. Because she owes the school some $8,000 plus. And obviously she can't pay that amount. Besides, she has two kids. As well, her boyfriend/husband is doing time behind bars.

Senator Conner is thinking about withdrawing another $8,000 from the bank for her. "Schola, let me get some cash from the bank before they close."

"Are you paying off another poor person?"

"In fact, I'm. She needs her transcripts to transfer to a different school. But owes her current school in tuition."

"Why does she have to transfer?"

"Shootings, suicides, and deaths. All on campus. Students who can, have transferred. Even workers are leaving. The place is no longer conducive for education."

"I see," Schola replies. "In that case, she isn't leaving the school on her own volition. She is forced out. This's what one might call constructive transfer. Not only does she not own the school anything, the school might have to cover the cost of transferring to another school. A visit to the school should be a gentleman thing to do. If they're still deaf, we file a suit with the courts, especially, since we are idle."

Senator Conner is very impressed. Problem is that they don't know the name or the address of this young, single mother. And they hope that she shows up tomorrow as she does daily.

The following day, the duo, the Senator and Schola, are at the soup kitchen an hour before it opens. And after two hours, she comes by. "There she's, the Senator points to Schola." At this point, Senator Conner knows exactly what she gets. So her order is all wrapped up.

Onlookers are surprise when Schola announces to the young mother that they are taking a trip to her school with her. We're going to get those transcripts for you. The girl thinks she's dreaming.

The entrance to the registrar's office of the college is dramatic. Those outside pause to take a good look at the two tall and athletic white men, both in suits, walking confidently with a black girl in their middle. The doors give way as the triumvirate file past. While inside, they don't even remove their sunglasses. With the shooting, people are shaken.

"I'm Mr Schola. I'm an attorney. This is my client, Ms err..., the girl answers, both men hear her name for the first time. She says her transcript isn't released to her. And she retains me to look into the matter. And this is my sniper. I hear you guys shoot at will."

The puzzled faces don't know how to react. Someone higher up is summoned. And in less than five minutes the official transcripts are released. "Official," the mark reads. They pay no dime.

"I'm all for schools and colleges doing well. Usually, you'll have to pay for the cost of her transfer to the new school. But we know you guys are having a tough year. So we understand." Schola consoles them.

Just like that. They make another person happy for the day. But they are still waiting for the jury to make them happy.

76

FIXING HER AFFAIRS

SHE'S DYING. SHE FEELS LIFE slowly, slowly leaving her body. She knows she's dying. She's beginning to accept her fate. Prior to accepting her impending fate, she fights hard. She knows that she has. She follows every medical prescription. She agrees to all their medical trials. She accepts to be the guinea pig of their frontice of medical ventures. But now, she feels the breath going out of body. Her spirit is departing her. The night of her life is nigh. And she knows it. She accepts it.

Professor Linda Duval is diagnosed of an advanced metastatic lung cancer a bit over a year ago. Before the diagnoses, she often feels strange. She often feels weak. She takes it to be nothing. And sometimes while driving, she feels dizzy and often stops to retain her total consciousness. But in the last episode, she completely passes out while on the wheel.

The resulting accident causes the death of a mother and two of her tender children; a boy and a girl. The accident leaves a poor widower and two young children – a boy and a girl as well. The guilt of depriving a husband of his wife and kids, and, the surviving kids, of their mother and siblings should wear heavily on a normal person. Not Professor Linda Duval. For up until now, Prof Duval had no soul. No conscience. No ethics. She thinks of it as an accident. She isn't at fault. And life is full of so many accidents and misfortunes. She doesn't accept any blame.

She nearly dies herself. Upon gaining consciousness, she's diagnosed of this deadly cancer. Doctors were examining her to treat her accident wounds. They found the cancer too instead.

Incidentaloma is the medical term for an unanticipated finding unrelated to the original medical examination. The cancer has been eating away at her for years now. According to doctor's prognosis, she would have died suddenly but for the accident that drew their attention to the malignant cancer.

At the time of the diagnosis, doctors think the cancer might be treatable, offering Prof Duval a glimmer of hope. They give her so much hope. Typical of Prof Duval, she even thanks her stars for the accident. For the accident leads to the discovery of the cancer and proffers a potential treatment. She doesn't care that a mother and two young lives pass on. She doesn't care a young man is rendered a widower. She doesn't care that a young man must balance work with raising two toddlers by himself. Professor Duval is soulless. Almost. Clearly, she has no conscience.

And likely for her, the police investigation doesn't establish that she feels dizzy or passes out occasionally while on the wheels. Such a finding might have meant that Prof Duval is guilty of involuntary manslaughter at least, a serious felony in the Commonwealth of Massachusetts. At first, she is more concern about the prospects of going to prison. She gets a lawyer. And incurs very little legal expenses because charges aren't pressed.

The truth is that she doesn't know that her dizziness poses enough of a threat to the public. The accident is her first time of completely passing out while driving. Though it isn't clear she would have stopped driving had she known that she is susceptible to unconsciousness while on the wheels.

Nonetheless, last week, she makes contacts with the widower and his children to apologize and seek their forgiveness for the deaths. The mourning, three-member family pity her. How could they not? She is almost lifeless herself. They leave Prof Duval's hospital feeling very sorry for her despite their grief and seething anger for killing three of their kin.

But she feels better after apologizing to them again. She really feels better. She's almost at peace with herself and ready to die but for one more apology. A sin worse than causing an accident. Prof Duval has been a very bad girl; she has been a horrible human being. Soulless. Until now.

77

FIXING HER AFFAIRS 2

IS EMINENCE, CARDINAL GEORGE GASKELL of New York, is flabbergasted. The Cardinal has seen it all and isn't easily surprised. But the Cardinal is surprised, even afraid. A dying woman at St. Anne's Hospital in Newark City pleads to see him. Cardinal Gaskell is a busy man, to say the least. Besides, Newark is not his jurisdiction. A bishop shouldn't really be tending to the flocks of another diocese without an invitation or permission from the bishop of that diocese, in this case, the Cardinal of Newark.

The call comes in again today for the countless time. And this time, Cardinal Gaskell's secretary says it is a doctor insisting to speak with the Cardinal. Cardinal Gaskell feels compelled to take the doctor's call.

"Please is this Cardinal Gaskell of New York?" the caller asks.

"Yes, peace and joy be with you my son. How may I help you doctor?" Cardinal Gaskell is impatient. Rightly so, he thinks.

"Thanks, your eminence for taking the call. This is Doctor Nelson Malus of St. Anne's Hospital in Newark." The caller introduces himself.

"Yes Doc., I explained myself rather adequately to the nurse who called on behalf of Prof Linda Duval. Since she isn't a relative, I either need to be invited or given the permission of my brother Cardinal of Newark to visit on a pastoral note."

"Yes, your eminence. I understand. I'm a Catholic. If truth be told, I was short of a year to ordination before I left the seminary twenty years ago."

"Oh, I didn't know that."

"Your eminence, I had you for Systematic Theology and American Catholic Thought at Catholic University of America in D.C."

"Ooh." His eminence is speechless."

"Please, I don't expect you to remember me. It has been two long decades. But you need to get down here. She doesn't have much time left. In fact, she could be gone at anything. She keeps asking for you. It's her dying wish to see you. She would die a sad person if she doesn't see you."

"Okay, I'm coming right away."

After hanging up, his eminence asks his secretary to get the car. They are heading to Anne's hospital in Newark.

"But Your Eminence, the finance committee meets in an hours' time," Fr David Hagarty, the cardinal's secretary and diarist protests. It's the duty of the secretary, amid competing attentions, to keep the cardinal to his schedule. Keeping the cardinal to his schedule is an arduous task. And one single interference, like the present one, throws the whole day, week, and sometimes even month out of order. An order that is badly needed to properly run the Catholic Church in New York.

"I know, but I need to attend to a dying person first."

78

CARDINAL MEETS DR MALUS

DOCTOR MALUS WELCOMES HIS FORMER seminary professor. Now a Cardinal, he's even considered a papabile. That is, a serious candidate for the office of Pope. The former seminarian, now a medical doctor, reaches to kiss the ring of His Eminence who declines but taps him on the back instead.

The two men walk to Prof Duval's room. His Eminence comes with anointing oil. "Has she been anointed yet," His Eminence asks.

"She isn't even a catholic," Doctor Malus replies. The cardinal stops in his tracks. Ponders for a while.

"This's really strange," the cardinal says.

While inside, Prof Duval asks to be left alone with the cardinal. The cardinal nods to Doctor Malus who nods back in reverence and leaves the room.

79

CARDINAL HEARS PROF DUVAL

THE CARDINAL IS IN THAT room for over an hour. More than Dr Malus expects, making the doctor worried. But His Eminence emerges from the room, eventually, much to the relieve of Dr Malus.

"How long does she have?"

"Not much time Your Eminence."

"I see. Then I must be going now. And please keep her alive until I return," the Cardinal Gaskell orders.

"And how is Johan?" The Cardinal asks of Dr Malus's wife.

Doctor Malus is very surprised by the question. Dr Malus nearly drops the stethoscope he holds. "Your Eminence I don't believe you still remember my wife. That was a long time ago." Dr Malus says.

"I don't forget my students, Nelson," His Eminence says and calls him without the title Doctor. "I don't forget, especially, my brilliant students, the Cardinal repeats with a look of deep admiration for his former student."

"Well, we're married with three kinds. Two of them in college now," Dr Malus says of the life he has so far built with the love of his life, Johan.

"Please you must bring the entire family for a visit when we take care of this whole Prof Duval thing. I will be in touch." With that, His Eminence is gone.

80

CARDINAL CALLS

CARDINAL GASKELL IS YEARS AWAY in thought from both his driver and priest assistant as they drive away from St Anne's Hospital. The Cardinal, in fact, is four years away in though from his traveling companions. The driver and assistant have no way of divining the reason and purpose of the unusual visit. And they'll never know why the cardinal is so distracted and saddened. The Cardinal is not susceptible to distraction. This must be big.

Guilt overwhelms the Cardinal. He oversees the entire investigation into the allegations against then Father Schola. He was the archbishop of Boston then. Father Schola was a professor at Harvard, Prof Duval's colleague.

Given the child abuse scandal, and the growing cases of sexual harassment in the country generally, Cardinal Gaskell, then, Archbishop Gaskell, leaned heavily towards defrocking then Father Schola. By way of evidence, Prof Duval didn't provide much, if any. Prof Duval, then a colleague professor of Schola's at Harvard accuses the priest of sexually harassing her. It's her word against his. Around the time, a woman, Ms Corell Woolsey immolated herself because nobody addressed her sexual harassment claims. Ms Woolsey leaves behind toddlers. Father Schola had to go. And the poor priest professor was discharged without due process.

Now, Cardinal Gaskell doesn't know how to make this right. A priest is wrongly dismissed and all his faculties as a priest taken from him based on lies. What's to be done now? Call him back to the priesthood? What if he is already married? There're more questions. And even more regrets. The sexual scandals of various forms push the Church to scratch clean its house and in so doing appears to have thrown some babies away with the water.

But first things first. Schola is to be contacted and if possible, summoned. Prof Duval wants to personally apologize to him. And she doesn't have much time, she tells the cardinal in their visit that just ended a while ago. So the Cardinal needs to hurry up. There is the next challenge. How does he get Schola? Is Schola even still alive?

81

PROVINCIAL IN NAIROBI

THE PROVINCIAL, FR ANTHONY CANTWELL, SJ, is in Nairobi, Kenya, attending a conference of world leaders of the Jesuits on "bridging new frontiers in today's world" when Cardinal Gaskell calls the curia in Manhattan to speak to him. Given the time difference, it's 1:45 a.m. in Nairobi. The socius, that is, the assistant to Father Fr Anthony Cantwell, SJ, tells the Cardinal that the call might have to wait a few more hours because "Fr. Cantwell is sleeping now." But the Cardinal insists that Father Cantwell be woken. The Cardinal's words were very somber; "someone is dying and needs to make things right."

When he is informed about it, Fr Cantwell decides to leave the conference right away for New York City. Fr Cantwell is as confused as he is sad. He remembers the allegations against Fr Schola. Fr Cantwell had just started his tenure as leader of the Jesuits in the states of New York, New Jersey, DC, Maryland. He remembers Fr Schola almost tearfully and painfully confessing his innocence. The archdiocese of Boston is involved. A potential scandal is on the brink of breaking if Professor Duval goes public with her allegations. Fr Cantwell feels his hands tied. Fr Cantwell decides that Fr Schola must leave when Ms Woolsey self-immolates in protest of denials of her sexual harassment claims just around that time.

The young priest, Fr Schola, pleads with him to allow him in residence until he figures out where to go. He doesn't have anywhere to go, Fr Schola begs. But it's decided that the diseased branch should be axed from the rest of the tree to save the tree. Cut off from what he comes to know and call home – the Society of Jesus – God knows where Schola goes. "Will he forgive," is what Fr Cantwell keeps asking himself in the long flight, even made more longer by the circumstances, from Nairobi to New York.

Fr Cantwell hopes and prays that someone at the Jesuit Center is still friends with Fr Schola. If Schola isn't found, this is a disaster. But there's another problem. Would he even forgive everybody involved in this?

Arriving at the Jesuit curia in Manhattan, Fr Cantwell goes straight to his office and dials Fr Petrus Mentor at the Holy Mountain.

"Hello, Fr Provincial, aren't you in Nairobi?"

"Yes, I was, Fr. Mentor. An emergency brings me back."

"I'm all ears and at your service, Fr Cantwell," Fr Mentor says, sensing the storm in Fr Cantwell's voice and ready to embrace the storm should he be deployed.

"Thanks. Do you recall Fr Schola, the young priest, the Harvard professor, that circumstances compelled us to send away four years ago?" Fr Cantwell asks and hopes for good news.

"Yes, Schola is doing very well. He's now an attorney. In fact, he's in the headlines. He is defending Senator Conner."

The line goes silent for a while as Fr Cantwell recalls Schola's piece in the New York Times, cautioning against judging the Senator before trial is had.

"Hello Fr Cantwell, are you there?"

"Yes, I'm here. So you are saying that we can get him to New York?"

"Well, we could try. But remember he's in the middle of a national trial. So I can't be too sure."

"Please Fr Mentor, get him to New York immediately. It's important that he comes right away." The line goes silent.

82

MENTOR CALLS THE GOVERNOR

FR MENTOR HARDLY CALLS HIS former classmate, Governor Schola, outside the major feast days and holidays. They talk on Thanksgiving Days; send cards on other festivities such as Christmas, Easter, and more importantly on the Feast of St. Ignatius, July 31st. When the other voice over the phone says that he is Fr Mentor, the governor is understandably surprised, if pleasantly. The Governor's instincts tells him that something must be amiss.

Schola is needed in New York as soon as possible, Fr Mentor relays the solemn message. The Provincial, Fr Cantwell, wants to see him right away. Fr Mentor is emphatic. Schola must leave for New York as soon as possible. The unprecedented and brief phone call ends.

A Jesuit never ceases to be one. The former Governor, former Jesuit, Spartman Schola, readies his Gulfstream for his adopted son, Schola, another former Jesuit to fly into New York even before contacting Schola.

83

CLOSING UP FOR THE DAY at the Soup Kitchen, Schola and Senator Conner aren't really surprised that the jury are still helplessly hung. The daily jury verdict over the past weeks is no verdict. So they part ways, hoping to return the following day. They've no idea that things have dramatically changed. Life continues to exist in twists beside the trial.

84

PROVINCIAL MEETS PROF. DUVAL/ SCHOLA VISITS NEW YORK

FR CANTWELL, SJ, THE PROVINCIAL, is a troubled man. Fr Cantwell isn't one easily troubled. But Fr Cantwell is a troubled man. If what Cardinal Gaskell relates to him about the recantations of Prof Linda Duval is true, he, Fr Cantwell, sins against an innocent man, an innocent priest, an innocent Jesuit and an innocent illustrious professor. Fr Cantwell feels profoundly nauseated. Then Fr Schola is shown the door out of the Jesuits on account of Prof Duval's charges that the priest-professor behaved improperly towards her, sexually. It must have been a very painful experience for Fr Schola. The provincial looks over the language of the letter mandating Fr Schola's dismissal: "He is to vacate all our residences as soon as possible. Not one more night." Harsh.

But as a Jesuit, Fr Cantwell sees the finger of God in everything. God is present in every single thing. Schola is now an attorney. Can you believe that? It even gets more unexpected. Schola is the lead counsel in the Senator Conner case. Fr Peter Krock, one of the assistants to Fr Cantwell culls newspaper's accounts of the trail: "The unknown lawyer took the scandalous case and turned it into a winning one," the *New York Times* declares. "For his lead lawyer's legal acumen, Senator Conner might just escape jail," *The Wall Street Journal* predicts. "Before trial, nobody had a reasonable doubt that Senator Conner wouldn't be imprisoned, the Senator's lead lawyer, an unknown attorney, is sowing lots of doubts in the minds of many, least of which, the jury" *Time* magazine concludes. God has a weird sense of humor, Fr Cantwell muses.

But where is the hand of God in all of this? Fr Cantwell wonders. The Church is struggling with its own legal problems in the child abuse scandal. Maybe, Schola could handle that too. Fr Cantwell has a problem entrusting documents of the Church to lay people. Not that he wants to hide anything. Fr Cantwell sees it proper that priest-lawyers should handle the Church's most sensitive legal issues. Schola might just be the answer. God uses every situation to his own good.

But first, Fr Cantwell wants to talk to the dying woman in question. Cardinal Gaskell strongly suggests that Fr Cantwell meets with the dying accuser. And after Fr Cantwell's meets with Prof Duval, the Cardinal and Fr Cantwell would meet Schola at the Cardinal's house in New York. The meeting is scheduled for the evening of today after dinner with the Cardinal. Fr Cantwell orders Father Petrus Mentor, SJ to be in attendance too.

85

THE TRIP TO NYC

SENATOR CONNER IS, UNDERSTANDABLY, AGITATED that Schola must leave Fort Wayne for New York when the jury could be delivering a verdict any time. The Senator fails to convince Schola to wait till the verdict is rendered. Schola assures him that he thought of it. In fact, he won't leave him behind. So Schola must find a way of taking the Senator to New York.

So the in-camera hearing in the judge's chambers is unusual.

"Mr Schola, do you realize that the jury's verdict might be ready as we speak," the judge tries to explain to Schola why he and his client can't leave Fort Wayne.

"But your honor, this's a matter of my client's life. His physician who moved to New York City asks that my client comes over for a quick check up. We'll be back tomorrow," Schola lies.

Eventually, the judge allows Senator Conner to travel to New York City for a medical review.

Senator Conner's opinion of Schola as the naïve, bookish person has all but eroded. Schola is shrewd. Schola lies to the judge to get him along for the trip. Senator Conner has no doctors in New York City. And the Senator isn't even sure that he knows any doctors there. But Schola manages to convince the judge that his client needs to see his New York physician. But the Senator is yet to find out why Schola needs to go to New York City.

The duo – Senator Conner and Schola – are the only passengers on the Gulf Stream that takes off from Fort Wayne to the Big Apple that afternoon. Senator Conner sits across Schola looking at his strange attorney. The Senator is trying in vain to understand him. Trying to know this man who is young enough to be his son. But who in several ways is much more mature than him. It's so clear that the thoughts of Schola are so far away.

"Why does the Cardinal want to see you," Senator Conner eventually asks when the speedy Gulf Stream starts descending the skies of New York. "Because he wants to excommunicate me for representing you," Schola replies. Both men laugh.

86

AT THE CARDINAL'S RESIDENCE

IS EMINENCE, CARDINAL GASKELL, ISN'T expecting an additional guest in addition to Fr Mentor, Fr Cantwell and Schola. And the cardinal's surprise is heightened on realizing that the additional guest is Senator Conner. But rooms are available for both men in the relatively spacious mansion of the Cardinal's residence. The conversation at dinner is terse. The aura is tense. The professional church men don't know how Schola is going to response to the new information. They didn't treat him well. Their guilt worsened when they learn that at the time of his leaving, Schola had nowhere to go.

Dinner isn't over when the phone rings. The caller asks to speak with Fr Mentor. And upon talking the call, Fr Mentor hands it over to Schola. Schola is startled for a while. The confusion is all over his face. The caller is the Governor. Schola's countenance is radiant on recognizing the voice. Schola assures the Governor that he's fine. Very fine. And would be home soon. The Governor misses him. Already.

87

THE MEETING

FTER DINNER, SENATOR CONNER IS excused. Cardinal Gaskell, Fr Cantwell, Fr. Mentor, and Schola go into the Cardinal's office for the meeting whose agenda is known only to the cardinal and the Provincial. Senator Conner decides to wonder about the cardinal's mansion.

Senator Conner finds the cardinal's residence very modest. It's a two-story building. Probably nine rooms. A chapel. No swimming pool. No bar. But a basketball court. It's smaller than the smallest of the Senator's mansions. Yet this man is the head of a whole diocese. A leading member of the Catholic Church in the United States. Two kinds of portraits are very prominent in this house. Pictures of the saints and pictures of poor people. Smiling children from Africa and Asia. Happy looking old people. Hospitals. And schools. And even more schools. That is what they do.

Senator Conner is experiencing something new this evening. He can't describe it. The Senator feels that he has been chasing the wrong things in life. But he isn't going to let this Schola guy out of his sight. He would employ him to run his company when this trial thing is over. No matter how the verdict goes. To be a happy man, he knows that he must wake up every day with an appointment with Schola.

Schola comes out of the meeting with the Cardinal, the Provincial and Fr Mentor visibly upset. Senator Conner has never seen Schola this angry. But the other three come out of the meeting very relieved. Looking far better than they go in. They unload their guilt. And ask for Schola's forgiveness. And also ask that he forgives Prof Duval. The work of the three is done.

Schola is angry. Schola wonders why the confession that exonerates him is coming at this time. A good four years after.

88

SCHOLA IS ANGRY

UNDERSTANDABLY, SCHOLA COULDN'T SLEEP LAST night after his meeting with Cardinal Gaskell, Fr Cantwell, SJ, and Fr Mentor, SJ. After the meeting, Schola seethes in anger. The suppressed anger of four years ago comes gusting out. All of it. In one night. The truth is now out. Schola is accused of something heinous, of, which he is as innocent as a child. He is subsequently humiliated and eventually fired from the Jesuits, his only true home, as well as from Harvard where his budding teaching career was taking a great shape.

He loves his former vocation as a priest. He loves his former life as a priest-professor who taught philosophy and ethics. He never for once thought of life outside of the Jesuits. And so he never for once engaged in acts that would derail his clerical life. But from nowhere, Prof Duval accuses him of sexual harassment. As Schola paces about in his room in anger, he wonders whether he has even as much as ever shaken Prof Duval's hands. They have never had physical contact.

Yet the committee listens to her story and believes her. Write a damning report. And relying on the committee's report Schola gets a sack. All of this, without anyone listening to him. He tells those few with ears for him that he is innocent. But he doubts anybody believes him. He doubts whether even Fr Mentor believes him at the time.

There's a knock on his door. It's Senator Conner. The Senator realizes that Schola is still in a foul mood, an even angrier mood than yesterday. The two men don't even greet. For there isn't a reason to ask how Schola is doing. Senator Conner just sits on the bed and watches Schola walk up and down the length of the room.

There's yet another knock on Schola's door. It's Fr Mentor. The two men exchange greetings. Senator Conner looks at Schola and concludes that the two men need to be alone. The Senator leaves the room.

Fr Mentor's message is that Prof Duval had a bad night and is still lucky to be alive. "If you want to visit her, it might be wise to do so right away," Fr Mentor advises. Schola has been thinking about that possibility since last night and this morning. And is yet to decide. Schola knows that a suggestion from Fr Mentor is always worth the try, even in these circumstances. But Schola is too angry to meet his accuser. Prof Duval ruins Schola's former happy and meaningful life.

89

SCHOLA MEETS PATIENT

WHEN FR MENTOR AND SCHOLA get to Prof Duval's room at St Anne's Hospital, a doctor and a nurse stand armed-folded over her. Their mood is sober.

"How's she?" Fr Mentor asks.

"It was a bad night," the doctor answers. The four stand there in silence for a while. The nurse broke the silence:

"Who is Fr Schola?" Fr Mentor and Schola look at each other perplexed. "She has been murmuring Father Schola all night," the nurse explains.

"I used to be Fr Schola," Schola answers with almost a chuckle. "I'm still Schola, but not Fr Schola," Schola attempts a joke. At the sound of Schola's voice, Prof Duval opens her eyes and is lucid at that instant. Her beauty has faded, Schola observes. She lays there, a shadow of her former self. But there is no doubt that she was once beautiful.

"High Linda, what're you doing lazily lying around here? You're supposed to be firing away at the bright minds at Harvard, Professor." Everyone, including Prof Duval laugh.

"You still have that cruel but harmless sense of humor," Fr Schola, Prof Duval remarks.

Prof Duval tries getting up. Schola walks to her and helps her up to a sitting position, allowing her to recline comfortably. Schola holds her two fragile hands. Those hands were once very beautiful. But frail now. The cancer has done its worse.

"Please forgive me, Fr Schola" she says tearfully.

"Please don't be sad. You did nothing wrong." Pointing to Fr. Mentor, Schola says: "This man has always wanted to fire me as a priest. You only gave him an excuse." The room is all laughter again.

And with that laughter, a cough seizes Prof Duval. And a choke follows. Then a seizure. And then silence. Eternal silence. She's gone. She goes laughing. Laughing at the joke of a former priest whose priesthood she ended. She dies happily. She dies in Schola's arms.

Sadness and relieve come over everybody. The doctor reports the time of death and the nurse writes it on a card. Fr Mentor says a prayer.

Leaving his cellphone number with Dr Malus, Schola asks that the doctor informs him of the funeral arrangement. Schola likes to attend as Prof Duval wishes.

90

CARDINAL AND SENATOR
AT BREAKFAST

"HONESTLY, I HAVE READ A bit about you in the newspaper," Cardinal Gaskell says. Cardinal Gaskell and Senator Conner are at breakfast alone at the Cardinal's residence.

"To be honest, I've never really been a religious person," Senator Conner says. "My parents never really went to Church. And I only go to Church when there is a funeral or when I'm campaigning. So I don't know much about the Church," the Senator confesses.

"It isn't the essential thing—going to church," the Cardinal replies, reaching for peanut butter. "When the chips fall, it's what's in a person's heart. Church can help clean up a heart. But it's one of the several ways of having a pure heart: A heart 'with malice towards none, and charity towards all,'" to paraphrase Abe.

"Who is Abe?" The Senator asks, thinking it's the name of a saint.

"Ooh, sorry. President Lincoln," the Cardinal says. I was quoting one of his famous speeches.

Senator Conner is ponderous at the Cardinal's remarks. The Cardinal isn't condemning him. He doesn't ostracize him. Even when he's the face of a public scandal, he breakfasts with the Cardinal.

And the Cardinal isn't fake about it. He feels that the Cardinal is genuine. He likes him. Sinner though he's. But who isn't a sinner? So the two eat in silence. The Senator feels very welcomed. The first ever since the scandal broke.

"I see photos on the walls. I see pictures of religious figures but mostly of children and mothers," the Senator remarks, half question, half statement.

"Yes, the core constituents of the Church –the poor— as Pope Francis would say," the Cardinal says. "Feeding, clothing, and educating the poor are dear to my heart," the Cardinal reveals, without a trace of arrogance.

That much is evident, the Senator thinks, but doesn't say it.

At that point, Fr Mentor and Schola walk in. They're a happy pair. For Schola, especially, a complete departure in countenance from yesternight and this morning.

"Your Eminence, I'm starving. I hope you haven't eaten everything." Schola says with a loud laugh.

"I've never heard that laughter before," Senator Conner says in surprise. His Eminence is equally surprise at Schola's happy voice. The miracle of forgiveness.

Fr Mentor isn't keeping them in suspense. "Prof Linda Duval died a moment ago. She dies with a radiant and a happy face and laughing even louder than Schola's."

"So she only stayed alive to see Schola before going," the Cardinals says thoughtfully, half a question and half a definitive statement. The room goes silent for the rest of the breakfast.

The Senator wonders what on earth is going on. The Senator will never know. Of all their shortcomings, Catholic priests take their vow of confidentiality seriously. One's sins and secrets are saved with Catholic priests. Priests die with secrets told them.

91

VIEWS OF THE CONSULTANTS

RIGHT AFTER BREAKFAST, SCHOLA AND Senator Conner are up in the sky in the Governor's Gulf Stream headed for Fort Wayne, Indiana. The unexpected trip to New York City temporarily takes their thoughts momentarily away from the impending jury verdict and its varied implications. But before the duo embark on their lonely flight back, Fr Mentor is sure – at the instruction of Fr Cantwell – to touch base with Schola in view of the unanticipated developments in the past two days and the implications therefrom.

And before Fr Mentor meets with Schola, Fr Cantwell has an emergency conference with his consultants – advisors – on Schola's standing vis-à-vis the Jesuits. The man is dismissed from the Jesuits and disrobed as a priest on very malicious grounds – albeit unknown at the time. As is often the case with contentious and sensitive issues, the views of the consultors on the question are different – and all passionate.

For Fr Burle O'Connor, SJ, what is done is done. God uses unfortunate situations for good. Schola should discern what the purpose of God is for him, that's, if he has not already done so. Coming back to the Jesuits or to the priesthood is out of the question in Fr O'Connor's view. In the past four years, Schola lives a life unmonitored by the Jesuits. They can't be sure what he has been doing all these four years. Bringing Schola back might cause problems for the Order in the future.

The youngest of the consultors – not yet ordained a priest – is the exact opposite of Fr O'Connor's take. Mr Castor Challoner,

SJ, argues that given the injustice done Schola; given the public humiliation with plucking him from his teaching in the middle of the semester at Harvard; and given God knows what troubles he faced since he left the Jesuits, two things are required. First, an unqualified apology must be rendered. And two, if he wishes to return, he must be welcomed back with open hands.

And in between these two extreme views are moderate views of all brands.

Then the issue arises as to whether Schola even still wants to be a Jesuit and a priest? Nobody in the room knows. For the main issue arises if he wants to return to the Jesuit Order. If he's happy where he's, let him be. That's the major concession.

Fr Cantwell brings in Fr Mentor for a moment to take his view on what Schola's posture is given the recent revelations. Does he still want to be a Jesuit, and a priest for that matter? Fr Mentor doesn't know either; he hasn't discussed the matter with Schola. However, Fr. Mentor makes one thing clear. Schola is and has always been a Jesuit at heart – thus, a man of obedience. He would do virtually whatever the Jesuits want of him.

In any event, Fr Cantwell tells his group of advisors that he thought that Schola should handle some of the legal matters of the Jesuits in New York and the other three states. The archdiocese of New York might want his help with their legal challenges, too.

So the status of Schola vis-avis the Jesuits is left unresolved for now. Instead, Father Cantwell tells Schola to return to New York for a discussion after the Senator Conner's verdict.

92

FLIGHT BACK AFTER
HOSPITAL VISIT

O
N THE FLIGHT BACK, SCHOLA is divining what talks Fr Cantwell intends to have with him after the verdict. He wonders what's on the provincial's mind. And he wonders what his responses to those views would be.

Senator Conner is used to a silent Schola. So for much of the trip, the Senator just stares at Schola. Usually, the Senator has dozens of girls onboard to warm the flight. But not with this Schola guy. No drinks, no babes. He's boring. Completely. What a wasted flight, the Senator thinks to himself.

Girls are great distraction during times like this. The verdict could be anytime. Even today. If guilty, he could be warded off to prison. For God knows how long. The loneliness makes the flight longer than it should be.

Soon enough, the pilot announces landing instructions. Both men reach for their seatbelts.

At the tarmac to welcome them is Mr Conkling, who also informs them that the jury is still hopelessly deadlock and now wants to see the video. The judge would be making a ruling on the jury request.

⬤

Schola plans to argue against the inclusion of the video on grounds that it might criminalize others beside Senator Conner, and probably expose the Senator to other charges beside the present ones. But Judge Kaufman already has her answer reasoned out. The video would be redacted, and the relevant parts shown to the jury. Problem with this approach is that the parties have no idea which portions would be erased, and which ones left for the eyes of the jury.

The Prosecutor, Ms Kast, renews her effort to see the entire video. She argues that she stands in a very disadvantageous position because she has no clue what's in the video. Again, Ms Kast's request is denied.

The video was in fact planted by an aid of the Governor in the residence of Senator Conner. It was an "opposition research project." Senator Conner has been a rising Republican in Indiana. The Governor's side of the Republican Party wanted to have much on Senator Connor as possible. So Mr Creel Dent, an aid to the Republican Chairman in Indiana at the time, decides to find some dirt on Senator Conner. Dirt that could be used to ensure Senator Conner's cooperation and compromise going forward. Truth is that Governor Spartman Schola didn't and doesn't know about this video. Such a dubious project would never have had the blessing of the Governor. And when incriminating evidence was gathered and shown to him, he asked the gatherers to destroy it. And he even nearly fired them. In fact, he fired one such dirt collector and recalled him after three months.

The video contains a lot of mostly careless talks. How the Mayor is very corrupt, for example. According to one guest, since the current mayor took over the affairs of the city, Democrat's businesses have been suffering. All the contracts are awarded to Republicans.

Even the governor isn't left out. Senator Conner takes a swipe at the governor's anti-immigration policies and how that is hampering his cheap labor. "You know these immigrants work harder than natives and they're even paid less," a guest of the Senator is heard saying. "And if they complain, I threaten them with deportation," Senator Conner says to a round of laughter. Everybody on that video looks pretty much drunk.

And the last part of the video shows Ms Larnage Pincus falling into the Senator's arms. And murmuring something.

93

SENATOR CONNER'S SEAT

WHEN THE FORMER SENATE MAJORITY leader, Senator Cornelius Conner Jr., resigns his post following the allegations, the Republican Party nominates John Tillis to finish up the rest of the term. Senator Conner considers the seat as his "stolen" seat; for his tenure is yet to run out. Politically, Senator Conner knows that he's done and over. Initially, he wants one of his political allies to fill his senate seat for the remaining term. But the GOP in Indiana overrules his wishes. And he has very few political allies left. If any at all.

When Schola delivers his oral argument, the Senator thinks to himself, the Senate of the United States could use such speeches. Since then, the Senator has been flirting with the idea of Schola running for the senate seat he considers his own.

Funds won't be a problem. The Senator is willing to give up all his wealth to retain that seat to enable him wield a semblance of political relevance in Indiana and beyond. But there're serious problems with Conner's idea of getting Schola to the Senate.

The least of these challenges is that Schola isn't a known figure within the GOP circles in Indiana. So Schola may not be allowed to run on the Republican ticket.

Even at that, Schola could run as an independent candidate. The odds of beating both his Democrat and Republican competitors are very grim if Schola runs as an independent in Indiana. But if that is the only option to stay politically relevant in Indiana, the Senator is willing to take the chance and pour every grain into it.

But here is the main problem: Schola: This unusual former priest is independent in thought. Schola can't be easily talked into enterprises that he has no conviction in. Besides, Schola doesn't show any interest whatever in politics. But once this trial is over, the Senator will have a serious chat with his lawyer. Schola must run for the Senate.

94

THE GOVERNOR'S MEDICAL REPORT

GOVERNOR SPARKMAN SCHOLA LOOKS AT the medical report again. The Governor knows that the resultant pain from his fall four years ago couldn't have endure this long. He knows that something is wrong with his body. The medical report confirms it now. This isn't good at all.

But the Governor is a happy man. He lives a full life of service to his people. Along his journey of service to his people, he makes mistakes and sometimes comes up very short. But he gives his time in public service his best. He gives it his all. And so he's grateful to have served his follow Hoosiers. The Governor is a happy man despite the damning medical report.

Nobody must see this report. He must first put his affairs in order before he joins the love of his life and their two daughters in the other world.

That reminds him, he hasn't sat down with Schola since the trial of Senator Conner. And Petrus summons him to New York City recently. The Governor wonders what's happening in the world of the young man who's now his son in every meaning of the term. Though Schola doesn't know it. Yet.

Schola continues to prove himself worthy in the eyes of the Governor. Schola continues to stay to his principles. When the occasion requires it, he balances his principle with pragmatism and reality. Once convinced, Schola swims against the current, no matter what and no matter how strong. Here's the mark of a man. A man who endures all seasons. A man that can be trusted.

The Governor couldn't have asked for a better heir to the fruits of his earthly labors. The Governor is grateful.

The Governor knows he must talk to Schola. The Governor looks at the medical report again. He has enough time to put his affairs in order. Governor Sparkman Schola has lived a full life. Now is the perfect time to depart the scene of this world. Governor Sparkman Schola is a happy man.

95

THE JUDGE MUSES ON SCHOLA

YET ANOTHER WEEK ENDS WITH no final verdict from the jury. Judge Kaufman's frustration is now palpable. Judge Kaufman doesn't care anymore about the outcome of the trial. She wants the case out of her bosom. Judge Kaufman prays the jury produces a verdict, no matter what it might be.

But from her experience as a judge spanning over three decades, she knows that a long jury deliberation usually settles on the defendant's favor. There're rare exceptions. But on the balance, such prolonged jury time will often end in a hung jury with the defendant freed.

That reminds her, that Schola of an attorney. Schola litigates beyond her expectations. Usually, the first trial of a rookie lawyer bleeds of vast areas of improvements. The confidence of the rookie is often low. The lack of experience shows. In rare cases, you see a beginning lawyer argue the case flawlessly. Schola belongs in this rare group. Erudite. Confident. Principled. But pragmatic. Unrelenting without compromising the code of ethics. Yet humble and respectful. Schola will go far. The signs of his greatness are palpable.

Judge Kaufman would like to see Schola so often in her courtroom. And probably, outside the courtroom, too.

96

MISTRIAL ANNOUNCED

THE JURY DELIBERATION TAKES LONG. The longest in recent times in Indiana. And about the longest in Judge Kaufman's court as far as she remembers. But when the jury announces its work done, the parties are surprise somewhat. All too soon, the trial of the century ends as must all things. Even Senator Conner who wants it all done with can't believe that it's over.

Schola can't believe it too. Schola's heart dances uncontrollably. Schola's breathing is becoming shorter and shorter. The verdict is at hand, and it could mean the end of the world for his client. It's equally a big reflection on his work as a lawyer. The first verdict of his new profession. No, his new calling.

Senator Conner is pale and blue. The Senator looks dazed. No matter what, the road is ending for him. He can't go back to politics and succeed. His business declines and his partners don't want him anymore. The Senator buries his wife whilst the trial is on. Though their divorce was in the works before she dies, it still hurts to lose her.

Like the first day of the trial, today, the day of the verdict, the courtroom is packed. Many of the Senator's enemies are in the courtroom, hoping the worst for the Senator. They just don't say it. The Senator looks to the far corner of his left. He is surprised who he sees. Ms Pincus. In a red dress. The Senator recognizes the dress. He bought it for her. When their eyes meet, Ms Pincus lips read: "I'm sorry." The Senator can't believe what he sees. The

Senator looks again. And this time, the lips are even clearer: "I love you Con."

The stress in the Senator disappears. At least, there's one person rooting for him. His accuser. The irony isn't lost on the Senator.

"Do you still love her," Schola says without looking at the Senator.

The Senator can't believe that Schola sees everything.

"What?" the Senator faints surprise.

"Do you still love Ms Pincus?"

The Senator is speechless.

"If you love her, now is the time to tell her," Schola suggests while looking ahead. None notices that he's even talking to the Senator.

"It's now or never," Schola says. "That's if you still love her."

The Senator turns to Ms Pincus's direction again, and their eyes meet again. This time their eyes balls lock for a while. And the tears drop from Ms Pincus's cheeks. The Senator smiles and winks at her. And she understands that she's forgiven. The heaviness leaves Ms Pincus. Ms Pincus prays the prayer of her life: God please acquit Senator Cornelius Conner, Jr.

Judge Kaufman walks in and perches on her high throne. The judge looks tired. Judge Kaufman does a great job of presiding over the most consequential political and sexual trial of Indiana. The judge pilots the trial skillfully through all the turbulences. Judge Kaufman is now bringing the plane to landing. No, while the judge pilots the plane, the jury now lands it.

"Does the jury have a verdict?" The judge asks staring at the jury direction with anticipation.

"Yes, your honor," the lead juror replies standing up.

"Please announce your decision to the court," the judge invites the foreperson.

"Your honor, I'm afraid the juror is helplessly hung after four weeks of deliberation," the forewoman announces the jury verdict.

"In that case, the law compels me to declare a mistrial," Judge Kaufman announces.

"Thank you, members of the jury, for your service to your state and nation" the Judge says. And banging her gavel for the first time in a while, she declares the court adjourned. She walks to her chambers, looking tired, tired than she looks at the beginning of the trial. Old as well. She wonders whether the time hasn't come for her to bow out. She truly wonders whether this's the right time to retire from the bench.

Senator Conner loses it all, except avoiding prison time. Emotions of all kinds gush through him. The Senator feels like riding a bicycle. She turns in the direction of the woman who taught him how to ride a bicycle, she has since left the courtroom.

Senator Conner realizes how much he misses her for the first time. "I love her," the Senator whimpers to himself in disbelief. The Senator decides to ride a bike that evening.

97

ANANDA IS WITH MOTHER

CHOLA AVOIDS THE MEDIA. PACKED in front of the court stairs, the media badly needs to hear from the unheard-of attorney who frees the Senator when convicting him was all but assured. But Schola evades the prying media. More important, Schola wears his success at the trial lightly. Nay, Schola doesn't wear his success at all. Mr Conkling cringes at schola's refusal to address the media. A beginning attorney builds his clientele with such apparently innocuous press releases after such landmark trials. But not this beginning attorney—Schola. What a waste, Mr Conkling thinks to himself.

Schola makes it to the Farm just in time for the 7 pm family meal with mother and father. Schola is truly tired and hungry. For the first time in months, Schola feels really hungry. He feels like he hasn't eaten since the beginning of the trial.

Upon entering the house, Schola thinks he hears two famine voices, Mother and one other person. Rarely do people visit the Farm. The Farm is designated as a family house. An occasional visitor comes every now and then. But strictly family. There's something about the new voice. It's familiar. It's inviting. It penetrates Schola's heart. Who could that be, Schola wonders.

"Son is that you," mother bellows from the kitchen.

"Yes, I'm hungry," Schola replies.

"I don't remember when you have never been hungry," mother replies with a laughter.

As a policy, the Scholas don't talk about work before or during the family meal. If at all, work comes up after dinner during tea time in the living room.

"We have a guest today," mother says. "Ms Stokes is visiting," mother says again.

When she walks from the kitchen into the living room, Schola is speechless at the sight of the goddess before him.

Schola could only stare.

"Honey, if you have suddenly become a statue, let me please have the bag in your hand while you stand," Ms Stoke says, taking Schola's bag from him.

"Thanks," Schola says handing the bag over to her.

Mother knows love when she sees it. And she loves a love that will last forever no matter what. Mother is witnessing one such love. Right there, at that moment, she decides that those two, Schola and Ananda, must be left alone.

"Pap," I have an emergency to take care of at Sparkman's place."

"An emergency?" The senior Schola is confused.

"Yes," Mrs Schola says.

"And what do you need me to do, sweetheart?" The senior Schola asks.

"Please drive me there," mother says.

Within moments that Schola walks into the house, he's left alone with Ananda. The two have the entire meal to themselves. Schola's hunger vanishes. And a different kind of hunger sets in.

Ms Ananda prays for this day. She sits across from Schola. Takes off her shoes. Lifts her left leg on Schola's toes. Schola pushes his toes towards hers so that her leg rests well. They try not to look. The fire in their eyes is uncontainable. Ananda lifts her right leg onto Schola's toes. Schola steadies her right leg on hers again. It's here that it is not certain who decides first. But their lips move toward each other, at the same time.

"I love you Schola," Ananda confesses in tears.

"I fully understand," Schola replies. He gets up, walks over to her side, and picks her outside to the emerging full moon across the skies. They both stare in silence at the moon as it emerges fully. No words. But they know they are meant to be forever. It's peaceful. Peaceful. So peaceful.

98

THE SENATOR

THE SENATOR REPAIRS TO HIS big mansion to great relief. He counts his losses. Six months ago, he was one of the most powerful political actors in the United States of America: The most powerful surviving republic on the face of the earth, meaning he was one of the most powerful political actors in the world. The Senator was much more than an important political actor: He was a massive political machinery.

As the majority leader in the US Senate, Senator Corner was almost the leader of the legislature. A bill hardly becomes law without his blessing. And with a clear GOP majority in the Senate—and with his great rapport with senators across the divide—Senator Cornerlius Conner Jr., was the US Senate: The Senator was the second arm of government of the greatest surviving republic on earth. The Senator was the world.

Then, the Senator was a leading Republican presidential candidate, too. He had commissioned a research team to gather data on the viability of his presidential bid in the next election. The research findings were positive and encouraging—he had a two third chance of winning the Republican primary if he runs.

The sexual allegation against him and its attendant trial cut short the planned research into his chances if he runs against the leading Democratic presidential hopefuls for the next presidential elections.

Senator Conner was the face of politics in the future in the US. The Senator has lost his political capital and promise. All of it.

In business, he was even more appealing. A billionaire. A member of the elite one percent. The Senator has an array of companies ushering in profits yearly like snow in Alaska before the advent of global warning. Money wasn't a problem. Sometimes he had no idea what to do with all the money that he had. But now, the Senator's business associates have cut him off or are cutting him off. Media outlets refuse to advertise his business.

The Senator was the face of successful business in the US. But the sexual allegations against him drained his business profits as climate change melts ice in Alaska. The Senator has lost that too. Lots of it.

Thanks to Ms Pincus, and women like her, the Senator's business went down with each new allegation. True, the Senator has a weakness for the fairer sex. And on numerous occasions, admittedly, might have crossed the line. But never with Ms Pincus. Never. The Senator becomes extra careful with women when it was emerging that he might be in the running for president one day. How ironic! His fall is a blow from the one woman he never wronged. The one woman …

The sound of his intercom interrupts his thoughts. "Senator, please there's a Ms Pincus here to see you?" The Senator's private security detail announces.

The Senator is surprise. Utterly. For a moment, the Senator wonders whether he should allow Ms Pincus in. Ms Pincus has always had nerves. "Please let her in, Mike, and thanks," the Senator says to his house security guide.

Upon entering the sitting room downstairs, Ms Pincus is torn between giving the Senator a hug or a hand shake or nothing. Senator Conner doesn't help the situation by standing stoic, emotionless.

Ms Pincus decides against both the hug and the handshake and sits, looking away from the Senator. The Senator looks across the miserable figure in front of him. She's to be pitied.

"Cony, please I need a place to stay for the night," Ms Pincus explains her presence. "I broke up with my mother a moment ago," she informs the Senator.

There's a long pause. Ms Pincus bites her figures while waiting for an answer to her plea for a place to stay for the night.

"Yes, the house is yours as I said in the past. You can stay in which ever room you want. And do whatever you want. It's your house," the Senator says without sarcasm and leaves for his study to pick up from where he left his thoughts earlier.

Ms Pincus breaks into subdued sobs. On hearing the sobs, the Senator turns and teases: "Should I take you to bed again?"

"You're a jerk," Ms Pincus replies.

"Happy to know," the Senator says and leaves for his study.

99

SCHOLA VISITS THE SENATOR

THE SENATOR ISN'T PARTICULARLY SCHOLARLY. The Senator isn't a committed reader, though, he reads often. But he maintains a study wherever he's domiciled. This study—which he restricts to almost himself—offers the private space for him to think, reflect, introspect, plan, strategize. His business plans are hatched in his study. And his political ambitions are plotted in his study. So when the Senator repairs to his study, it's for serious business.

"What's left of my life?" The Senator paces up and down his study in introspection. He isn't so enthused about business now. And his pension is good to see him through the rest of his life. But as an ambitious man, the Senator isn't contended with a life that isn't engaged and impactful.

The Senator isn't happy with the way he is plunked from politics. He's sacrificed to make the Republican Party look good. The Senator wants to retain his senate seat and his control of the GOP in Indiana and the Midwest. Since he can't run for office, he needs a surrogate. Someone he can fully trust. He just finds out—thanks to the trial—that there's no such person in his former friends and associates. No single person.

Except for this Schola guy, his lawyer, the Senator has no confidante. Schola first writes in the *Times* in support of him. And then he agrees to represent him at trial. And he eventually frees him. The guy has everything in a politician. But will Schola agree to run for political office? The Senator wonders. Throughout the trial, Schola for once, never mentions politics. If Schola agrees to run, the Senator is ready to fund him and reactivate whatever is left of his political might and machinery for victory.

That reminds him, he hasn't even paid Schola any legal fees. And Schola hasn't ask him. What is wrong with this Schola guy? The Senator wonders. An attorney with no interest in attorney fees. What kind of attorney is that?

The knock on the door pulls the Senator from his thoughts, again. "Yes Mike," the Senator asks annoyed now. "Please, a Schola is here to see you," Mike says. "Please let him in," the Senator says promptly.

The Senator is pleasantly surprised. As he makes his way down from his study to meet Schola, the Senator scents an aroma from the kitchen. And wonders who now cooks in his house. Nobody cooks here, as far as the Senator remembers. The Senator then recalls that Ms Pincus is around. Could she be the one? The Senator wonders.

100

THE CHEF

"SENATOR, YOU DIDN'T TELL ME you had a skilled chef?" Schola says as the Senator descends the stairs.

"And you didn't tell me that you hang out with Ms Ananda Stokes," the Senator teases upon seeing Ananda's arm around Schola's waist. "Aah, and somebody also had an additional motive in convincing me to bring in the opinion author of the Times," the Senator teases again, referring to Ananda's repeated appeals that Schola should be brought in to help with the case.

"I see. So it wasn't the Senator who reads the piece and asks to see me?" Schola asks in genuine surprise. "Ma'am, what else don't I know?" Schola wonders loud. Ananda pretense she hasn't heard any of this. She pitches Schola on the back. Schola wrings from her pitch.

"Please Senator, who's in the kitchen?" Ananda changes the subject.

"I honestly have no idea," the Senator says. "I'm intrigued to find out as well," the Senator says. The three work into the kitchen.

"Ms Pincus," both Ananda and Schola shout in disbelieve.

"I'm sorry, I forgot that she's around" the Senator apologizes.

"You forgot!" both Ananda and Schola shout again at the same time.

"Do the two of you always think and speak at the same time?" Ms Pincus directs the question to Ananda and Schola.

"What're you talking about?" both Ananda and Schola shout again at the same. Now Ananda and Schola look at each other in disbelieve.

"How long has she been living here?" Schola asks on his way out of the kitchen with the Senator. Ananda remains in the kitchen with Ms Pincus.

"She comes in less than an hour ago" the Senator answers. "That's why I forget she is around. She says she moves out of her mother's and has no place to stay."

"I see," Schola says, while looking far away and thinking.

"I have something to discuss with you," the Senator brings Schola back from his thoughts.

"Yes, you can tell me anything," Schola prepares to listen.

"Not here, in my study," the Senator says.

101

THE WILL

PROF LINDA DUVAL IS THE only surviving issue of her late parents. Well, she was the sole surviving issue of her late parents until her own death. Her father dies when she is fifteen. Her mother hustles and puts her through college. After which Prof Duval goes back for graduate studies at Cornell. Prof Duval's mother dies before she finishes her graduate studies and assumes her teaching role at Harvard where Schola will join her later.

Prof Duval pays the mortgage before the accident that eventually leads to her death after her period of sickness. Given that Prof Duval isn't close to any of her relatives—she barely knows them even—the question of whom to give her properties to—the natural objects of her bounty—isn't straight forward.

Then she thinks about Schola as a beneficiary. The idea of willing everything of hers to Schola massages her resurrected conscience. Initially, she plans on surprising Schola. That's, Schola will be notified of his luck after her death. But then, as the cancer takes a toll on her and death becomes imminent, the guilt becomes more pronounced. That's when she decides to call in Schola to confess.

Prof Duval hires an attorney who draws up her Will. Prof Duval looks over her Last Will and Testament and is pleased. The beneficiary of her Will would be utterly shocked. Schola would be shocked. But Prof Duval is so overwhelmed by the lack of vengeance in Schola's countenance when they meet that she forgets to mention the Will and dies almost immediately. Peacefully.

102

IN SENATOR'S STUDY
WITH SCHOLA

THE SENATOR WALKS UP THE stairs of the apartments of his Range to his secluded study with Schola. Walking behind the Senator, Schola notices the man is beginning to regain qualities the scandal expunges from him: Confidence, Pride, Purpose, and Direction. At the entrance to his study, the Senator opens the door and ushers in Schola. Schola has never seen a private study this massive and well decorated. Schola thinks that the book collection could be bigger, however.

"You've a paradise to yourself here," Schola remarks to the Senator.

"Yes, I love it in here. I allow very few people inside. Not even my wives are permitted," the Senator says as a matter of fact.

"I must be lucky then," Schola says with a smile.

"No, you are special Mr. Schola," The Senator replies with a serious face. "The previous visitor to my study before you is our current president."

"President Albert Ruggles?" Schola asks, very surprised.

"Yes, President Ruggles. He came to thank me for my support—financially and otherwise—in his re-election campaign." The Senator informs Schola.

"The two of you are very close friends," Schola says, half a question, half an answer.

"No, we were friends," the Senator says with anger and hurt in his voice.

"Forgiveness is also a manly virtue, Senator," Schola reproaches the Senator mildly. "When was the last time you forgave someone?" Schola asks the Senator.

"I just forgave Ms Pincus." The Senator says proudly.

"No, that is called love. You love her. And love conquers all."

"Aah," the Senator says, surprised.

"When was the last time you forgave someone you have no reasons at all to forgive?" Schola asks.

The Senator is speechless and stares at Schola.

Schola decides to change the topic. "You say something important needs to be discussed."

"Yes." The Senator says while directing Schola to a seat. When the two men are seated, the Senator clears his throat and begins.

"First, thanks for agreeing to fight for me in court and for doing a good job." The Senator begins. Schola nods in understanding. In line with that, we never discussed your fees. The Senator says, waiting for Schola's reply.

Schola looks at the floor and stares for a while. He breathes in heavily. Schola remembers the promise to himself at the beginning of the trial not to accept payment from the Senator for his services to him in this trial. Schola reasons that even if the Senator is innocent of Ms Pincus's claims, it's more than likely that the Senator might have offended numerous women in the past in his rather remarkable reckless escapees with females. But Schola has to frame his response carefully so as not to be seen as part of the sea of people condemning the Senator.

"In retrospect, I should be thanking you, Senator. Representing you gave me experience in an area of law that I had no interest in and never would have had any experience of. So I should thank you." Schola says and allows some time.

"Regarding the fees," Schola continues, "I'm in less need of money than Mr Conkling who partnered with me. I understand he has some really big financial crisis that, on the main, let to his disbarment." Schola says and stares towards the stairs of books in the Senator's study. "Mr Conkling is a good man. I'll like you to help him," Schola pleads on behalf of Mr Conkling.

The Senator could sense Schola's line of suggestion. But the Senator wonders what else he can do for Mr. Conkling, besides giving him money, since Mr. Conkling can no longer practice as an attorney.

"But you say he can't practice again?" The Senator asks Schola.

"Yes, but we can attempt getting him re-instated," Schola replies and continues. "If he's able to pay back whatever money and obligations he owns his former clients and law firm, we can petition the Supreme Court of Indiana to give the man a second chance," Schola suggests.

"That's no problem. Just tell me how much debt is in question here. I will clear everything. No problem."

"Thanks a lot Senator," Schola profusely thanks the Senator, shaking his hands.

When the hand-shaking is over, a gratitude that amuses the Senator, the Senator moves on to his second, the most important, reason he summons Schola to his study.

Mr Schola, the second thing is so important to me. You might need to think it over. But you need to give me an answer soon enough to enable me start strategizing.

Schola is bewildered and can't think of what the Senator needs him to do before the Senator strategizes. But Schola is a good listener and does well to conceal his confusion. As a former priest and a former professor, Schola knows only too well that a parishioner or student would discontinue with a line of thought if the priest or professor appears overly concerned and anticipatory of the emerging disclosure.

The Senator waits to see any initial signs of approval or otherwise but senses none. So the Senator continues, "I'll like you to run for Senator in the upcoming elections."

Schola's stoicism departs him at the proposal and he chuckles. But the Senator remains serious and undeterred, refusing to join in Schola's attempt at belittling his crucial proposition.

"As I said, give it some thinking and get back to me as soon as you can," the Senator says with a stone face. Running for the senate requires some planning and strategizing.

Schola realizes that this isn't a joke. Schola knows that many a great undertaking first comes as a ridiculous idea.

For the first time since his encounter with the Senator, Schola doesn't know what to say. Schola never sees this one coming. Schola is speechless. It's the speechlessness, the reactionlessnes of a girl whose closest male friend suddenly asks her to marry him. The girl never knew the guy was in love with her. She thought they were just friends.

But the response to such sudden suggestion is critical. It can ruin everything. Or it may be the beginning of a new, unknown adventure.

The phone in the Senator's study goes off again. "Yes, Mike," the Senator says, unhappy with the interruption at this critical moment.

"The ladies say dinner is served," Mike relates the information to the study.

"Thanks, Mike, tell them we're coming down," the Senator says putting down the phone.

With that, Schola's first visit to the Senator's secluded study ends, enlisting Schola in yet a list of the distinguishables. Schola is invited to where only presidents hold counsel.

103

RENEWED MR CONKLING

MR BARFOOT CONKLING IS THE luckiest man in America. A month ago, his ever increasingly miserable life is all but over. Mr Conkling loses it all: family, profession, friends, and finances. Above all, Mr Conkling finds no meaning in life again. He concludes that death is preferred to his pointless existence.

So he decides to kill himself. But on the day he sets out to make arrangements for his own burial, Mr Schola, an acquittance of four years ago whose path crosses his when Mr Conkling's world begins clashing down, calls. Schola asks Mr Conkling for help with the trial of the moment. The trial of Senator Conner, former Senate Majority Leader.

Mr Conkling accepts the unusual and unexpected offer. Mr Conkling, really, makes almost zero impact on the trial. Or so he thinks. But the Senator is acquitted. His side wins. A big win. An unexpected win.

Though Schola and the Senator don't know, it's really Mr Conkling's win. In acquitting the Senator, the jury acquits Mr Conkling of his keep-on-hold suicide plan.

Also important, Mr Conkling survives the monthlong trial without as much as a smell of his best friend—drinks. And this morning, the morning after the jury delivers its verdict, Mr Conkling empties his room of all the vodka, whiskey and other bona fide members of this class of bottles. All. And Mr Conkling resolves never to touch a drink again in his remaining years on earth.

Mr Conkling gives himself a fresh shot at life again. He will begin small. He'll get a job. Pay his bills. Live a small life of his own. He'll find a new meaning in this life. He will make a comeback. Mr Conkling is sure of it. He can feel the fire for success within him. His heart is on fire.

Mr Conkling is enmeshed in these hopeful thoughts of a new beginning when Schola visits him at home. Unexpectedly. But pleasantly. Mr Conkling is happy to see his partner of the last month, and the man who calls him an old friend.

Mr Conkling goes to his freeze to offer Schola something to drink but finds nothing. Not even water. Except Schola wants to drink from his tap. Schola says he is fine and goes straight to the point of his visit.

"I'm sorry we didn't discuss fees before you joined the team. I wonder how much we owe you for your month of dedicated service," Schola begins the purpose of his visit.

Mr Conkling doesn't know what to make of his continuing luck with Schola. In fairness, Mr Conkling should be paying Schola for saving him from suicide, from alcoholism, from a pointless existence. Schola doesn't know and will never know how he claws back Mr Conkling from the jaws of death.

"That's very thoughtful of you, Mr Schola," Mr Conkling begins. "But as you know, my role was very minimal and doesn't in fairness warrant any form of remuneration at all. None." Mr Conkling emphasizes.

"Thanks for your generosity, Mr. Conkling," Schola says, and brings out a cheque from his breast pocket. "Nonetheless, the Senator is pleased with your minimal role and wants me to deliver this check to you," Schola says, handing Mr Conkling a check of $250,000.

Mr Conkling stares at the lottery he wins with disbelief. Mr. Conkling's emotions are numb as they have been for some time now. But Mr. Conkling feels his emotions coming back to life.

Mr. Conkling feels resurrected. Mr. Conkling again stares at the check in disbelieve. It's amazing what money can do in a man's life, Schola thinks to himself after seeing Mr Conkling transform instantly.

"Also, the Senator and I'll like to attempt to renew your license as an attorney." This second offer jolts Mr Conkling from his Disney world. "The Senator will pay all debts to your clients and former law firm. When the debts are settled, we will petition the Indiana Supreme Court for your re-instatement as an attorney," Schola says and rises to leave.

When Mr Conkling closes the door after Schola leaves, Mr Conkling weeps like a baby. Happy tears. Tears long in need of pouring over. A great therapy.

104

THE GOVERNOR, HIS AFFAIRS

THE GOVERNOR GLANCES AT HIS schedule for the next two weeks. Critical affairs need taking care of. Great care must be exercised.

The first is the Governor's memoir. Schola talks the Governor into chronicling his life in politics and business as well as his spirituality in the form of a memoir. The Governor has been working on the manuscript for the last four years. But the chapters still need fine-tuning before Schola will have it in his skilled literary hands for comments. The Governor is happy with his Memoir but yet to settle on a title.

Also, on his schedule is the disclosure of his terminal cancer to his family and closest associates. The Governor isn't too sure how his aged but active parents will receive the news of his impending death. For months now, he has avoided his parents, his mother especially, who is talented in detecting things the Governor wants hidden.

The Governor is surprised that, so far, his mother hasn't suspected that something is wrong with him. But since the Governor tragically lost his beloved wife and children, the Governor's wish for privacy heightened and his parents respect this privacy.

Even more concerning for the Governor is how Schola will receive the bad news. Schola finds stability and anchors much of his life on the Governor. The Governor finds Schola's deep attachment to him pleasing. Unmoored from the Governor's family, Schola has no family to turn to. Schola is the Governor's de facto son. Plans are far advanced to transform this de facto status into a de jure one. This brings out the final but critical question of his Last Will and Testament.

The Governor is tilting towards willing his entire property to Schola. The Governor's parents will have no use for his wealth, especially, once he is gone. But in Schola, the Governor is sure, his parents will find new meaning in life. In fact, they have already. Schola and the three are inseparably. And Schola spends much time with them at the Farm than with the Governor in his plush Range.

The Governor gets up, walks to his most private drawer in his study and brings out his previous Last Will and Testament. The Governor looks at the signature of his attorney and the two witnesses. The document is flawlessly prepared and duly executed. It's valid. It meets all the requirements of a valid Will in the state of Indiana.

Sparkman Schola is the richest man in Indiana and one of the richest in the United States. The list of his holdings loudly shows his vast wealth.

The Governor owns a chain of real estate across the United States and beyond. The biggest of these is the Governor's range in Florida, which he bought from Warren Buffet, the richest man in the world. The Governor's Florida range values at $865 million.

Besides the Florida range, are five other ranges. Two in California with a combined value of up to the value of the Florida range. Another in New York of half the value of the Florida range. And the last one in Indiana where the Governor currently resides.

Besides these ranges, the Governor owns over a hundred mansions and houses totted over the world with a minimum value of $59,000 and up to $500,000.

Then the flee of aircrafts. Seven in all: two Boeing 828 jets, a Gulfstream IV, a Cessna 680 Citation Sovereign, Challenger 850,

Bombardier 700 and a syberjet SJ 30. The Governor looks at his lists of flying birds and shakes his head in shame. The Governor doesn't even like flying. The planes were needed for various operations at some point.

Prominent on the list of properties is the slew of businesses: Schola Clean Energy (formerly, Schola Oil Group), Schola Law/Audit Firm, the World (the daily newspaper), Schola Farm, the Schola Basketball Team, Schola Plastic Renewable, the Schola Publishing Co. Ltd., and of course the Schola Group of Hospitals and Laboratories.

Of special concern for the Governor is his study and the books and collections therein, as well as the much bigger collection in the Schola library, totaling over five million books and art works. Some of these books are rare books, of which the library of Congress doesn't even have copies. For example, the Codex Makolana. The Governor knows that of all his earthly vanities, it's the books and related collections that would hold dear for Schola. The Governor's deceased wife, Anna, was a librarian.

The governor looks at his holdings in paintings. The paintings are the fruits of Anna's passion. Anna loves her collection of paintings. And Anna's knowledge of the great hands in the field from Leonardo da Vinci and Vincent Van Gogh to Pablo Picasso amazes the Governor. The Governor puts the list down and reminisces the good times with his deceased wife. The Governor can't wait to join his beloved wife in the next world. The Governor is grateful for his cancer. The cancer will take him to his beloved Anna.

That reminds the Governor. Mother mentions in a previous visit on the day the jury tenders a verdict in favor of the Senator that she thinks Schola is in love. The Governor wonders how mother's claim is possible given the bookish, monkish, and largely secluded life of Schola in the last four years. But the Governor is excited for Schola and longs to meet the young woman in question. Ananda, mother says, is her name. Ananda Stokes.

And over the phone the other day, mother speaks so highly of Ananda. Ananda moves into the crowded Farmhouse and isn't complaining. Ananda settles in comfortably and looks happy.

The Governor is a bit worried that Schola hasn't as much as a word mentioned Ananda to him. The Governor ...

Ms Harvanet knocks on the door of the Governor's study, interrupting the Governor's thoughts.

"Rosa, please is that you?" The Governor asks, sure that only Ms Harvanet would knock on the door of his study at this time.

"Yes, Governor, you have an impromptu guest," Ms Harvanet announces her purpose.

"I'll be down in the guest room then," the Governor replies. But before Ms Harvanet replies, Ananda is already in the Governor's study.

"I can't wait any longer to see you Governor. So I'm ushering myself into your study," Ananda says and hugs the Governor.

The Governor is surprised. Even confused. And yes delighted. The warm hug reminds the Governor of his deceased wife. Such fire in a simple touch. The Governor sits and smiles almost sheepishly.

105

ANANDA AND THE GOVERNOR

MS ANANDA STOKES IS ALARMED by the heat from the Governor's body. Ananda takes a second look at the man her love, Schola, is never tired of singing praises about. The Governor looks sick to Ananda. Doctor Forman Stokes, Ananda's father, and Laura, her mother, have vast experience in the medical field. Ananda's mother was a nurse and is retired now with her own clinic. The late Doctor Forman Stokes was a well-respected physician.

Growing up, Ananda, an only child, often feels that the home was a medical school. Ananda knows a lot about the human body and its sicknesses by age 18 that going to medical school was a waste of her time. Hence, she goes to law school instead. But the home-taught medicine has never left Ananda. So Ananda knows a dying man when she sees one.

The Governor is pretty alarmed when the goddess approaches him closely the second time. Ananda hits the Governor in the abdomen and the Governor gives out a loud moan, which the hit and its attendant sharp pain induced. The Governor looks at Ananda, speechless. Ananda looks at him wordless.

And with tears, Ananda says, "you're dying." More of a statement. No, a sure prediction.

The Governor looks at his crying daughter-in-law and is a happy man. The Governor smiles with profound happiness. Sure enough, the Governor's wealth will be in good hands with Schola and Ananda.

"No, I'm not dying. I'm joining my late wife and our two children. And I'm in a haste to join them. I'm not dying." The Governor says smiling with an unmistakably beautiful radiance.

"You're a bastard like Schola," Ananda says. Ananda approaches the Governor, assesses him closely with the tenderness of the Governor's late wife. The Governor relishes in his new caretaker. While Ananda keeps saying, "you're dying. You are leaving us. You knew about it and refuse to seek a cure."

"Of all the good things they say about you, they didn't say you are a great physician," the Governor says after Ananda is done with the physical examination and sits down facing him. Ananda stares at him, oblivious to the compliment, thinking about what can be done. In as much as she likes the Governor to live, the cancer is pretty much advanced, beyond cure.

"Please let me show you something," the Governor says, pulling Ananda up to the room and the closet of his late wife.

106

DEAN AS PRESIDENT

THE COLLEGE OF PRESIDENTS, THE high-profile chief executives of the various Schola Group of businesses and organizations meet typically biannually, save emergency sessions. The first time Schola attended such meeting, albeit an emergency session, the presidents summon the Governor and ask him to join the race of White House hopefuls. This was four years ago when Schola first arrives in Fort Wayne to hand-deliver Fr Mentor's hand-written letter to the Governor. When Schola is around, he attends these meetings as an observer at the behest of the Governor. The other presidents have over the years come to accept—and even respect—Schola as an unofficial member of the College of Presidents.

Today: 9 th October 2020, the College has the full complement of its members for the last cabinet meeting of the year. The rectangle seating in the conference room of the Governor's Fort Wayne townhouse, the nerve center of the Schola Corporation, is hosting this crucial meeting with a single agenda: Each president will give an Annual Report to the College with a roadmap going forward.

At the helm of the rectangle seats is Governor Sparkman Schola in his black suit with a spotless white shirt and deep red tire. Though radiating happiness, it's obvious to closer associates of the Governor that something important and unprecedented is on the Governor's mind.

The Governor opens the meeting with a prayer by Schola. The former Jesuit priest calls on the Holy Spirit to inspire and guide the late morning deliberation as to serve the greater glory of God.

To the right of the Governor is the Dean of the College of Presidents who is as well the president of the Schola Law Firm. Dr Devlin Dingell, on behalf of his colleagues, thanks the Governor for summoning the meeting and Schola for the opening prayer. Dr Dingell proceeds to present the report of the top law firm. "Profits are all-time high and morale is even highest at the firm," Dr Dingell reports to nod of approval around the table. "The number of pro bono cases and hours that the firm offers to residents of Indiana and beyond is the highest and the best in the country," Dr Dingell reports to the heart delight of the Governor.

To the right of the Dean of the College, Dr Dingell, is the president of the Schola audit firm, Mr Cotton Dodge, a renowned financier. Mr Dodge in his report dabbles in figures and statistics that very few understand and even fewer in the room are interested in. But the bottom line of his report is that the sizeable wealth of Governor Schola is well invested and the returns are ample evidence of his wise investments over the years and in this past year.

To the right of Mr Dodge is the president of Schola Green, formerly, the Schola Oil Group, Mr Koskinen Kendrew. The Governor's vast fortunate flows in large part from his oil exploration around the world. But in the last five years, and following global concerns and trends, Schola Oil purges itself of fossils fuel. The replacements, wind and solar energy, are proving even more profitable. Every continent, country, state, province and community is turning to wind and solar powered energy. Schola Green is the leading entrepreneur in this new field with lots of prospects. Mr Kendrew, turning to a projector, forecasts the financial flow of the new industry in the next decade, and the returns are in the trillions.

To the right of Mr Kendrew is the president of the Schola Farm. She presents her report.

To the left of the Governor and down the rectangular table is Dr Custor Ewell, president of the Schola Foundations, a multi-non-profit organization of the Schola Hospital, the Soup Kitchens, the Schola Community Colleges and two High Schools. These are the expenses side of the Schola Group. The other groups serve as the cash cows of these charity groups.

The last president to present his report is Mr Plater Post, the President of the *World*, Schola's major daily newspaper. With the rise of digital literacy, the *World* is on a campaign to increase its digital subscriptions in the coming year. The experts are hired and the base for the massive campaign is up and running in full throttle. The plan is to overtake the Wall Street Journal in the newspaper business in the next five years.

The Governor receives each Annual Report before these meetings. So the Governor, unlike the other presidents, knows what each president is presenting. The Governor has never been so happy with the progress of his top lieutenants and their associates.

While the presidents present the reports one after another, the Governor's mind is far away. Fifty years away in the past. Fifty years ago when he parted ways with the Jesuits. Taught classics—Latin and Greek—in high school for a year, then decides to become a lawyer.

In the second year of law school, the Governor marries his law school sweetheart, Anna. After law school, the couple start these businesses together. And God blesses the fruits of their hands.

If only Anna were still alive to see what has become of their efforts of fifty years ago. The pain in the Governor's abdomen surges and he nearly gives off a mild cry. Yes, I accept Lord, the Governor says to himself. The Governor can't wait to join his wife and their two sons in the hereafter. The Governor is in a haste to go and to end the meeting.

Everybody turns to the Governor after Mr. Post draws down the curtail on the Annual Reports. The Governor is forced to return to the meeting from his prayer of joining his late family.

"Thanks so much for your hard work evinced in the great feats achieved over the year. Truly, thanks so much. I'm eternally grateful to all of you for serving humanity in various ways," the Governor says to a round of applaud, lasting almost forever.

"But before we close this executive session for the end of year dinner, I have one final announcement," the Governor says, drawing the full attention of everyone. "After much prayer and discernment, I retire as president of the College."

Nobody expects this. Even Schola who seats outside the rectangular table almost behind the Governor is surprised. Schola senses the Governor appears weak and departing but couldn't be too sure.

"The Dean of the College acts as president until the new President assumes office," the Governor finalizes his announcement. The Governor looks around the Group he hand-picks for his service to humanity and is grateful for God's blessings. The Governor leaves the conference room and yearns to join his beloved Anna and their cherished children.

107

INDIANA SUPREME COURT

MR BARFOOT CONKLING PETITIONS THE Supreme Court of Indiana the state's judicial body charged with attorney's disciplinary matters. The petition seeks a review of Mr Conkling's disbarment. Schola, of course, is Mr Conkling attorney for the ethics hearing scheduled today, October 23, 2020, at the conference room of the Supreme Court building in Indianapolis, the state's capital.

The Senator accompanies Mr. Barfoot and Schola for the ethics hearing with the Supreme Justices of the State of Indiana. The Senator insists that they jet from Fort Wayne into Indianapolis with one of his private jets. Schola refuses the unnecessary luxury. As a compromise, the three make it for the hearing in one of the Senator's limousine. Even the limo was unnecessary in Schola's view.

Mr Conkling can't believe his luck. Judging from his appearance, he's truly a new creation. Thanks to the Senator. No, thanks to Schola. Mr. Conkling's former law firm is incredulous when Mr Conkling tells them he is going to refund them for the financial lost his reckless practice caused the firm.

As well, Mr. Conkling settles all the clients he owes, plus interest on their debts, to their utter disbelieve. The check the Senator issues him for being part of his trial is just about enough to settle all his debts. All his debts.

Meantime, the Senator gives Mr. Conkling one of his mansions in Fort Wayne to stay until he buys a home of his own. In return, Mr Conkling is giving the Senator informal legal advice in efforts at reclaiming parts of his business empire lost and boosting the remaining parts, an endeavor involving lots of legal and corporate transactions, Mr Conkling's comfort zone as is criminal law.

Reclaiming his lost law license is a jewel on the crown of Mr Conkling's unexpected fortune. The man who saves the Senator from an inevitable prison time is leading Mr Conkling's lost law license reclaiming party. This's an impossible mission, even for Schola, Mr. Conkling knows. But Mr Conkling knows very well that in life everything is possible.

Usually, the ethics committee denies review of the type Mr Conkling submits. But it's the untypical name of the petitioner's attorney, Mr Priestley Plusbriuschola, that catches the fancy of the preliminary reviewing law clerk of disciplinary petitions. Like herself who just started clerking for the Chief Justice of the Indiana Supreme Court, this new lawyer is new to the profession. Yet Mr Plusbriuschola is the lawyer in America, having removed the disgraced Senator Connor from the tight prosecutorial claws. The law clerk is intrigued. She wants to know more. She wants to meet Schola.

The clerk shows Schola's petition to his boss, Justice Wendy de Brito, the Chief Justice. She looks the petition over. Sure it's a no. But … there's something about the lawyer. The new toss of the Indiana Bar Association.

"Please let me think about this," Justice de Brito tells her clerk. Two days later, the clerk reminds Her Ladyship.

"Okay, let's hear them out," Justice de Brito says. "But you know we're never going to re-instate Mr Conkling?" More of a statement than a question.

The hearing this morning is thus about Schola more than it is about Mr Conkling.

108

THE DISCIPLINARY HEARING

THE HEARING TAKES PLACE IN the conference room of the Supreme Court. The five Justices aren't robed as they do in public trials. But they still look official and intimidating enough.

The Chief Justice is the first to fire off at Schola and Mr Conkling. "Mr Schola, what's your mission as a lawyer? Excuse all the guilty people from the consequences of their actions?" Justice Wendy de Brito asks, not smiling.

"Very far from it ma'am," Schola rises up to answer the question. But he's told he can sit down. So he sits down. "So far from it, ma'am," Schola repeats upon resuming his seat. "I serve the rule of law. That the law applies to everybody equally, both the good citizen and the bad citizen," Schola says.

The Chief Justice follows up with another question. "That's my point, Mr Schola. Since called to the bar, how many innocent and good citizens have you defended?"

"Ma'am, since called to the bar, I have never turned down a request for my legal expertise. The supposedly bad ones are the only ones asking for my help. I will happily …"

Justice John Covici interjects Schola. "Supposedly bad ones?" Justice Covici asks cynically.

"Well my Lord, the rule of law, of which our nation is so proud of, presumes the accused innocent until proven otherwise," Schola answers the question and is not sure how to proceed.

Justice David Alvord saves the awkward silence. "Mr Schola, you think Mr Conking is fit to practice law?"

"My Lord, it isn't in my place to judge who is fit to practice law. A grave judgement I have no clue what to look for in a woman or a man. But I know this. Mr Conkling disgraced our noble profession not so long ago. Subsequently he was disbarred, rightly so. But the dynamics have changed as Mr Conkling is now a completely changed man. He has learnt the lesson of his life. More importantly, Mr Conkling has discovered that the only thing he cares about is practicing law. It's his only love. Without which, Mr Conkling has no life. So we're here to inform you of this new change."

Justice Dan Malory, who like Justice Peter Bernays, is quiet all this while, suddenly speaks up. "Mr Schola, just what are these changes in the man who defrauded his firm and clients?"

"Thank you my Lord for the question. First, he used to be an alcoholic. He's no longer one. And he doesn't desire to have a drink for the rest of his life."

"Second, the most important things for him in life, then, were things that money could afford. A luxurious life. Having learnt the fragility of our mortal life, Mr Conkling is rededicated to making our society more just with or without a law license."

Even Mr Conkling looks surprise at Schola when he utters the phrases "with or without a law license." And the Justices look surprise, too.

Justice de Brito asks the final question: "So if Mr Conkling can make the world a better place without a law license why are you here Mr Schola?"

"Because the law license will give him a better tool for making our society fairer," Schola says, smiles and leans back. The Chief Justice smiles. This new lawyer is in his own world, the Chief Justice thinks to herself. And his world is quite an interesting world.

"Thanks for your submission Mr. Schola. Our verdict is forthcoming in the weeks ahead." Justice de Brito says, indicating the end of the proceeding.

"Thank you, my Lords, for the opportunity to be heard. Thank you." Schola says with a genuinely weeping voice, stands, bows to their Lordships and leaves with Mr Conkling.

109

GOVERNOR UPDATES WILL

MR RAY KOUSSER, GOVERNOR SCHOLA'S personal attorney, is surprised, but pleased that the widely admired former governor of Indiana asks to meet with him in the office. When the Governor visits Mr Kousser in the office, it is solely official and business. Apart from the Governor's Will, Mr Kousser can't think of what official business needs attending to.

Few years ago, after the Governor buried his beloved wife and children, the Governor updates his Last Will and Testament. This revoked Will largely benefits the Governor's natural heirs: his two sons and wife. After the demise of these three, the Governor updates his will, benefiting mainly his parents and a few other bodies. Mr Kousser isn't aware of any significant changes in the Governor's life requiring him to alter his current will.

But Mr Kousser is a patient man. The Governor would soon visit. Mr Kousser would soon know the purpose of the visit.

110

UPDATED WILL

THE GOVERNOR IS A HAPPY man. Yesterday he visits his personal attorney, Mr Kousser, to make changes to his Will. The Governor holds a copy of the codicil in his hand. The entire document is some twelve pages.

The Governor is a happy man. He looks over every page of his most recent Last Will and Testament. His intent is clearly expressed. His two attesting witnesses have signed in the presence of each other. The Governor duly executes the will in the presence of his two attesting witnesses.

The Governor is a happy man. The main beneficiary of this Will, Schola, would be shocked. For overnight, Schola joins the elite group of the one percent: an exclusive club of the most prominent billionaires. The Governor looks over the devise that would most pleased Schola—the library and its vast holdings. The Governor looks at his signature on the last page of his will. This might be the last time the Governor would be required to sign a document.

No. The Governor has one last important document to sign before he joins his family in the hereafter.

Better now, than later. The Governor calls Ms Harvanet over the intercom. Please Rosa, are you able to bring me a piece of white paper from the printer?

Ms Harvanet goes to the printer. Opens the printer. Brings out several pieces of paper. Ms Harvanet guesses that the Governor probably wanted to write someone important. So in addition to the white papers, she goes to the Governor with white foolscaps official papers, too.

"You asked for white papers, but I think these might be better," Ms Harvanet says, holding out both set of papers, one in his right hand, the other his left.

The Governor is a happy man. He smiles at the wise woman in front of him. And wishes he could take her along to join his family in the next life. The Governor looks at her again, and smiles. An infectious smile that overwhelms Ms Harvanet, causing her to look away shyly while returning the smile.

The Governor takes the foolscap paper, a single sheet. And smiles again. No words between the two. But Ms Harvanet knows that the Governor is grateful. She is happy when the Governor is happy. Happiness has been threatening to leave the Governor ever since the Governor's entire immediate family died.

Just when Ms Harvanet is almost out of the Governor's sight, the Governor remembers. "Rosa, would you please ask Priestley to come in tomorrow?"

"Sure. At what time do you want Mr Schola here?" Ms Harvanet asks.

"No hurry. Anytime, as long as it's tomorrow," the Governor replies.

The Governor is a happy man. Ms Harvanet knows that the Governor is a happy man. And so Ms Harvanet is so happy as well.

111

SCHOLA TO DELIVER LETTER

THE GOVERNOR HAS A LETTER for his life-long Jesuit friend. The Governor insists that Schola uses one of the jets to Rochester, NY, to deliver his hand-written epistle to Fr Petrus Mentor, SJ. Schola, of course, declines. Instead, Schola decides to travel with Greyhound, the same way he comes four years ago at Fr Mentor's behest.

As was four years ago, Schola is required to hand-deliver the Governor's letter personally to Fr Mentor. Schola wonders what it's with these two friends and their hand-written and hand-delivery letters. But Schola has other important concerns as he makes the relatively long trip to the Holy Mountain.

Schola wants to go with his love, Ananda. But Ananda flatly declines to go with him. This's the first time Ananda refuses to do something that Schola earnestly asks of her.

Schola had wanted to introduce his newfound meaning in life, Ananda, to Fr Mentor. Schola believes Fr Mentor would love Ananda. Schola badly needs the two to meet and get along.

That reminds Schola, since Ananda comes back from her visit to the Governor, she has been low. Ananda says there's nothing wrong with her. But Schola senses a change in his love. Sadness of sort.

But the Governor calls him after the visit and is all cheers. The Governor loves Ananda as Schola anticipates. The Governor is full of praises for her.

Something doesn't add up, Schola concludes of Ananda's refusal to join him for the trip and her change of mood after the visit. Schola wonders whether Ms Harvanet said something annoying to Ananda. Ms Harvanet runs a tight ship up there. Schola blames himself. He should have warned Ananda of Ms Harvanet. Ananda should know that Ms Harvanet carries no malice. Ms Harvanet does it to protect the Governor.

Schola introspects on the revise journey four years ago. There were lots of unknown four years ago. A lost in meaning four years ago. A lost in purpose four years ago. A lost in direction four years ago. A complete lost four years ago. Schola had reasoned that God dumped him. Schola was angry at God for enduring what he was wrongly accused of doing.

Schola feels guilty for doubting God four years ago. It has all worked out. At least, it is working out. Schola is grateful for the evil visited upon him four years ago.

Schola isn't any less happy than when he was a Jesuit. Schola is grateful to God. Grateful to Fr Mentor. Grateful to Governor Schola. And most important, grateful to Prof Linda Duval.

That reminds Schola. He is scheduled to attend Prof Duval's funeral next week.

112

ANANDA AND GOVERNOR

THE NEXT MORNING AFTER SCHOLA goes to Rochester, NY, to hand-deliver the Governor's handwritten letter to Fr Mentor, Ms Stokes pays the Governor a surprised visit. It's an early morning visit.

The Governor can't contain his joy upon seeing Ms Stokes. "There you are, Ananda!" the Governor exclaims on seeing her. Ms Stokes stands and looks at the Governor in amusement. "How're you so happy when you are dying soon?" she asks.

"Here's the problem with your observation. I'm not dying. I'm joining my family in the next world," the Governor replies, smiling.

"What about your family here?" Ms Stokes asks.

"They would be fine. They are strong. They would be fine." The Governor says and goes towards her. Grabs her and gives her a tight hug. Ms Stokes doesn't want to let go of the Governor. So they hold each other so tight and for so long.

"Let me get Ms Harvanet to get us some breakfast," the Governor says, breaking away from Ms Stokes.

"I prepared some breakfast before coming up to your bedroom," Ms Stokes says.

"Ananda, you remind me so much of my late wife," the Governor says with nostalgia in his voice.

"This's why you shouldn't die," Ananda says, looking the Governor in the eyes.

"Exactly why I should die," the Governor replies to a loud laughter from the two.

"You're a bastard," Ananda says, hitting the Governor quite hard on the back.

The Governor chuckles and replies; "my late wife use to tell me that a lot."

The pair walk down to the dining room, holding hands in a physical space that they know would be no more in months or weeks or even days. It could be any day.

When they are seated, the Governor is surprised to see that his plate is already filled with eggs of some sort.

"What is this?" the Governor looks into his delicious plate and asks.

"Scrambled eggs," Ms Stokes replies. The Governor's joy is uncontainable, and he digs in. Savoring every bite in his month. Ananda pours him a glass of fresh juice. The Governor takes a gulp and beams with happiness. The lemon flavor refreshes the Governor.

Ananda gets up from her seat and moves over to the Governor's side. Sits next to him. Her left arm wraps around him. She eats from the Governor's plate.

The two eat in silence. They eat slowly. Breakfast takes over an hour. The Governor eats far more than he is used to. The Governor is too full.

"Ananda, I'm too full that I can't do anything. Please take me to my room. Let me take a little nap." The Governor pleads with Ms Stokes.

"No. We're going for a walk in the garden," Ms Stokes replies. The Governor hasn't taken a leisure walk in a while. He likes to walk in the refreshing garden outside.

And within a minute, the two are promenading happily in the green garden of the Range. Holding hands. Tightly.

Governor Spartman Schola is a happy man.

113

SCHOLA MEETS PROVINCIAL

SCHOLA HAND-DELIVERS THE LETTER TO Fr Mentor yesterday. Schola has no idea of the content of this second letter as he has no idea of the content of the first letter four years ago. He's just a bearer of letters. Letters from one long-time friend to another. Letters that are hand-written. Letters that must be hand-delivered. Just a letter.

After Schola delivers the letter, Fr Mentor tells him that Fr Cantwell would like to meet with him in Manhattan. Almost immediately.

Like the meeting with Fr Cantwell four years ago, Schola emplanes from Rochester to New York City and is completely lost in thoughts during the journey. But at peace this time.

Tempus fugis. Time flies. Schola says to himself as he walks into the Provincial's office. Schola takes the same seat as four years ago. The Provincial takes his same seat as four years ago. The room is still the same. Same paintings in the same strategic places. Same tables and furniture.

But unlike the previous meeting of four years ago, the room is less sad and less tense. In fact, the room is filled with delightful expectation. The provincial senses no malice in Schola's countenance and decides that any apology is a mere formality. Not necessary. The man is carrying no grudges.

"Given the new development in the last weeks, I wanted to touch base with you and see how you feel about all of this," Fr Cantwell says.

Schola doesn't know exactly how he should articulate his feelings about all of what happened four years ago. Schola thinks for a while. "It has been God who allowed it all for a greater good. I'm yet to discover what this greater good is." Schola says.

"I'm consoled by the meaning you attach to all of this. On my part and in retrospect, I acted out of the toxic atmosphere at the time. I didn't have all the facts." Fr Cantwell struggles a bit with an explanation.

"I'm really grateful for the experience. It has brought a lot of wonderful people into my life. People from whom I draw lots of happiness. Specifically, I'm in love with a young woman whom I met during the Senator Corner's trial. Apparently, she was my student at Harvard. I didn't know her at the time. But she knew me very well. We're living together now. We're thinking of building a life together. I truly love Ananda Stokes," Schola concludes.

Fr Cantwell allows the new information to sink in. So the question of whether Schola might want to return to the Jesuit Order is settled. Schola has forgiven all the parties, including Prof Duval. All Fr Cantwell can do is wish Schola well.

"Well, thanks for the understanding. And we wish you well in your new vocation. I have no doubt that you would be happy." Fr Cantwell says to conclude the meeting.

"Please whenever you are in town, do well to visit us. The Jesuits are still your family," Fr Cantwell says.

"Thanks for the invitation Fr Cantwell," Schola says, rises and shakes the provincial's hand.

Yes, there was something not right about the goodbye of four years ago. This's a better goodbye. The two men look at each with mutual respect.

114

RULING ON MR CONKLING

THE DISCIPLINARY COMMITTEE OF THE Indiana Supreme Court hears the re-instatement petition of Mr. Barfoot Conkling and is ready with its decision. On the trip from Fort Wayne to Indianapolis, Mr Barfoot can't believe the change in his fortunes. A change manifests in the fact that he drives his own car. A change manifests in the fact that he lives in his own house. It's amazing how one's fortune can change overnight. Unexpectedly.

The verdict on his petition is far from a likely favorable one. Mr Conkling knows it. Mr. Conkling is even surprised that the Justices take up his petition. As Schola says before he left for New York, "the odds are heavily against us."

But Mr Conkling is consoled in numerous ways despite a likely refusal to re-activate his attorney license. The Senator is filling Mr Conkling's schedule with jobs of all sorts. Transactional law, stuff that he's beginning to re-engage with and enjoying. Hence, a license enables him to fully and confidently handle all of the Senator's transactions in his vast businesses.

As well, the Senator has been generous to Mr Conkling. Mr Conkling could invest some of his earnings without having to work as such. So the picture is not so bleak. Thanks to a young man—Schola—that he meets four years ago. Mr Conkling is about losing his attorney license as well as his marriage then. And he subsequently loses both.

During those turbulent times, Mr Conkling spends quite some time praying in the Church. Schola spots the troubled man and decides to reach out. Their two weeks' meetings end abruptly when Schola leaves for law school.

And when Mr Conkling has all but given up in life, Schola comes back into his life, resurrecting it. Mr Conkling is grateful to Schola as he drives to Indianapolis to receive the ruling on his petition. No matter the outcome as Schola tells him, he must be grateful to the Justices for hearing him out. Gratitude is thus Mr. Conkling's attitude no matter how the verdict turns out.

Mr Conkling gets to Indianapolis an hour before the courts open for business. So he breakfasts at Diners, not too far from the State House where the Supreme Court is housed. Mr Conkling feels grateful as he eats his breakfast. He is happy and grateful no matter how unfavorable today's verdict turns out.

115

GOVERNOR/MS STOKES TOUR HOUSE

MS STOKES IS FULL OF tears. Her tears are galloping down her cheeks unto her chest as the Nile flows into the Victoria Falls. Strongly and constantly. Unceasingly.

The Governor is taking Ms Stokes through Anna's, the Governor's deceased wife's, wardrobe. It's amazing how two people can look alike. You look just like my former wife, the Governor keeps saying. Do you know that she used to hit me on the back just like you. But not as hard as you do. This latest comment receives another hard hit from Ms Stokes. "You are a bastard," Ms Stokes says upon each hit. The Governor just laughs. The Governor is happy.

"I got this diamond ring for her on the tin anniversary of our wedding," the Governor says pulling yet another drawer of accessories. Another cough and Ms Stokes hands the Governor the bottle of water that she holds. "Sorry, please drink a bit," Ms Stokes says, nurturing the Governor tenderly. "Thank you, Ananda," the Governor says. And smiles. Ms Stokes smiles back.

"Has she ever worn any of these?" Ms Stokes asks, gazing at the impeccable jewelries.

"Never," the Governor says. Anna never touches any of these. She was fond of her African beads, though. "Come let me show you," the Governor says, pulling Ms Stokes to yet another round of drawers. "She wore these. We bought these from Cape Coast, Ghana, when we went to visit the castles that slaves were held en route to the Americas," the Governor says, pointing to a bunch of traditional African neck and hand beads. "Anna loved these and worn them often," the Governor says.

The African beads induce the most pleasure in Ms Stokes since the tour of jewelries. She smiles and puts a bunch on her neck and a few on her hands.

"Amazing how two people are alike," the Governor says again. "So of all the jewelries I have been showing you, it's these that capture your fancy," the Governor asks smiling.

"Yes, they are the most beautiful," Ms Stokes says and goes over the mirror to admire herself. Beaming away in happiness.

The Governor looks at the young woman, the wife of his son, his daughter-in-law. She's happy. And so the Governor is happy. The Governor would tell his wife when he meets her in the next world that he left the family in the hands of worthy people. Good people. Schola and Ananda.

"Ananda, come," the Governor pulls her again. "Let me show you the room of the boys. I have not entered it in a while now." The tears resume in Ms Stokes face. She struggles to wipe them away. She feels the pain of a man losing his beloved wife and two sons. It must be a horrible experience.

While in the boys' room, the two remain silent. For the first time, Ms Stokes feels movement within her womb. She has missed her monthly period. She wants to be sure before telling Schola. As if the baby can feel that this's the room.

"Governor, I'm pregnant," Ms Stokes says. The Governor chuckles. The pain and sadness of memories of his late sons are defeated. The Governor is overjoyed. "I haven't told Schola yet," Ms Stokes says.

Ms Stokes proceeds to open the drawers. Looks at the wardrobes. Mrs Schola was very organized. The room of the boys is immaculately in order. The clothes of the boys from their birth well-preserved. Mrs Schola saved the clothes of the first baby for the second one. Mrs Schola could conserve. This despite all the money at her disposal. I wouldn't have to buy new clothes for my baby, Ms Stokes says. "Thanks, Mrs Schola," she says.

The moment in her womb kits again. Ms Stokes is taken aback by the action of the unborn in her womb.

They might have been in the boys' room for a while. For Ms Harvanet comes to check on them yet again. "We're fine," the Governor remarks. "We're fine," the Governor repeats. The Governor is a happy man.

Ms Stokes looks over the room again. She now understands why the Governor is in a hurry to join his wife in the next world. It makes complete sense. And it's fair.

"Let me show you one last place," the Governor says, pulling Ms Stokes out of the boys' room.

116

VISIT TO THE FAMILY CEMETERY

THE DUO, THE GOVERNOR AND Ms Stokes, step out of the massive house into the family shrine, where the late Mrs Schola and the two sons are buried. They walk hand in hand. At the sight of the tombstones, the two stop on their tracks upon the sight of a figure squatting before the three graves.

"Is that not Priestley," the Governor asks Ms Stokes.

"Yes, that's him," Ms Stokes replies. "I know he's due back today, but I didn't know that he would be back this early," Ms Stokes says.

Both continue to the graveside. Schola is praying when they get there. Schola appears oblivious of their presence. The two stand hand in hand and watch in silence as Schola prays.

After about fifteen minutes, Schola takes the bundle of flowers that he bought initially for Ananda and lays each on each tombstone. The Governor assists in laying the flowers. The Governor beams with happiness after laying the last bundle of flowers. The Governor is a happy man. The Governor joins his family soon in the next world. So the Governor is a happy man.

The three walk back into the house.

"Sorry I didn't inform you guys that I was coming back earlier than anticipated," Schola apologizes. "Instead of waiting for the bus to set off this morning, I decided to come with the night bus," Schola explains. "We got into Fort Wayne this morning and I decided to visit the Range first before going to the Farm."

"Priestley, you look tired. Let me get you something to eat," Ms Stokes says and heads to the kitchen to fix lunch, leaving the two men along.

"Fr Mentor has another letter for you," Schola says, puts his hand in his breast pocket and brings out a letter for the Governor.

"Petrus, Petrus," the Governor says with anticipation upon taking the letter.

"Please permit me to freshen up," Schola excuses the Governor and goes to the room he first sleeps the evening he delivers a letter to the Governor four years ago. Schola is not surprised to see that Ananda is using the same room. She uses Schola's room. This, too, doesn't surprise Schola.

117

GOVERNOR READS THE LETTER; LUNCH OF THE THREE

THE GOVERNOR READS THE LETTER from his Jesuit classmate and friend the third time. "Petrus has always been thoughtful," the Governor says to himself. Fr Mentor's words console and refresh the Governor. Happy tears stroll down the Governor's face. The Governor quickly wipes his tears, ensuring that nobody sees him crying. The Governor is a happy man.

It's the sweet aroma that summons both the Governor and Schola to the dining room. Both enter the room almost at the same time. Ms Stokes look at them in surprise and laugh. "I'm sure the same DNA runs through the two of you," Ms Stokes says.

The men go to work. They bring out the plates and set the table. The trio dig in after praying the grace as soon as the food is set down.

"How was New York," the Governor asks.

"Great," Schola says, washing down mashed potatoes with a glass of water. "I met with Fr Mentor. We had a great meeting as usual," Schola reports.

"Yes, Petrus is always a good companion," the Governor says with sweet memories of the elderly Jesuit priest.

"Who is Petrus," Ms Stokes asks.

"Sorry, Fr Petrus Mentor," the Governor explains. "Petrus and I entered the Jesuit novitiate the same day and have since been friends," the Governor explains.

"By the way, he likes to meet you as soon as you are able," Schola informs Ms Stokes.

"And how am I going to make it to the Holy Mountain," Ms Stokes asks.

"We shall visit the Mountain on our way back from Prof Linda Duval's funeral," Schola explains.

"And who is Prof Linda Duval?" Ms Stokes asks.

The two, the Governor and Schola, look at each other. Schola doesn't know how much to tell Ms Stokes or even to tell her at all.

"Prof Duval and Schola were colleagues at Harvard," the Governor reveals. "She dies recently. It was her dying wish that Schola be present at her funeral," the Governor finishes.

Ms Stokes stops eating and gazes far away in wonder. After a long pause, Ms Stokes asks: "And when is the funeral of this Prof Duval again?"

"Next week," Schola says.

The Governor realizes the two need time alone. The Governor gets up, takes his desert of fruits puddy and goes to his study. "Keep the fight decent," the Governor admonishes as he leaves the two alone.

"And when were you going to tell me about Prof Linda Duval? Ms Stokes blast off as soon as the Governor leaves the room.

"And when were you going to tell me that the Governor is dying?" Schola fires back.

"What?" Ms Stokes asks in surprise. "How do you know that?" She asks again.

"I overheard your conversations when he was showing you around. You calling him a bastard because he was leaving us," Schola explains.

"He compelled me to take a vow not to tell you until he tells you himself," Ms Stokes explains.

"And secrets now exist between us," Schola rebuts.

"I'm sorry, Honey," she apologizes. Schola looks at her with love and a bit of shame for been hard on her.

"Fine. I understand," Schola says.

"Now back to this Prof Duval," Ms Stokes renews her point. "Why must you be at her funeral?" She asks.

"Because it's her dying wish that I be at the funeral," Schola explains.

There's a long pause. With no further explanation forthcoming, Ms Stokes feels that she has no choice: "Was she the reason you had to leave the priesthood?'

Schola laughs at the question. "I doubt I ever as much as shook hands with Prof Duval when I was at Harvard," Schola explains and continues, "in spite of the numerous sexual advances she made at me. But yes, she accused me of sexually harassing her. Given the charged atmosphere regarding sexual harassment at the time, the Jesuits were compelled to let me go without much of due process," Schola finishes up.

"Sometimes we convict the innocent only to realize our mistake ..." Ms Stokes quotes Schola's opinion that the New York Times published three months ago.

"Yet you attend her funeral?" Ms Stokes says, much as a wonder than a question.

"And you, my dear wife, will attend as well," Schola replies.

"Saint Schola," Ms Stokes teases. A tease that appears to her quite plausible.

"Come let me show you something," Schola pulls Ananda to his own study at the Range.

EPILOGUE

It's a somber morning: 23rd October, 2021.

The crowd is rather lean. But the fire is quite a scene to behold. It engulfs the entire body, and within minutes the inferno chaffs the remains into ashes. Prof Linda Duval is finally cremated as is her final desire.

Few are in attendance. No Harvard faculty members. Their absence is telling, Schola observes and thinks to himself. Two persons represent the family. Their relationship to Prof Duval isn't obvious. Some distant relatives, maybe.

The Jesuits in attendance are the provincial, Fr Cantwell, and Fr Mentor, director of the Holy Mountain. Of course, Schola and his love, Ms Stokes, complete the list of the handful mourners.

The presiding minister isn't too sure what to do. The crematorium only brings this minister to officiate when the deceased or his family fails to make religious arrangement for the final funeral rites, but it appears the deceased or the family won't mind a religious rite.

The ad hoc pastor sees two men in clerical collars—Frs Cantwell and Mentor. The pastor hesitates for a moment. Eventually, the pastor makes up his mind and approaches Fr Mentor. "Please do you mind presiding?" Fr Mentor is surprised. Fr Mentor looks to Fr Cantwell for approval and gets a quick nod in approval. As a priest, Fr Mentor is ever ready for such unplanned sacerdotal duties: The holy water and stole are in his pocket as is holy oil, just in case.

So Fr Mentor steps forward to bless the remains of Prof Linda Duval. Before the fire is set to the body, Fr Mentor says a few words about Prof Duval. Fr Mentor remembers her as an honest person who tells the truth when it matters the most. Her ability to tell the truth heals and frees others. "She was a brave and honest woman," Fr Mentor says.

Fr Mentor invites anybody who might want to share a word with others. Everybody looks at the two family members. They decline the invitation politely.

"Saint Schola, won't you say anything at your wife's funeral," Ms Stokes pinches Schola in the back as she teases him quietly.

"Prof Linda Duval and I were faculty members at Harvard some few years back. As I remember her, she was very human. She exuded the weaknesses typical of human beings. She was ambitious, wanting to get ahead in life. She was supercompetitive. She was smart as well." Schola pauses and continues.

"But when the stakes are high and the most important things in life beckon, Prof Duval doesn't hesitate in being brave and truthful. I'm grateful for knowing her. Her life blessed mine beyond measure." Schola finishes his sincere encomium of Prof Duval.

The thoughts of Fr Cantwell are four years removed from the events right in front of him. Fr Cantwell recalls the mournful Monday morning that Ms Corel Woolsey self-immolated. And the chain of events that her self-immolation excites and leaves in their wake. Today ends one of those events.

The fire of four years ago of that mournful Monday morning was quite a scene to behold as is the case presently. The fire engulfs the entire remains of Prof Duval, and within minutes the fire chaffs her remains into ashes.

Schola takes some of the ashes to the family shrine in Fort Wayne, Indiana, in remembrance of Prof Duval. If he hadn't, Prof Duval would have had no such honor among the living; for none of the two family members present thought it worthwhile to take her ashes with them.

Fr Cantwell watches in wonder and praises God from his heart. Truly, in the design of divine providence there're no coincidences.

THE END

Printed in the United States
by Baker & Taylor Publisher Services